Marriage Building Blocks

A Practical Guide to Christian Marriage

Branford Yeboah

2012

 New Generation Publishing

In an age where the marriage institution is being endangered, evidenced by the downward spiral of divorce throughout the world. Can the Christian marriage be a lamp that will lighten the darkness divorce has caused to the institution of marriage? Can the Christian marriage be a shining example to the institution of marriage when one in every two marriages breaks down? Is the Christian marriage a good ambassador for Jesus Christ to the institution of marriage? When the world looks at the Christian marriage, what do they see? **Love and submission?** The reasons we marry will either take us down the road that leads to divorce or **make the Christian marriage an effective witness for Christ.**

Table of Contents

Acknowledgements 6

Introduction 7

1. Effective Communication in Marriage 13

2. Identifying Problems in Marriage 31

3. Decisions and Problem-Solving 41

4. Christ the counsellor 59

5. Marriage Flavours 72

6. Building a False Image 87

7. Disappointments 98

8. The Family Relationship 119

9. Sex outside Marriage 128

10. Children 155

11. Unfaithfulness in Marriage 158

12. When the Wife Becomes the Second Wife 176

13. Divorce: Who Is To Blame 191

14. Remarriage: What Does The Bible Say?.... 215

15. The Power of Love in Marriage 234

16. Forgiveness in an Imperfect Marriage 264

17. The Power of a Praying Husband 317

18. The Power of United Prayer in Marriage .. 345

19. Broken promises....................................... 357

20. Providential 427

21. In obedience to God 443

Bibliography 451

Acknowledgements

I am deeply thankful to my dear wife Mary who gave me all the support and encouragement without which this book would not have been written. When I felt like giving up, she edged me on. Behind the scenes, she played a great role to making this book available to its readers.

Then to Emma Rowley-Ashwood whose brilliant guidance and editing has made all the difference. I am also thankful to the following: Dr. Cecile Hoareau and Betty Kenney who have read the manuscript and returned excellent feedback.

I am also thankful to James Rowley-Ashwood for his enormous wisdom, support, guidance and his brilliant creative design of the cover that makes it so attractive in the eyes of those who buy this book.

Introduction

I hope this book will be a source of spiritual and physical blessing to those who are married and those who are about to marry. Welcome to the world of insight into Marriage Building Blocks, a new generation of study into what Christian married life is. Its purpose is to help you discover ways to relate to the Word of God in the eyes of God who created the institution of marriage.

Its aim is to raise awareness of the damage divorce is doing to the Christian marriage. This book makes it easy to bring the Word of God and prayer into your marriage by taking you right into the world of Christian marriage as the Bible speaks of it. The Christian marriage was meant to be priceless and a means of evangelizing to the world.

The study of this book will help you to get a clear understanding of what marriage is about by focusing on the Word of God and examining carefully what Scriptures say about how to live a Christian marriage. Considering the examples in this book will get you thinking about how to relate the teaching of the Word of God to everyday married life.

The examples in this book raise questions about what it means to live as a Christian wife or husband in a world where marriages are failing. Are they failing because marriage has lost its value? What is the believer's role in a world where divorce has become a common household word? In addition, how can the believer's marriage touch the married lives of unbelievers? What role can the Christian marriage play in a world where marriage has become like a commodity we can get rid of if we no longer need its service?

You will discover that people are not much different when it comes to marriage now than they were thousands of years ago. Moreover, you will see that God's Word is more useful in marriage than you ever realized. Explore the pages of this book and take a closer look at what it says about marriage and its building blocks, what it can do in your marriage and how it may work for your marriage.

You will find this book to be exciting reading because it is very practical and intriguing. You will feel at home, as you are reading it. Within the pages of this book, you will find many resources for your married life. The result of this book is an excellent material that will enrich your married lives and development of your day-to-day married life.

All the characters in this book are real people. Some are very close friends whilst others I know through friends. Their life experiences are real and I have personally witnessed them. Some of them weathered the storms and came out victorious and others failed. They have given me permission to write their life stories so that others might learn from the path they took.

Whilst some of them made decisions independent of God, which resulted in failure, others included God in their decision-making, which ended well. I have deliberately substituted their real names to protect their identities. In addition, I have changed the names of locations where events took place in anticipation that local familiarity will be lost.

What matters is that others may learn from these life experiences. Apart from two people, the rest of the characters mentioned in this book are Christians, people who have really experienced the redeeming grace of Jesus Christ and have been baptised in the Holy Spirit, people who know the word of God and live by the Word.

Their experience goes to show how fallible we are in spite of our faith in God. The fact is, without

Christ, we can do nothing. In a world where we are exposed to carnal desire, it is only in total dependency on God that we can overcome our weakness. This book deals with practical issues in marriage.

It examines some of the problems in marriage and seeks to resolve some of them. The author does not claim to hold all the answers to the causes of divorce. However, it examines issues relating to decisions and choices people make before marriage. It also looks at the reasons behind decisions some people make. It deals with choice and what factors influenced them.

The book discusses mistakes committed by married couples, then examines them carefully to find out why those mistakes were committed and how to help those contemplating divorce. One of the reasons for writing this book is to help young couples going through marital problems.

This book examines the reasons why some men beat their wives at the slightest provocation when they know there is no justification for spousal beating. We must agree that there are no known Scriptural verses to support this kind of behaviour in marriage. A husband who respects himself will never lay a finger on his wife.

It is heart breaking to know there are many Christian wives suffering in silence because they do not want to expose their husband's abusive behaviours. As a result, some of them endure years of battering at the hands of their husband who are **pastor, elder or deacon. A Christian husband who abuses his wife brings shame to the very faith he claims to profess.**

Can an abusive Christian husband, who holds a responsible position in the church counsel a battered woman in the Church? Certainly not, his abusive behaviour towards his spouse disqualifies him from counselling. Christian husbands who hold a responsible position in the church should endeavour to be good ambassadors of Christ.

This book does not have the answers as to why some men subject their wives to years of physical abuse; neither does it seek to claim it contains magical formulas, which, if followed, can cure the canker that makes some men beat their wives. It takes an amazing love for a devoted and loving wife to endure years of abuse from a husband who is a complete tyrant.

The only thing this book stands for is to ensure that those who are about to take marriage vows know it takes love, unity and faith in Christ through prayer to experience the presence of the power of God in marriage. It takes prayer, the word of God, love and submission for a marriage to succeed.

The author views love and submission as the most effective building block for any marriage. Again, love and submission are the pillars that support the structure of any marriage. Marriage can only be built upon this foundation. Love and submission are partners in marriage and are so closely allied they cannot be separated.

If spouses can love each other as Christ loves us, then there will be no reason for separation or divorce. The Scriptures are centred on God, Christ and the Holy Spirit. Similarly, marriage is centred on Unity, Love and Submission. These three are the main marriage building blocks.

1. Effective Communication in Marriage

"Come now, let us reason together." (Isaiah 1:8).

Married spouses are always involved in communication. It is the process and art of transmitting a message. Communication is made up of three essential parts. First, the source person has an intent, or meaning. This may be an idea, a feeling, or information. Then, there is the receiver to whom the meaning is sent.

The receiver is a person who has preconceptions, which may affect how he receives the meaning. When the communication process is clear, the receiver understands the meaning exactly as the source person intended. In communication we must have a clear, objective idea of what we want to say.

Use correct, precise language and not vague terms that may sound as if you want to conceal something from your spouse. Use words that your spouse will understand, avoid words such as "you know what I mean; I hope you understand, this is what I mean." These strange and complicated terms will not impress your spouse.

Do you find it difficult to communicate effectively with people? What do you do when others say things that make you uncomfortable? How do you communicate your feelings? How do you react when you hear words that make you feel uncomfortable? This is what King Solomon says. A man's wisdom gives him patience; it is to his glory to overlook an offence. (Proverbs 19:11). Through patience a ruler can be persuaded, and a gentle tongue can break a bone. (Proverbs 25:15).

Exploring the above questions would help us to deal with the issues some people have. Communication is no doubt the most important thing in marriage. It takes love and respect to communicate effectively, to maintain healthy and long lasting marriage. The language of love is communication, and he who knows the act of communication knows how to keep trouble out of his marriage.

By using effective communication skills in your marriage, you will be creating a healthy atmosphere in your marriage. Let us look at a scenario now. Your wife comes home after a bad day at work with a colleague and finds you lost in a telephone conversation. She says, "Hi! Honey," but you do not take notice of their presence.

Again, she says, "Hello love!" and you respond by raising your hand in acknowledgment, and you keep on talking until your conversation is over. This brief interaction is called the NEGATIVE MOMENT OF TRUTH. The negative impression the colleague has formed will be passed on.

Now let us take another example. Your wife comes home with a work colleague and finds you busy talking on the phone. You say, "Hi honey," you walk to your wife and plant a kiss on her lips and tell the other person on the phone. "My wife is here and I will call later." You welcome the guest with a hug and smile, making them welcome. This is called a POSITIVE MOMENT OF TRUTH.

TYPE OF BEHAVIOURS IN COMMUNICATIONS:

1. Making eye contact: - Making eye contact is very good in communication. It is the only indication that you are interested in what your spouse is saying. It reassures your spouse of your love and affection. Eye contact is what makes communication interesting in marriage.

2. Stating clearly what you want instead of going round and round and ending the conversation in a dead end. 3. Involving your wife in all decisions, 4. Acknowledging your wife's viewpoint, this is

very important in marriage because it reassures your wife that you value her decisions. This is called ASSERTIVE BEHAVIOUR, (positive behaviour).

COMMON BARRIERS TO COMMUNICATION:

Sometimes communication in marriage requires hard work to make ourselves clear and to get ourselves understood by our spouse. The following are known to be barriers to communication: lack of motivation to listen to your spouse due to discomfort, illness pain or cold.

Emotions may interfere in the communication process; there may be a clash of personality between spouses. The husband may jump to conclusions instead of waiting, hearing and understanding what the wife has to say. Only then will we accept what our spouse is saying.

When married couples are communicating, the husband or the wife should not regard his or her opinion as fact. This can lead to a barrier in communication, which can make the other person in the marriage feel that he or she is being put down.

When communicating we must differentiate between what is subjective and what is objective.

Subjective thoughts are based on your own ideas or opinion rather than fact. This can sometimes create barriers to communication when a husband or wife wants the spouse to accept what he or she is saying as being right. This can create friction in communication due to its unfairness.

On the other hand, objective communications are not based on personal feeling or opinions but only on facts. Here you are able to communicate convincingly to clear every cloud of doubt. If what we are communicating can be proven because we have evidence, then what we are communicating will lead to a sound conclusion.

The impact of communication on every marriage has the power either to hold the marriage together or break the marriage apart. In communication, we must watch the words we say to our spouse, because incorrect words can upset your spouse and lead to quarrels. In Proverbs 15:1 King Solomon said, "Hash word stirs up anger." On the other hand, kind words can inspire a feeling of joy. A strong marital relationship requires effective communication. Love is what keeps communication alive.

In Ephesians, Paul teaches the effectiveness of true communication. Let every husband and wife read these words. "Instead, speaking the truth in love, we will in all things grow up into him who is the head, that is, Christ. From him the whole body, joined and held together by every supporting ligament, grows and builds itself up in love, as each part does its work." (Ephesians 4:15-16).

Communicating in marriage is expressed as speaking the truth in love. In communicating, we must always speak the truth to our spouse. This is very important because trust can only be earned through speaking the truth. The last thing you need in marriage is to lose your trust because you cannot be trusted to speak the truth. See Proverbs 8:7, "My mouth speaks what is truth." By speaking the truth to your spouse, you are obeying the Word of God.

Communication in marriage can be expressed in two forms. Married couples communicate either verbally or nonverbally. By nonverbal communication, we are talking about gestures. Married couples can use gestures to communicate purely for their own understanding.

Married couples can use facial expressions to communicate without anybody knowing what they are saying. This can be done through the movement of the body, eye contact or moving the mouth and the hands simultaneously without uttering a word. Communication in marriage is the process of speaking the truth with love.

When married couples are communicating, it should involve the total person and not half of the person present and the other half of the person wandering away. Bad attitude in communication is when the husband's body is present but his mind is wandering very far away. This can cause frustration and lead to a breakdown in communication.

In communication, the body and mind must be present. It must involve the total person. Women are very good communicators so they pay particular attention to what goes on during communication. What interests a woman in communication is her husband's undivided attention. Therefore, the husband must give his wife undivided attention when they are communicating.

Communication is essential in a marriage that needs healing. Communication is the means for renewal and healing. A failing marriage is a marriage that has lost the spark that can reignite the love that once existed between the couple. The renewal of a failing marriage can only be restored through communication, beyond this there is nothing.

Running around for advice will do both of you no good, because some advice can worsen problems. Besides, in our desperation we turn to accept whatever advice we receive without sieving through to find out if such advice can restore healing in the marriage. You will save yourselves time and money by communicating instead of running around for help.

Communication is the catalyst that can turn a failing marriage into a happy marriage. If a marriage has lost the spark, the way to re-kindle love is through communicating. To reignite the love in the marriage, couples should not borrow a matchstick from outsiders. Borrowing a matchstick will do you no good because matchstick are not designed to reignite love. Matchstick in this context are the people you go to for advice.

A failing marriage is like a withered plant with a nutrient deficiency. You will not find the cure from the chemist shop or a health shop. The only prescription recommended is communication that costs nothing. The greatest form of healing in every marriage is through communication because it is the only healing remedy available. Marriages fail because of lack of communication.

A failing marriage is a sign of breakdown in communication. The only solution is to restore communication in your marriage. Communication is the music of love in marriage and every effort must be made to keep the music going. Communication keeps married couples dancing to its tune. It is free and costs nothing. It saves time and money. Never allow this music of love to stop because it inspires love.

Effective communication in marriage is choosing to be responsible in expressing our feelings honestly and receiving our spouse's feelings in the same way. Anything short of this will lead to a breakdown in communication. One of the key problems in marriage is the lack of acceptance of spouses' views on issues concerning the direction of the marriage. This lack of acceptance creates what are called roadblocks in communication.

Communication in marriage is a process of giving in love and receiving in love. Alternatively, we must communicate in love and listen in love. Acceptance must be with love. Without love, acceptance is not sincere. Similarly, giving must be with love, without love giving is not sincere. Where there is love, spouses communicate in love. Love stimulates communication in marriage. In a marriage where there is no love, a husband and wife hardly talk to each other.

Grandmother once said, "Marriage communication rests on the foundation of trust and is supported on a pillar of truth." This is the reason why if your spouse cannot trust what you are communicating, then half of her faith in you is weakened. It is weakened because you are not communicating the truth.

Telling the truth is one of the most important guidelines in communications, communication between married couples depends on a bond of trust. For example, if you are talking to your wife and she believes you are telling the truth, but later finds out you lied to her, then you are likely to lose her truth.

Your spouse desire to listen to you means she trusts in you. However, if she believes you are lying to her she will no longer accept or be interested in your communications. Telling the truth simple means avoiding deliberate lies, an honest and sincere husband will not try twisting facts during communications.

Dishonesty in marriage is a breeding ground for lies. In addition, lies discourage communication because the recipient has lost interest in what you have to say. Lies indicate that something is lacking in what you are communicating. Truth is what you are not communicating. If you love your spouse, you will not lie when communicating. In marriage, a lie conceals the truth and weakens trust.

Transparency in marriage depends on truth, that the communicator is communicating nothing but the truth. Moreover, the receiver has absolute faith that the message being communicated is truth. This depends on trust. Love is the only thing that can make married couples communicate truth meaningfully, and it comes from the heart and not from the head. When a spouse is communicating the truth it means he or she is honest.

Love holds the key to unlocking marital problems. It is the foundation stone in marriage and must be guided with the heart. Love is the foundation stone the marriage builder cannot reject. Love is the cornerstone that holds marriage together. Communication is built on love; this is the reason why those who want to see the power of love being demonstrated in their marriage must not stop communicating.

The only visible sign of expressing love is through communicating. In communication, love is expressed practically and not theoretically. Married couples who communicate effectively grow to love each other more and more. In communication, love must be seen in action in both spouses. Active love is genuineness; this means being transparent and truthful in our communication.

Seeking what is good for your spouse is an expression of love. This kind of love brings healing and wholeness to our marriage. Wholeness here means something complete. Our married life must be complete, until then something is lacking in the marriage. Only communication can bring about renewal.

As married couples, we must communicate in truthfulness, in this way we demonstrate active love. Communication is the only thing that can spice up marriage. Communication is what creates laughter in the marriage. Communication stimulates affection in marriage. A husband who holds deep affection for his wife will love communicating with her.

Communication is an important nutrient in marriage that helps it to blossom. Breakdown in communication leads to breakdown in marriages. Married couples should do everything possible to keep communication alive in their marriage.

Grandfather once said, "One of the reasons married couples are unable to communicate effectively is that they get so caught up living busy lives that they do not have time to communicate with their spouse." A busy life is like building a marriage on quicksand. Situations like that can sink the marriage, so if you value your marriage walk away from a busy life. A busy life is the quickest way to divorce.

Resentment builds up where there is no communication. This puts emotional strain on the marriage. In a world where people live under constant stress and pressure, communication is the only way married couples can be relieved from stress-related problems. Give it a trial and you will know it is worth communicating with your spouse.

Communication is the oil that keeps the flames of love in marriage burning. Communication is the oil that lubricates the wheel of marriage. Communication in marriage is what keeps friction out of the marriage. Friction in marriage is due to luck of communication. Therefore, to avoid constant friction in marriage, we need to stimulate communication.

Communication stops from the day a husband stops loving his wife or a wife stops loving her husband. When something outside the marriage stops spouses from communicating with each other, that same thing will separate them. Whatever stops spouses from communicating is what will break up the marriage.

The person responsible for the breakdown in communication in the marriage should examine himself to see if he is doing something outside the marriage that is shutting down the lines of communication. The spouse affected by the breakdown in communications should begin to ask questions. A breakdown in communication is the first sign of trouble in a marriage and a wake-up call.

To prevent a rusty marriage, keep the lubricant in. Whatever stops communication in marriage should be lubricated to prevent a rusty marriage. The dreadful thing in a marriage is to have a husband and wife not talking to each other. A situation like this can be very painful and distressing to both spouses.

The process of spouses not talking to each other is called **silent trade.** Situations like this call for an urgent solution before things get out of control. **Silent trade** in marriage is like a road that leads to a dead end. **Silent trade** kills love in marriage. Spouses who tread on this path will find themselves fighting each other in a divorce court.

The only thing to benefit from **silent trade** is **divorce**. Divorce is a bitter pill that is sometimes forced down the throat of a spouse who refuses to communicate. Silent trade is what can excommunicate love in marriage. Stop it before divorce kills and buries your marriage.

Silent trade is bad for marriage because it drives a permanent wedge in the wheel of marriage and keeps spouses farther apart from each other. Therefore, kill **silent trade** in your marriage before it kills your marriage. Allowing **silent trade** to choke communication out of your marriage will send you knocking on the doors of marriage counsellors.

This will allow poisonous people who should never have been involved in your marriage to start showing their ugly faces. To avoid these kinds of people showing their faces in your marriage, listen to this advice by grandmother, "Talk together, reason together, and bin the problem together." She said, "If we keep to this advice, the wheel of communication will continue revolving."

What keeps a train of mesh gears working perfectly is lubricant. Take the lubricant out and the gears become overheated due to friction. This situation can cause the gear teeth to break and the car to grind to halt. With hindsight, we must avoid situations that will cause problems in communication.

Run a gearbox dry without lubricant and you will receive a massive bill by post from your mechanic, similarly if you run your marriage on **silent trade,** be prepared to receive the divorce summons from the clerk of court via the mail carrier. Most marriages do not work because spouses do not know how to communicate effectively.

Communication is a vital ingredient in all marriages, without it there would be no marriage. Communication spices up marriages. Effective communication surmounts and removes all obstacles in marriage. It overcomes every difficulty and rises above any mountain that will stand against your marriage. It stands steadfast in the midst of invisible hindrances.

Communication brings hope from the realms of despair, whilst creating success where neither success nor its preconditions existed. Communication is a formidable weapon in marriage, but it is sad that most couples lack the skills to use this weapon in overcoming the problems in their marriage.

If you kill your marriage with **silent trade** the sole beneficiary will be divorce. Be warned, nobody will weep and sympathize with you. The only word of encouragement you will get is, "As you prepare your bed, so you lie on it." Going the extra mile is very crucial in any marriage undergoing difficulties.

Communication is a vital ingredient in marriage. Therefore, married couples must do everything to keep communication alive in their marriage. Breakdown in communication is the canker that destroys a happy marriage and leaves both spouses bitter enemies with double-edged swords in their hands.

Married couples who stop communicating are creating a situation that will influence the behaviour of their children later in life. Children who are caught in a war of words between their parents watch and monitor the strange behaviour. We must do every thing possible to prevent children from being exposed to **silent trade.**

The final advice is if you cannot communicate the truth, then be silent. Its better not to communicate than to communicate lies. Communicating lies in marriage is unhealthy, therefore unacceptable in marriage.

Communicating lies breeds mistrust amongst married couples. This then leads to deception, and when deception has gained root in the marriage it bears the fruits of anger, bitterness, fits of temper and fits of rage. Anger, bitterness, fits of temper and fits of rage are all symptoms of divorce that can destroy the healthy root of marriage. They gain root in marriage because mistrust acts as a fertile environment.

2. Identifying Problems in Marriage

My dear brothers, take note of this: everyone should be quick to listen, slow to speak and slow to become angry, for the man's anger does not bring about the righteous life that God desires. (James 1:19-20) and Ephesians 4:26 Paul says, "In your anger do not sin": Do not let the sun go down while you are still angry. An angry man stirs up dissention, and a hot-tempered one commits many sins. (Proverbs 29:22)

Those who are able to identify problems in their marriage put themselves a step ahead of the problem unlike those who cannot read the early warning signs of problems in the marriage. This is the reason why we must be sensitive to what goes on in our marriage. The following are some of the things we have to look for:

Identify or define the problem: The first step is to know what the problem is. It is possible that the real problem is not what you are thinking. When you identify the problem, state it in specific terms. You must identify the problem more precisely than to say, "This is what I feel about the situation." For example, the car will not start because the battery has run down. Therefore, you now know why the family car would not start.

Analyze and describe the general situation. You must state and examine all the facts related to the problem. In this process, you can determine if the problem is urgent, serious, or tentative, and you can decide whether to act immediately or wait for a while. Nevertheless, waiting is not a good option because it is dangerous and can worsen the problem.

Establish criteria for solving the problem: The value system of the decision-makers will determine the criteria. In the Christian marriage, this will involve both the spiritual and physical. Show your spouse that you are concerned. This will give her the assurance you care for her. Also, show that you are willing to help in the marriage.

Consider alternative solutions: Sometimes this called "brainstorming," where the wife and the husband say just whatever comes to mind with no restrictions. This is a chance to propose the merits and demerits of several solutions, and each one proposed is evaluated on its merits. The approach to each problem is very important because if it is approached with the wrong motives you are bound to have difficulties.

Select a course of action and decide on procedures: Do you know the facts? If you think, you have the facts; make sure the facts can be proven. Then, you will need to choose the right place, time and a mood that will be helpful to both of you. A spouse who makes mistakes and keeps changing his or her mind cannot be trusted.

Communication problems: To avoid troublemakers infringing onto your marriage, you have to be very careful in your choice of words. Let us sound a word of warning: marriage is not about "you", it is about "us," which means the interest of the husband and wife is what you must both seek.

In marriage, we must very careful how we use "linking verb," A linking verb shows a relationship between the subject and the predicate complement, which follows it. The linking verb is called a joining verb. It does not assert action; it expresses a static condition or a state of being.

For a clearer understanding, we shall restrict ourselves to conversations about marriage. In marriage, we speak using the plural, for example; we are, we were, we shall, we have been, we had been and we shall have been. In marriage, we do not speak using the singular verb, I am, I was, I shall be, I have been, I had been and I shall have been.

Remember it is about you and your wife or you and your husband. When in-laws are around you must be very careful of how you choose your words, when to say them and how to say them. Compliment each other by showing unity in the marriage. Do not give reasons for anyone to suspect there are problems.

Do not use selfish expressions like, "I did that." Instead say, we did that; I bought this "should be" we bought this and finally "we do things together." Positive statements in marriage will keep troublemakers out of your marriage. Whatever is acquired in the marriage belongs to husband and wife.

Lack of motivation: Interest and unity are qualities that create motivation in marriage that allow spouses to take a keen interest in what the other has to say. Curiosity is sometimes a means of arousing interest. Interest often precedes unity; a factor that motivates married couples to listen to each other.

Discussion: The atmosphere must allow good interaction between husband and wife to participate in the discussion. In addition, there must be enough time for a discussion you both know will need it. During the discussion, you must take note of what issues made the discussion longer than intended.

Attitude: An attitude of loving, caring and friendliness helps to produce good teamwork in marriage. In a marriage where husband and wife have freedom of expression without any hostility displayed, both spouses live in a wonderful married relationship. It takes love and affection to accomplish this in marriage.

Do not judge: The marital home is not a place for the blame game to operate. Do not use words that will hurt your wife or husband. Your actions and intentions must be without judgement. Instead, they should motivate your spouse. Spouses must refrain from actions that appear to be very rude.

Disagreement: When you disagree with your spouse on an issue you consider very important, you must respect the viewpoint of your spouse, because you may be wrong. Calmness of tone in disagreement is a sign of affection. On the other hand, a high-pitched tone in an emotionally charged disagreement creates anger and fear in marriage.

Body motion: Facial expressions can either compliment your spouse or reveal a bad attitude toward your spouse. In addition, your facial expression can reveal interest in your wife or husband. On the other hand, it can reveal the disagreement you are brooding over which you have allowed to create a barrier in your marriage.

Love or rejection, happiness or sorrow, pleasure or pain, surprise or disgust, sympathy or antipathy and like and dislike. All these emotions can be expressed through facial expressions without uttering a word from the mouth. Facial expressions can make your spouse respond when you are saying something he or she does not agree with.

I am the Boss! Who made you the Boss? Husbands who makes themselves bosses in the marital home do no permit disagreement, make high demands and as a result do not realise his wife has developed a negative feelings toward him. A bossy husband is a dictatorial husband. These kinds of attitudes are bad for marriage and disrupt communication in marriage.

A dictatorial husband makes decisions in the marital home concerning what, how and when things are to be done. Whatever he says is right and should be accepted as right in the home, in addition he rarely accepts his wife's opinion or ideas. He fails to recognise the wisdom in what his wife is saying. Checks and balances in the marital home are indications of a good and a happy marital relationship.

Aggressive behaviour: Shouting and screaming at your spouse is bad for marriage. Spouses who behave in this manner have no self-confidence and turn to suspect their spouse is up to something they cannot prove. This can causes anxiety in some people. Their inability to prove their case causes constant angry arguments. This situation can make one of them accuse the other of being quarrelsome.

Threatening behaviour: Is the worst behaviour in marriage communication, which can split up spouses. Besides this kind of behaviour is demeaning, and does not give respect to your spouse. Only a husband who has little respect for his wife or a wife who has little respect for her husband will behave in this way.

The blame game: Blaming your spouse for everything that goes wrong in the marriage shows signs of weakness. Insecurity is another factor that causes a spouse to start blaming his spouse for the slightest mistake. In marriage, we share the blame rather than shifting it on the other person.

Who are you married to? Marriage is something we cannot predict the outcome of because you may not really know the person you are marrying until you wake up after the honeymoon and find out the person you are married to is nothing but a DICTATOR. A spouse who insists his will rules in the home is nothing but a DICTATOR.

Every woman is married to one of the following men. A husband who is a PROTECTOR, a husband who is a NICE GUY, a husband who is WEAK, a husband who is a JUDGE and a husband who is nothing but a BULLY. Can you identify your husband from the above list?

A negative self-concept: We choose a spouse who can bring purpose to our marriage, bring potential to the marriage and to do the best for the interest of the marriage. However, a spouse with a negative self-image will cause brokenness in the marriage, will create a sense of false security in the marriage and is insensitive to his wife's needs.

On the other hand, a husband with a positive sense of self is a mark of spiritual and physical maturity. He gives his wife a sense of worth and a reason to be loved. A sense of worth in a marriage is a mark of a happy marriage that puts a smile on the face of every married woman. Give your spouse a reason to believe you care. Please do not give your spouse a reason to believe you do not care.

Lack of love: Lack of love in marriage is the cause of broken hearts and wounded spirits that has caused untold hardship in marriages. A husband is responsible for love in the marriage and any lack of it is a sign of irresponsibility on the part of the husband. If you look at the description of love in 1 Corinthians 13: 4-7, you will find that there are fourteen verbs there. The love Paul is writing about is love in action. That is **seeking your wife's highest interest.**

Subjective truth: In marriage, truth means that you are real and genuine, not false or artificial; genuineness in marriage means being transparent or truthful in how you relate to your wife. When I said, I love you; I meant every word of it. I do not have to hide my true feelings to you. The husband you are seeing is real; I do not have to mask my face.

My love for you is without question. It is said, "Love is the key quality in marriage and love is the highest of Christian virtues." See Ephesians 5:23-33 and 2 Peter 1:3-11. Psychology and theology both confirm that the most powerful healing force man has ever known is LOVE. Love is the only thing that can bring healing to a sick marriage.

Anger: The Christian husband must learn to express anger in a loving way. He must know how to use his anger for the good of the marriage. the Christian husband should direct his anger towards Satan and not his wife because he is the one who stirs anger and not the spouse, therefore direct your anger to Satan.

3. Decisions and Problem-Solving

"There is a way that seems right to a man, but in the end it leads to death." (Proverbs 14:12). What this verse means is that the decisions you have made may not be the best. This calls for rethinking over the decision or taking it to the LORD in prayer. Then wait until you have heard from God.

Decision-making: In terms of looking for a spouse, is the act of determining in one's own mind to work with God in choosing one person out of the number of people you meet. It involves making a selection based on criteria. Criteria in this context do not refer to the physical aspect of the person but his or her spiritual maturity.

Evaluation process: The purpose of evaluation is to determine what is lacking in the spiritual life of your future spouse, his public image, character, is he someone you can trust. By comparing his character to yours; look out for his temperament, his likes, dislikes, and question if there is anything about him or her that raises doubts about his or her suitability as a suitor?

In spite of his spiritual maturity, is he someone I can spend the rest of my life with? Although spiritual maturity is one of the major qualities one should look for in the prospective spouse, we should be mindful of his character and attitude, because being spiritually mature does not make one an angel. Again, you need to find out if you are compatible with each other.

Some mature Christians are very quick-tempered and for some unknown reason have no control over their quick temper. It is very important that if you spot this beast in your future husband then be bold and confront him with what you think about him. If he admits his ugly side, then work with him to find how to get rid of that bad temper in him.

Then you have two options: one, suspend every arrangement you both have made towards the engagement, and put him on trial observation. During this period, he (or she) is on probation. Ask him to seek both spiritual and physical help. Prayer changes things, so take it to the LORD in prayer and God who knows our weakness will set him free from the yoke of bad temper.

You will be better off dealing first with monster in your future husband than going ahead with marriage that will turn your home into a battleground. Taming the monster in your suitor will be important for your marital home. Suitors who admit they have bad temper do make strenuous effort to tame it.

Marriage is a lifetime commitment and the man or woman we choose as our future spouse should become an ambassador of Christ to the marriage institution. A suitor who behaves badly in public will be nothing but a disgrace. Good public behaviour is very important for spouses who are ambassadors of Christ in marriage.

You need to evaluate and assess the spiritual maturity of the man or woman you want to spend the rest of your life with before committing yourself. This takes time, and requires spending time with the LORD in prayer. Watch out for his reaction when it comes to prayer. Check for his spiritual involvement in the Church.

Does he look like someone who likes praying, does he take active part in Church activities? Find out all you need to know about him from his pastor, elders, deacons and trusted friends in the Church. In your quest to know who he really is, you must leave no stone unturned. The waiting time is a problem for most people, but if you wait on the LORD, the answer will come.

Grandfather once told me that, "choosing a husband or wife is not an easy matter. The choice of life partner must be made with one's life because marriage is a lifetime commitment." This requires time, careful consideration, and above all praying and waiting on the LORD to answer.

William Carey, the English missionary to India in the eighteenth century, has given us this stirring challenge: "Our God is a great God. Expect great things from God, attempt great things for God." We need to remember these words. If our plans are always small, then God does not need to become involved.

Prayer gives us a great source of power and insight in choosing our future partners. This is all-important because marriage is a lifetime commitment. God is the one who sees what we cannot see in a person. If you need a woman of virtue then trust God and expect Him to give you what you ask in prayer.

We must accept that some of the reasons for higher divorce rates in the Christian community are due to bad decisions. When we make decisions independent of God, we end up putting God out of our decision-making. This is where the problem starts, and once it starts without God, it runs out of control.

Therefore, we must guard against neglecting God in our decision-making. Alone with God in our decision is far better than so many people's advice. On this note, it is imperative that Christians thinking of getting married must work with God in their decision-making. The two key words to take note of are Decision and Problem-solving.

Decision-making is a special part of problem solving. For example before a person takes that final decision to get married. Whereas problem solving leads to specific results, decision-making leads down uncertain paths. Decisions involve options in life in which the variables are less subject to control and the outcomes are more uncertain.

The outcome can be uncertain because no two people know each other well enough to draw a conclusion on any future relationship. Marriage, for instance, is a decision, not a problem. A person can control his or her own problem-solving choice but cannot control the results of a decision in which another person is involved.

As a result, much care needs to go into decision-making. Likely results of the decision must be considered, and the strengths and weaknesses of different kinds of choices must be carefully weighed. For example, should I remain single or shall I marry? Could I best serve the Lord as a single person or in marriage?

If you make a decision and halfway through the courtship and you realise you have a made a mistake, then put things on holds immediately. It does not matter now how far you have reached with your courtship. It is better to make sure you have the right person as your spouse than to live the rest of your life with a person who will turn out to be a thorn in your marriage.

The following examples are decisions that close friends of mine made and what happened after. The path each of them took has a great lesson to teach us. Whilst some of them sought the will of God, others tried to help God to make things happen in their favour. Those who forget the story of Samson are bound to go down the same road.

Example one: This is a true account of an event that led a young to marry a woman God personally chose for him. Phillip was a young man praying for a beautiful wife to bring joy and happiness into his life. In the mindset of this young man, only a beautiful woman could make him happy.

Take a careful note of his request and see if there is something you can learn from it. Examine carefully the reason why this young wanted to marry. In our choice of wife or husband, we become so blind that we fail to see and understand the reason why God set up the marriage institution.

Until we understand why God instituted marriage, we are bound to commit serious mistakes in our married life. For the Christian such a mistake will bring shame and dishonour to the very institution God established to unify man and woman. If we allow the veil of beauty to blind us, then we will stumble into headache and pain.

For Christians to avoid a troubled marriage, they need to search the Scriptures to find the main reason why a man and a woman must come together as husband and wife. The Bible is the marriage manual Christians have to turn to for guidance when things start going wrong in the marriage institution God established.

For three good years, Phillip prayed that God would grant him his heart's desire. Then one night in a dream, a man he was walking with asked him, "What kind of a woman are you looking for to marry?" He told his companion he was looking for a very beautiful woman to marry. At this, his companion told him "God is going to give you a woman with the beauty of Jesus in her.

The beauty of Jesus will be seen in her, and all who see her will see the beauty of Christ in her." This brother must be a special person to God. Against this, he asked his companion for a sign that would enable him to know the woman. Then, his companion asked him" What are you holding in your hand?" "A Bible," he said. Then the man asked him. "Since you bought your Bible, has any woman touched it?" He said no.

Then his companion said, "The first woman to touch the Bible will be the woman God has chosen for you, she will bring joy and happiness to your life". At this, he awoke from his dream, pondering over the words of the companion. After careful thought, he realized when it comes to choosing a wife God had a different plan for him.

Phillip wanted a woman of outward beauty, but God wanted a woman with the beauty of Jesus for him. God would not impose this woman on him; it was a decision he had to make. Nevertheless, remember a person can control his or her own problem-solving choice but cannot control the results of a decision in which another person is involved.

First Phillip wanted a woman of his own choice he could present to God. Second, he wanted God to accept his perfect choice. Finally, he wanted God to bless the marriage. Christians like these will always put God out of their decision-making. We do not ask God to bless what we have chosen but we ask God if what we have chosen is the right choice.

Because God had given him a sign that would identify the woman, he set out to play games with words. Armed with the information given him in the dream he walked into every gathering looking around to see where beautiful young women were sitting.

And then he would go and sit by them, and deliberately get up, leaving his Bible behind, hoping one of the beautiful women would pick up the Bible, thereby fulfilling the sign God had given him in the dream. In many ways we all fall victim to this act of treachery. We all have what we are looking for in our future spouse, some look for good character, while others look for beauty.

It is clear that when it comes to looking for a bride, beauty surpassed character and integrity in this man's quest for a wife that would make him happy. Whilst this man is blinded by beauty, others are blinded by love. What a contrast. In our quest to look for a spouse, should character and integrity play the crucial role?

This young man could decide where and when to leave his Bible but the power to make any of the women pick up his Bible lay neither with him nor the women but only with God. God who is the Lord on earth and in heaven reigns supreme; He fashions and rules by His word, makes things happen to fulfil what He has spoken.

One day, a Women's Christian Fellowship invited him to speak on Christian evangelism. What great opportunity for him to sample and make a choice. He arrived at the meeting early and sat in the back row surveying the women as they walked in.

Suddenly he spotted a group of very beautiful women sitting in the middle row. He made a move towards where the women were sitting. He greeted them with a charming smile on his face. Frankly, Phillip is a handsome young man; any unmarried woman looking for a husband will find his advances irresistible.

The women were more than happy to have such a handsome man sit with them. There is a saying that "He who marries a woman purely on her good looks invites trouble into his home." I wish all Christian men would give a careful thought to this proverb. If you heed this advice, it will be a great asset in your choice of a future wife.

Phillip was so busy talking to the beautiful women around him that he did not notice the young woman God had chosen for him sitting directly behind him. God planned the seating arrangement. It is certain no man can outwit God. The Lord had prevented him from noticing her. For if he had seen that particular woman he would have moved seats.

God knows our thoughts and our deceptive schemes even before we put them into action. When he got up from his seat to go and give the speech, he got up without his Bible. However, this time he genuinely forgot it. All the beautiful women who sat around him saw the Bible. But, for some unexplained reason none of them could touch or take it to him.

Then the young woman destined to be his wife got up, stretched her hand between the two most beautiful women in the hall and picked the Bible. Then she called out, "Brother Phillip, your Bible." What a blessed way to fulfil God's word. This is clearly the Power of God at work.

At this, he became motionless like a lifeless statue. In his own words, he said, "I wished the ground had opened and swallowed me instantly." God will not answer such misguided prayers. What God has said He will do He will do and no one can stop Him. Yes, there is nobody who can.

God does not make mistakes. He keeps watch over His Word. Moreover, He has His eyes on those He has called to carry His message of Salvation. Some men and women of God in the ministry, especially in the choice of wives and husbands, have committed too many mistakes. Frankly, Eva became the driving force and the backbone behind this young man's ministry. God blessed the ministry because of her.

Although she was older than Phillip, she submitted to him and called him "My lord." This is a story of a man of God who set out to alter God's decision concerning his future wife, because God was about to give him a wife he considered physically unattractive. Therefore, he tried to do something very fast, by trying to be a step ahead of God.

What this young man tried to do is very common to most Christians. We make our decision and then take it to the Lord in prayer. Then, we ask God to accept and bless the choice we have made, without finding out if that is God's will for us. When it comes to marriage, we must be very careful that our emotions and feelings do not override God's will for us.

When God is silent over our prayer requests then we should know there might be some serious question marks over those requests. His silence could be an issue with what we are asking for, or He needs time to deal with some issues concerning the request. Our impatience towards God allows the devil to step in and answer our selfish prayers. Then we think God has answered our prayers.

It is worth noting that not all answered prayers are from God. This is the reason why it is necessary to crosscheck an answered prayer to ascertain if it is of the Holy Spirit. God will bless and help us prosper us better if we wait for Him. A classical example of this statement is in the pages of Scripture. It tells of the experiences of men and women who waited for God and prevailed.

One classical example is the story of king Uzziah. The Scripture tells us that, "As long as he sought the LORD, God gave him success." If we would seek God and include Him in all our decisions, He will give us success. In the Bible, you will find that all those who asked for the counsel of God before doing anything succeeded.

There is more to gain by waiting patiently for God than walking away because of impatience. Walking away can lead to untold headaches and regrets. In many cases, we walk away before the blessing comes. These tragic mistakes often befall many Christians. There are many reasons for unanswered prayers and only God knows why.

The problems most Christians encounter in marriage are the results of bad choices they made which were not in the will of God. When we fail to double-check answered prayers and allow ourselves to be carried away by our emotions, we will only have ourselves to blame.

The story of Samson's marriage is very intriguing and worth reading, not only to refresh our memories but also to serve as a warning. **Samson went down to Timnah and saw there a young Philistine woman. When he returned, he said to his father and mother, "I have seen a Philistine woman in Timnah; now get her for me as my wife." (Judges 14:1-2)**

Samson's decision to marry a Philistine woman against his parent's advice brought nothing but pain and headache that finally lead to his blindness and death. Not only that but also those close to him also suffered because of his **Decision-making.** When it comes to choosing a wife, some Christian's behaviour is not different from that of Samson.

The behaviour of Samson's choice of a wife reminds me of a young woman who went and found herself a husband and presented the man to her parents. When the parents objected her choice, she insisted, "It was either him or no one." When the parents reasoned that their daughter would not take no for an answer they gave in to her request. At the request of the parents, her boyfriend's parent came to ask her hand in marriage.

Before the ceremony started, her father in-law looked straight into her face and said, "Young woman, this is my son but he will certainly not make a good husband for you. You deserve a better person." At this the young woman jumped in defence of her boyfriend and said, "I don't care what you lot think about him because whatever you see in him I don't. Let's get on with what we have come here to do."

It is evident that love blinded this young woman. Some young people never learn when they are in love. I have witnessed countless young Christians' marriages that have ended in divorce, some barely six months or a year after their marriage. This is because there were things about their spouse they did not know and never thought it was worth finding out because of love.

Those who allow love to blind them are bound to go down this way. When it comes to choice, the behaviour of most Christians is no different from this young woman. Even if God were to send an angel with a message about their choice, they would rather hold on to their choice than give a thought to the angel's message.

What we have here is a woman who has seen what she wants and nothing is going to change her mind. When a person is blinded by choice, he or she fined it difficult to reason with those who oppose that choice. There is a warning from King Solomon to people who fall in this group:

"There is a way that seems right to a man, but in the end leads to death." The problem with some Christians is that they do not listen to the voice of the Holy Spirit. As we continue to resist the Holy Spirit He leaves us, and as a result, we drift away from Him to our peril. Unless we change our course of direction towards Him, there is nothing He can do to help us.

When it comes to marriage, I doubt whether some Christians really listen to God. From personal experience with people I have met, I can say without doubt that some Christians do not listen to God. Some Christians try to make up their mind concerning the type of suitors there are looking for, and this could explain the high divorce rate among Christians.

Another example is a story of a young Cuban Christian woman who fits the description of Christians who refuse to listen to God when they do not like what they are hearing. This young woman once asked me to remember her in my prayers concerning her choice of a future husband.

Unknown to me God had already answered her prayers, but she kept it to herself without telling me. After several months of praying, I asked her if she has heard from the LORD. At this she said, "Oh! Yes the LORD did answer me but I don't like the revelation." "What is it about the revelation that you do not like?" I asked.

What she said was typical of a self-centred Christian. She said, "God has revealed to me who my future husband is, and has also revealed it to the man. We are both fully convinced that this is the will of the LORD for us. But there is a problem." "What is the problem?" I asked. In response she said, "The man is too short and I don't like short men therefore the LORD should change his mind."

"What if the LORD does not change His mind" I asked, she said, "I insist the LORD must change

His mind" This is a woman determined to hold on to what she think is good for her irrespective of what God wants for her. The question we should be asking this young woman is, when it comes to marriage, should we accept what God gives us or reject His choice?

Two months later, we met again. I asked her "Have you changed your mind about God's choice for you?" "Nothing has changed, my decision still stands and nothing will change." Then she asked, "Can I come with you to your Church please! May be I can find what I am looking for." I told her, "I am sorry for all the men in my church are short men."

At the time of writing this book, she is still not married because she is waiting on the LORD to change His mind. Well, the LORD will never change his mind concerning the man He has chosen for her. What the LORD can only do is to give the man to another woman. A word of caution: if you reject what God has chosen for you then the devil will step in and give you what your heart desires.

4. Christ the counsellor

"For your love is ever before me, and I will walk continually in your truth." (Psalm 26:3).

One of the greatest problems in the world today is anxiety. It has caused disease and destroyed marriages. It has divided families and kept the offices of psychologists and psychiatrists crowded. Are there any solutions to these problems? Yes! Prayer is the only answer to anxiety.

When the Church has lost it divine power and authority to exercise deliverance and healing for those in the Church who have mental problems as the result of stress and anxiety, then the Church sends them to a mental hospital. The mental hospitals do not even have the answer to some problems.

What will you do when trouble raise its ugly head in your marriage? The only way to show it the exit is to put love into action, and not into words. In marriage, anger is put into words and not into action. By putting love into action, you will be cutting off the power supply of the troublemakers in the marriage.

Under no circumstances should married couples discuss any problems in their marriage with anybody else. The person you are going to discuss the problem with is not part of the problem. Therefore, he or she cannot be part of the solution. Going to marriage counsellors should always be the last option. That is, if it is becoming impossible for the two of you to resolve your marital problems.

Sitting down as a married couple to find ways of repairing the damage in the marriage is far better than seeking external help. Nevertheless, choosing a good counsellor will ultimately lead to a good solution and a happy marriage for both of you.

There are very good and experienced counsellors who can be of great help in dealing with very difficult marriage problems. A good marriage counsellor is a good asset to every sinking marriage. A good marriage counsellor is one that helps in the diagnosis of the actual problems in the marriage. A good marriage counsellor guides his clients in identifying the exact problem in the marriage.

A married counsellor is better than an unmarried counsellor in dealing with practical issues in marriages. To be able to deal with practical issues in marriage, couples should seek help from experienced counsellors. Married counsellors are better equipped in dealing with marital problems than unmarried counsellors are.

Why seek help from a married counsellor? The reason is simple; he or she might have experienced similar problems to the ones you may be going through in your marriage. By sharing his or her experience with you, will get you a head start in resolving your problems, although this may not always the case.

Marriage problems are practical and they need practical solutions and not theoretical solutions. To apply theoretical solutions to a marriage going through difficulties is like trying to fill a bucket of water with a basket. Marital problems can best be solved by husband and wife and never with a third party.

Seeking external solutions is never the best option but can be the last resort when every other avenue is exhausted. The Bible should play a central role in resolving Christian marriage problems because the Bible is the final authoritative word of God on marriage. Therefore, married Christians should seek counsel from a qualified Christian counsellor, never from the secular world.

Why should Christians not seek help from the secular world? Again, the reason is simple. Do you think a counsellor who is not a Christian can pray with you before the session begins? Do you think such a counsellor will seek God's guidance in resolving your problems? Do you think such a counsellor would use the Scriptures as a basis in guiding you to a godly solution?

Counselling must be both spiritual and physical. Spiritual in this context means working with the Holy Spirit to bring healing and restoration to the marriage. When love burns itself out in marriage, it causes a lot pain that can lead to anxiety and stress. Seeking counselling from the secular world should be the last resort, only used where there are no qualified Christian counsellors available.

However, any advice given you should be committed to the LORD in prayer because God is able to use the advice of the unbelieving counsellor to resolve marriage problems. The solutions to someone else's marriage problems may not be an answer to your marital problems. They should only be treated as a guiding principle and not as an accepted rule. This is because we all differ in the way we approach issues in life.

Now let me show you an excellent way. That way is Jesus. This can be found in John 14:6; when

Jesus Christ told Thomas, "I am the way and the truth and the life." The prophet Isaiah sums this up beautifully when he said this about Jesus. He is the "Wonderful Counsellor" (Isaiah 9:6d).

If Jesus Christ is the wonderful counsellor, why seek counselling from elsewhere? If we arm ourselves with these two Scriptural verses, our marriage will hold fast and will never fail if we depend upon the wonderful counsellor. By seeking the LORD'S counsel, He will speak to you through the Holy Spirit.

Before you take your marriage problems outside the marital home for help, ask yourself these questions. Is this person someone I can trust? Can I trust this person to keep the discussions away from other people's itching ears? Two things to take note of before seeking advice: can the person you are seeking advice from be trusted? Can he help to resolve your marriage problems and restore happiness to your marriage?

There is the possibility that he or she may succeed in destroying your marriage because of bad advice. It is the responsibility of every married couple to filter through any advice given. This ensures such advice does not inflame the already volatile situation. Watch out, what Satan does not want you to know is that you are able, with the Holy Spirit, to resolve your marital problem.

Watch out, there are people within the family and outside the family who are envious of your marriage and are waiting to pour cold water on your marriage if you ever come to them for advice. Therefore, it is preferable that marriage problems be resolved between the husband and wife. This does not mean you cannot seek external help if you both feel it is the only way to resolve the problems in the marriage.

Sometimes seeking help can lead to resolving the problems you are going through. However, in seeking external help the following factors must be taken into consideration. The maturity of those you are seeking help from is very important. They must be married, have experience in marriage, and above all, they must be matured Christian couple.

This advice was given by grandmother when we came to the age of marriage. She said, "When there is a problem in your marriage wake up at 05:00. And in the quietness of the morning call your husband or wife before God and discuss the problem." Before you start talking, place a Holy Bible between the two of you. The Bible is to remind you of the presence of the Holy Spirit in your midst.

God will be listening to the two of you. Therefore, each of you must speak the truth before God and not lie to each other, for it is written, "You must not lie." Do not lie to each other because it creates mistrust between spouses. It is the first sign of trouble in marriage. You must know you are in the presence of the God and any lie will not help with the discussion. Speak nothing but the truth to each other. Speaking the truth brings out the love and affection we have for our spouse.

These words of King Solomon are worth memorising. "The LORD detests lying lips, but he delights in men who are truthful. (Proverbs 12:22). Married life is all about truthfulness, where there is truth, trust reigns supreme in the marriage. Truth is what makes marriage so beautiful and admirable.

Nothing must be withheld from each other. Truth and transparency must be the keywords. Both of you must trust each other to come clean. In between the discussion, you can stop to pray if you both notice the talk will end in stalemate, and then resume the discussion under the guidance of the Holy Spirit.

God who instituted marriage will guide both of you to a peaceful solution. God can lead us in resolving the problems if we tell the truth. If we withhold vital information from each other, God will not help us. Confessing is the keyword that will lead both of you to resolving the problems, which leads to forgiveness.

One of the contributing factors in marriage problems are gossip. King Solomon said that speaking badly about others (gossip) could have a disastrous effect on them. Besides, it betrays the confidence they have in you. Gossip can separate close friends. Gossip does not build bridges; rather it destroys the foundation of marriage bridges.

Gossip in marriage fuels quarrels and destroys relationship. Damage done by gossip can be irreparable because it leaves lasting pain among married couples. This is how grandmother described a person who tries to repair broken fence because of his or her gossip. She said, "It is like a man who takes a pillow filled with cotton on a windy day and empties out the contents. Then he realised he had made a mistake and wants to correct it by gathering the cotton back into the pillow. The task ahead of him will be absolutely impossible because no human can do that."

Let us ask the Lord to help us not to engage in harmful talk about other people's marriage. God wants us to set guard over our mouths so that we will instead speak all the good we know about someone's marriage problems. Christians should not turn their mouth into a breeding ground for gossip, rather let what comes out of your mouth be a blessing to those who need blessing in their marriage and a healing for those who need healing in their marriage.

A restoration for those whose marriages are going through difficulties and need restoration, and comfort for those who need to be comforted because of their marriage problems. An uncontrolled tongue raises question as to whether a person is a child of God. The tongue is the most dangerous weapon in the world, so do not discourse your marriage problems with people who will turn out to be gossipers. Gossipers are troublemakers who will spread your marriage problems.

The tongue is a storm in the sea. It is more dangerous than a charging bull. In many ways, we all stumble. Similarly, the tongue can spread suspicion, therefore be very mindful of what you say about your spouse to others. Nevertheless, when the Lord controls our tongue, its word will smooth and heal marriages that are going through difficulties.

Watch out for our tongue: it reveals what we truly are. When a fire finishes burning through the material it feeds on, it goes out. Similarly, when gossip reaches the ear of someone who will not repeat it, it dies. Gossip, like other sins, is like "tasty trifles", (Proverbs 26:22). We like to hear it as it "tastes" good.

Gossip is rooted in our need to feel good about ourselves. As we bring others down, we gain the illusion that we are moving upward. That is why spreading gossip about someone's marriage problems is so difficult to resist. Nevertheless, be sure your tongue will one day expose your hypocrisy and everybody will know whether you walk with Christ or the devil.

It takes prayer and God's grace to bring us to the point where we refuse to pass it on or even hear it even under the guise of personal concern or a request to pray for a marriage in trouble. The safe rule is to meditate on the word of God, instead of gossiping. Gossip will only make friends drift apart instead of uniting them.

We must ask God for the wisdom to know when to speak, what to speak about other's marriage problems, and when simply to keep our mouth shut when gossip rears its ugly head. For "In the multitudes of words sin is not lacking, but he who restrains his lips is wise." (Proverbs 10:19).

However, if we must speak, let us talk of those things that encourage and move others closer to God, not those things that will discourage and hurt them. "The tongue of the wise promotes health" (Proverbs12:18). The book of Proverbs has a lot to say about gossip: Gossip separates the closest of friend (16:28) and keeps family strife boiling (18:8). It pours fuel on the coals of conflict, feeding the flames of hut and misunderstanding (26:21-22).

We fool ourselves into thinking that those juicy, whispered comments here and there about someone's marriage are harmless. But gossip leaves behind a wide swath of destruction and is never a victimless crime. Destroy gossip by ignoring it. Read Proverbs 26:20-28. If you are filled with the Spirit, you walk moment by moment under the control of the Holy Spirit.

On the other hand, the way we speak about other people's marriage behind their backs clearly indicates your hatred for them. A Spirit-filled Christian who bears the mark of Christ will never gossip about other people's marriage. Besides, as a Christian, we have no good reason to engage in gossip about what goes on in someone's marriage.

The Scripture encourage Christian to desist from gossiping. Those of us that claim to have the imprint of Christ on our life must keep our ears away from gossips, and our tongue from gossip that hurts others. A person who spends his or her entire life in the Church gossiping and yet wants people to believe he or she is a Christian will make others question his or her state of mind.

Your uncontrolled tongue, your attitude and behaviour towards others will put you on the hot spot where others will examine your spiritual radiance. No decent person will take a gossiper very seriously. A Christian gossiper weakens his testimony and his ability to be a good councillor and a good ambassador for Christ.

A person's tongue will always expose his or her hypocrisy. Do not tell people you have been baptised in the Holy Spirit. Instead, tell everyone that you have stopped gossiping. What matters most is: is Jesus real to you? May Jesus be real and may you walk in his presence and in obedience to His Word.

How can a person go to Church, sing and dance to the glory of God, lift his or her hand towards heaven in adoration of God and say, "Praise be to God from whom all blessings flow" then live a life of gossiping that is not consistent with Scripture? The Church is a divine institution in the mist of an evil world. She is in the world but not of the world.

Those who fan the flame of gossip about other people's marriage deliberately design it to inflict maximum pain on the marriage intended to brake-up the marriage. Behind every gossip is a sinister motive, and behind that motive is the spirit of Satan.

5. Marriage Flavours

"Everyone lies to his neighbour; their flattering lips speak with deception." (Psalm 12:2). The folly of a fool is deception." (Proverbs 14:8). Beware of your friends; do not trust your brothers. For every brother is a deceiver, and every friend a slander. Friends deceive friend, and no-one speaks the truth. They have taught their tongue to lie; they weary themselves with sinning. Their tongue is a deadly arrow; it speaks with deceit. With his mouth each speaks cordially to his neighbour, but in his heart he set a trap for him. (Jeremiah 9:4, 5, and 8).

Deception is a devious sickness. It hides the truth and parades a lie in beautiful words. Some people live their lives this way, and it is unfortunate that some Christians behave in this manner. On what basis can we trust a person is telling the truth? Sometimes this can be based on experience.

This reminds me of young couple's marriage I attended. During the ceremony, it so happened that there was only one wedding ring for the ceremony. This is unusual since marriage ceremonies began. Something was not right here and what was not right here is deception. When it came for the marriage vows to be taken, the groom's wedding ring was missing.

The groom deliberately came to the wedding without a wedding ring. His bride knew about it yet she went along with it because she did not want to rock the boat. This is the case of a stubborn fly being buried with the corpse. The groom's reason for coming to the wedding without ring was that he did not want to wear a wedding ring on his finger.

Surely, a groom who does not want to wear a ring on his finger should not be taking a bride as a wife. The wedding ring is the symbol of marriage and it is the only physical evidence that a man or woman is married. In Jeremiah 17:5, the prophet wrote, "Cursed is the one who trust in man,"

Watch out! Just as marriage has different flavours so there are Christians with different kinds of flavours. For example, there are Christians with Bible knowledge flavours, Christians with speaking-in-tongue flavours, and Christians with holy appearance flavour, the list is endless. Therefore, keep your eyes open and watch out for those who parade themselves to be holy men and women of God.

You will never know which of the flavours you are marrying until you end up saying "I do" to the wrong flavour. Do not be deceived by their flavours. Some of these flavours come in a form that appears to make them spiritual. Until you have time to sieve them with the Word of God, only then will you know the truth of their spirituality.

A man looking for a bride will use every flattering word to walk her down the aisle. Then after the wedding, those flattering words suddenly disappear from his heart through the mouth. Flattering words do not make a good marriage. Marriage is not about words, it is about demonstrating practical love and good character.

A marriage that began with a poor foundation during courting will crumble under the slightest storms. It will crumble because there were cracks during courting days. A crack they may have deliberately turned a blind eye to, hoping things will work out naturally during marriage.

Whatever we fail to put right during courtship will turn out to be the Weakness in the marriage. If there are problems during courting, it is imperative that you put wedding plans on hold until the issues are resolved. If problems are resolved by, burying them then be sure certain chains of events will resurrect the problem you thought had been hidden.

Most couples are blinded during courting. They are blinded by love and the joy of knowing that they are getting married. They become blind because they do not want to rock the courting boat, so they create the impression all is well and perfect. This kind of impression is wrong and may create problems later in the marriage.

However, what you see here is a picture of an imperfect man who within a twinkle of an eye has suddenly become perfect in order to win the woman of his dreams. Deception is a common practice among some couples planning to get married. They seem so much in a hurry to get married that they would say yes when they should be saying no. Waiting is very important for those who are in a courting relationship.

I have had the opportunity of talking to newly married couples who have regretted marrying their husband or wife. When asked why, most of them said, "This is not the real person I married. I did not see this character during courting." Deception is the appropriate answer. People who are in hurry are more likely to be deceived than those who are willing to wait on God.

The problem here is that when people are in love they fail to check for character references. What interests them in the curriculum vitae is the word LOVE. However, the love you see in the C.V. is deceptive love. It has the wrong flavour, it is weightless and the wind will blow it away when he or she has had enough of you.

Man cannot attain perfection because the first man God created destroyed what would have made us complete. If we see ourselves as Christians who must be perfect in all areas, then we cannot admit that we have weaknesses. This makes us vulnerable, because a man who does not know his weaknesses is really in trouble.

Knowing ourselves realistically is very important, although it is impossible to know everything about the person you are going to marry. This is the reason why it is necessary we train ourselves in waiting on God. Those who are able to wait on God will receive the best from Him.

It is worth not rushing into marriage until you have studied carefully the character reference. Read the C.V. repeatedly and do not be fooled by religious flavours. Only God knows who a Christian is. Most people lie on their C.V. to get what they want. Some people have preconceived ideas of what they are looking for in a C.V.

Keeping the other person waiting can bring out the lies in the C.V. Waiting can provoke issues that can resurrect hidden things you do not know about the person you are going to marry. Some Christians have a very bad character and a temper. You will never know until it is too late.

This reminds me of Silvia, Christian sister from Hon Kong. Her fiancé had kept her waiting so long because the young man had certain doubt about the relationship. When I asked the young man, why he had put the wedding plans on hold? This is what he said, "Anytime the issue of the wedding comes to my mind I become afraid, when I start to pray concerning the coming wedding I become afraid, when I am with her, I become afraid, the more I pray for her and the coming wedding the more I become afraid."

Against this, the Christian sister came to my office and said; "I can no longer wait for Paulo" This is a typical utterance of a Christian who has lost patience with God and man. In many ways we all fall victim of this kind of behaviour. Frustration, impatience, self-centeredness and egoism are the trademark of burnout Christian.

As Christians, are we suppose to wait on God or wait on man? This is where Sister Silvia missed the point. The Scriptures clearly state that we are to wait on God and not man. Isaiah 30:18 clearly states that "Blessed are all who wait for the LORD." Christians who cannot wait on God usually have "Plan B" and the "plan B" will only lead them to trust in man. Plan B in this context simply refers to what you intend to do if God does not answer your prayers.

Sorry, when it comes to waiting on God there is only Plan A and no plan B, therefore we have to until the answer comes. When Silvia became impatience with God and her fiancé, she walked away and married a young man from a different faith. On this note, I will advise Christians who want to know God and His dealing with the human race should study the Old Testament.

Being honest and open during courting is very important. There is no good reason to hide anything from each other; if you do, you may live to regret it later in the marriage if the other person finds out from other sources. Being honest is the first indication that this person can be trusted in a relationship.

Being honest and open is a way of providing a safety net around your marriage. It helps to safeguard against our past life which others know about, but which we want to hide from the other person during courting. Be very careful, for an old scare that suddenly turns into an open wound can be very painful.

It is dangerous and we must resist the temptation to hold back. There is nothing to be gained by trying to slide a lid on what is already in the public domain and pretend it never happened. Love is about trust. Trust that in spite of all my weakness, my failings and my shortcoming I can depend on this person.

Marriage is a union of two imperfect people who have decided to live together. Therefore, neither of them should expect perfection from the other. There is no perfect marriage. God knows we cannot be perfect living in this body. Therefore, we should not create the impression that we are perfect.

During the first year of marriage, two people from different family experiences and value systems begin to discover one another. Differences surface in areas such as finances, sexuality, use of time and habits. Each difference affords an opportunity for conflict, and hopefully growth.

Marriage is about two people from different backgrounds, different cultural backgrounds, different beliefs, different home training, different educational backgrounds with different taste and choices, different appearances and different environments. Some because of good home training are very neat and tidy.

Whilst some are very dirty. You may never know how dirty a man or woman is until you both settle down under the same roof. This can create serious problems if care is not taken. In addition, even some may not have been brought up and trained by their biological parents. Others too may have grown up in foster homes while some grew up in single parent homes.

Some are fast eaters whilst others are slow eaters. Moreover, some even have very bad table manners. In some marriages, you will find the woman to be more talkative whilst the man sits with his tongue glued to his mouth. You may find the man too dull and boring whilst the woman is very active, lively, lovely, jolly and charming.

Again you may find the woman to be very friendly and outgoing whilst the man may be unapproachable. A married woman who finds herself with this kind of husband will need the grace of God to make people welcome in their home. What will you do in situations like these?

This is a scenario where the wife did not see these habits during the courtship. With hindsight, it seems the husband suddenly became what he was not by suppressing his bad manners in order to win the woman. It is obvious something was not right, yet the fiancée could not spot it until after the wedding.

Here the man faked his C.V. by garnishing it to make it appear genuine. On the other hand, the woman did not take time to study the character reference before her. Studying the character reference of the man or woman you want to marry is very important before you commit yourself to a marriage that will turn out to have nothing but problems.

This man failed to realise that bad habits and bad manners we grew up with cannot be suppressed forever. Eventually they will show up. Therefore, it is better for your future wife or husband to know all the things you want to hide. Tell the truth because what you are not cannot be hidden forever; it will eventually come out one day.

Some people have a high sexual drive, whilst others have low sexual drive. Our sexual life differs from each other and if care is not taken, it could create problems later in the marriage. We face this complex situation in marriage. We need patience in understanding each other.

I know of a pastor whose wife wore two pairs of trousers to bed because of the husband's high sexual drive. This woman found herself with a husband who demanded sex every night. Whilst she preferred it fortnightly, the wife's behaviour towards the husband's sexual demands caused infidelity in the marriage.

This woman did not understand the complexity of sexual variation in marriage. Would you say this woman is selfish? The consequences of these kinds of attitude toward a husband who demands sex every day can create unfaithfulness in marriage if care is not taken and we have to be prepared for it.

The Apostle Paul in his letter to the Corinthians reaffirmed mutual sexual fulfilment in marriage, "The husband should give his wife her conjugal rights, and likewise the wife to her husband." (1 Corinthians 7:3). It is very important for married couples to understand each other's sexual demands and know how to meet those demands in order to avoid temptation.

There are various ways married couples can satisfy each other's sexual demands without having full sexual intercourse. Sex is one thing in marriage that should not be denied each other. A woman is free to deny her husband his dinner, but not his sexual demands. Sex binds married couples together in love and in unity. In sex, a man and his wife become one flesh.

Sex is good for the body because it takes away stress and relaxes the muscles. It is also a source of healing for married couples. Married couples should not deny each other this wonderful gift from God, except in sickness or health problems. Enjoy sex ONLY with your wife or husband.

What will a woman who finds herself with a husband who demands sex every day do? Alternatively, what about the husband who finds himself with a wife who demands sex every night? In situations like these, understanding each other's feelings is very important in order to prevent temptation.

Sex is the most important part of every marriage. Sex is the only thing that unites married couples. Sex brings happiness in a marriage. Sex can keep trouble out of marriage if it is well enjoyed and satisfying. Take sex out of marriage and there is no marriage. Sex is what joins a woman to her husband or a man to his wife. Sex is the binding cord in marriage. Sex is like a light that illuminates and brightens marriage. It is like fuel that powers an engine.

Issues concerning sexual demands should be resolved amicably. Sex is one thing that binds husband and wife together; it brings happiness to the home. Do not ignore issues concerning sexual demands. Issues concerning sexual problems should be treated with urgency to avoid infidelity in the marriage. If not resolved it can cause bedtime quarrels that can lead to so many troubles in the marriage. Sex makes marriage enjoyable with only the person to whom you are married.

When problems about sex come up in the marriage, they should be resolved between the couple. Under no condition should married couples take their sexual problems outside to be resolved by others. Sexual problems in marriage should not go beyond the marital home. A woman should not discuss sexual problems in her marriage with friends.

The only person you can discuss such problems with is your mother. Besides there are numerous books available in bookshops which married couples could study together. Pre-marital sex is never a solution to find out if your suitor is the right sexual partner for you because it can lead to disappointments, besides it is a sin against God. In marriage, it is love that comes first and not sex although sex binds and seals the marriage.

In looking for a suitor, we must make sure we have the right person because the Mr Right you have chosen to live the rest of your life with may not be a perfect man or woman. Mr Right or Miss Right refers to the man or woman you have chosen to live with. The big question is how long have you known this man or woman that you are convinced he is good enough for you.

Whatever you saw in a woman that made you choose her above other women should make you love her for the rest of your life. Whatever you saw in a woman that caught your attention and drew both of you together like magnets must forever remain the same. Whatever you saw in a woman that attracted you to her should remain the binding cord that holds the two of you together as husband and wife for the rest of your lives.

Whatever brought married couples together should keep them to together forever. Whatever attracted you to the woman you once saw as the most beautiful woman must forever remain in your heart and mind for the rest of your life. It must never fade. Marriage is falling in love repeatedly with the same person you have chosen as your wife or husband.

Marriage that grows in the soil of love and submission will blossom and not wither. True love blossoms and does not fade. When a marriage begins to wither, it shows the two most important nutrients in the marriage are lacking. The two most important things in every marriage are love and submission.

6. Building a False Image

"Kings take pleasure in honest lips; they value a man who speaks the truth." (Proverbs 16:13).

"Love me and tell me the truth" is what grandmother told us when we started introducing our fiancées to her. Can you love your fiancée and tell her the truth of who you really are? Truth is one of the most important foundation pillars in marriage.

Where there is truth, there is trust in a marriage. They are birds of the same feather, which flock together. People who fall in love with an image will end up building their marriage on sandy soil. This is the reason why, when marriage storms begin to blow the marriage would have nothing to hold onto.

Imaging is a method of relating to someone dearest to you, which does not show love. Imaging has nothing to do with love; rather it is a crafty way of being dishonest with someone you claim to love. A dishonest person will always put up a false image. Be very careful of image-builders because you will never know their true character.

A young man in love will create a false image because he is afraid his fiancée will not like who he really is. This may be the reason why some people build false images. We must agree that sometimes it is much harder to be honest in a relationship. Can we say emphatically we are always honest with our spouse?

Because sometimes we hold back for reasons known only to ourselves. Jack V. Rozell in his book 'Christian counselling' wrote the following about building an image: "A young man spends money during courtship, even though he does not feel he can afford to spend it. He does so because he wants to project a good image of himself.

When the pair wakes up after the ceremony, his new wife discovers that, he does no have the inexhaustible bank account that he seemed to have during the courting. He fell into the error of building an inaccurate image. People fall in love with images rather than people. Marriage is often the process of finding out who one really said, "I do" to.

What this young man did is not new to most of us. He wanted his in-laws to know their daughter would be financially secure and thereby keep their respect. This cheap publicity will lead to a dead end. Be advised not to go down that road. Good in-laws are more concerned about the happiness of their daughter than what money can buy.

Marriage is about being open and sincere with each other. During courtship, you must love the other person enough to tell her the truth. A decent woman will prefer a man of integrity than a man who is wealthy or appears to be wealthy. Although wealth will give the best things in marriage, yet it is never the reason for happiness in marriage.

Do not shower each other with expensive gifts that you know your bank account cannot sustain. The problem with this kind of imaging is that it will eventually be exposed, not by anybody but your bank account. To build your marriage foundation on deception is bad for marriage.

It is bad to pretend you can sustain expensive gifts, when your conscience and bank balance are telling you otherwise. It is bad to raise the hopes of your fiancé by making her believe that she is marrying a man from an upper class background or middle-class. If she finds out after the honeymoon that you are not what you made her believe you are, you will lose her trust and this could cause problems in the marriage.

This is foolish pride and deceptive showing-off. When your bride and in-laws find out who you really are, you will lose their respect. It is imperative the person receiving the expensive gifts should summon some courage and ask the following questions. Does he look like someone who can afford these gifts? Will the gifts be sustainable during the marriage? Are the gifts a mere show-off? Are the gifts meant to impress me?

The receiver must be able to ask some intriguing questions. It is only when you summon the courage to ask such questions can you fully asses the genuineness of your fiancé. When asking such questions watch the reaction of your fiancé, also take a good look at his or her facial expression, and then listen to how he or she answers your questions.

Let us be honest, when it comes to receiving gifts some women have an unquenchable thirst. Moreover, they use their unquenchable thirst to demand diamonds or solid gold rings on their hand before they even consider marriage. You would be well advised to walk away from a burden you cannot carry.

They choose the type of wedding, and plan everything from the beginning to the end. They do not even care if the man can afford the extravagant wedding they are planning. Their attitude goes beyond the extreme and that extreme could be the Achilles heel in the marriage. We must learn to be content with what we have.

We must also ask ourselves this question: Can we afford this type of wedding? Can we afford to go abroad for the honeymoon? You both need to sit down and talk this over carefully. Jesus said something in Luke that is worth mentioning. He said, "Suppose one of you wants to build a tower. Will he not first sit down and estimate the cost to see if he has enough money to complete it?" (Luke 14:28). The Word of God is the only guide to the Christian.

However, those who want display a spectacular wedding and have their guest gasping for breath will have a lot of thinking to do after the wedding. Of what use will it be after an impressive wedding only to find out after there is a mounting debt waiting for you? A woman demanding this kind of wedding should ask herself what happens when the music stops. I think women who demand this kind of wedding can bring joy to marriage by looking into the future.

Every man must resist the temptation of taking a bank loan to finance his wedding. It is unethical to start married life with creditors on your heels. It is better to start a married life with only a few things, than to start a marriage with all the good things of life. The most important thing in marriage is love and not good things.

What shall it profit a man if he finances his wedding on a bank loan? Is there anything to be gained by furnishing your matrimonial home with all the good things the world offers? A man who follows this path will go to bed thinking of how to keep debt collectors from infringing on his marriage.

Taking a loan to finance your wedding is like placing a time bomb in your home with the clock ticking. "Cut your coat according to your size." This proverb can be a good advice to help young courting couples who want to empty their purse to impress their fiancé.

Courting is when prospective couples can both sample each other. Therefore, do not leave any stone unturned because you are about to make a crucial decision that will affect you and the person you are intending to spend the rest of your life with. Some people try to hide their true character during courtship by suppressing their bad habits for fear of being ditched.

You will never know the true temper of the person you are marrying until after the honeymoon. The breeding ground for deception is when couples are courting. This is the time when some people lie about who they really are.

In addition, everyone seems to be able to control his or her temper, anger and fits of rage. However if you keep your nose to the ground you will smell a rat. Grandmother once said, "Character is like a smoke, you cannot hide it." This brings back the memory of a young West African woman called Ruby.

One day she came to my office with a young man and introduced him as her fiancé. He was handsome, tall and muscularly built. The next day she came to see me without the young man, and asked me what I thought of her fiancé. I said, "What a charming young man you have." However, whether this man would make a future good husband I cannot tell, because a man's good looks and personality alone are not enough to make a good husband.

I told her to take a very cautious approach before committing herself to the young man and not to be fooled by his good looks. Grandmother once said, "I would be happier with an ugly husband who will keep my blood pressure normal than a handsome husband who will raise my blood pressure very high because he cannot keep his eyes off women."

For some unknown reasons she felt very uncomfortable when the date of the wedding was fixed. When asked why she felt very uncomfortable she said, "Fear, fear and nothing but fear makes me keep changing the wedding date." Again, she said, "Something within me kept telling me to put off the date." She said worrying thoughts kept coming to her mind.

When the date was changed from March to November she saw the ugly side of her fiancé, the dormant temper the fiancé had been trying to suppress finally snapped. This made the young woman consider carefully the thoughts that kept coming to her mind. In her own words she said, "I am beginning to think God is trying to speak to me."

As a result, the young woman changed the wedding date for the second time, giving her ample time to look out for things she might have overlooked. Then she began to ask herself why her suitor was trying to rush through the wedding. Delay, it is said, can expose the ugly character in a person.

She was right in delaying the wedding. The fiancé was nothing but tyrant and dominating man who would not on take other's opinion. When the young man finally realised his fiancé knew who he really was he quickly changed from Mr Bad Character to Mr Good Character. He suddenly became like an instant tea.

He started showcring his fiancé with expensive gifts. The gifts were meant to make-up for his bad attitude. He kept buying gift after gifts so that this young woman thought this young man must be from a middle-class background. Therefore, it was worth giving him a second chance. By this, she blindly stumbled into a marriage that would turn out to be nothing but pain. She signed her divorce papers before even the wedding began.

Instead of this young woman fasting and praying to seek God's counsel, she blindly fell for his charm. She later said, "Things had reached such an advanced stage that I could not cancel the wedding and walk out on him. I was hoping that once we got married he might change." Such thoughts are the thoughts of a child who thinks it is possible for an empty sack to stand upright.

They got married in a colourful wedding, but five months after the wedding the marriage was over. If this young woman had given a careful thought to the doubt she had, she would not been in muddy waters. Sometimes the thoughts we try to ignore are the very thoughts that will prevent us from getting into muddy waters.

Why some Christians cannot see the warning signs is what baffles me. In Jeremiah 33:3 the prophet wrote, "Call to me and I will answer you and tell great and unsearchable things you do not know." Only God knows the heart and mind of everyone, therefore no one can deceive Him. If you call on Him, He will reveal the nature of the heart and the state of the mind of your fiancé to you.

During courtship, we see the very best of each other, but we never see the bad side of each other. The reason is simple: only the best of me must be seen by the person I want to marry. Only what is good in me must be seen by the person I am getting married to. This is the way deception works.

Bach and Wyde said in one of their books that most marriages get into trouble from the very first time people meet because they engage in behaviour called "imaging." When a person acts his best, shows his best side—he is building an image.

It is always good for couples who are preparing to get married to know each other's weaknesses and bad habits so that they can work towards changing them. You have nothing to gain by hiding your bad habits and attitudes. Rather you stand to gain if you allow him or her to know who you really are.

This is the reason why couples should not rush into marriage until they are sure their fiancé is a person who can control his or her temper. **A bad temperament is a sickness that can destroy a happy marriage.** The only medicine for bad temperament is self-control. Pray that God will take away from you the bad temperament and grant you self-control.

7. Disappointments

"Do not be yoked together with unbelievers. For what do righteousness and wickedness have in common? Or what fellowship can light have with darkness? What harmony is there between Christ and Belia? What does a believer have in common with an unbeliever? What agreement is there between the temple of God and idols? For we are the temple of the living God. As God has said: "I will live with them and walk among them, and I will be their God, and they will be my people." (2 Corinthian 6:14-18).

The value of marriage does not lie in wealth or material things. How long a marriage survives does not depend on what one can provide for his or her spouse. The value of marriage does not depend on academic excellence. Rather love is what makes marriage valuable, not wealth.

This means loving your wife as yourself, **seeking your wife's highest interest** and seeing your wife as the best woman who has come into your life. Marriage is all about love and nothing else. How long marriage lasts depends on the spouses' affection towards each other. Do you show much affection to your wife? Do you have a great affection for your wife? Do you respect your wife? In addition, how affectionate are you towards your wife?

Can your wife complement your affection? The object of marriage is not receiving but loving. The aim of seeking a wife is not for sex but rather being affectionate towards her. The object of marriage is arousing your wife's attention to your presence in a way that will make your wife feel your love.

Why are so many Christian marriages breaking down? The reasons could be many. The answer to this question lies in what grandmother once said, **"Marriages break down because of the reasons for which we marry".** Against this, it will be worthwhile to ponder over the reasons why you want to get married.

We all go into marriage with a shopping list in our hand. Just as we walk around the supermarket picking and choosing the items on our shopping list, so it is with marriage in the eyes of some people. Only the best is good enough for them.

When we pick a jam from the shelves, the first thing we do is to read the label to see if we like the ingredients. Similarly, we shop around for a prospective husband or wife with a long list. We choose whoever meets our criteria. Our criteria can sometimes be our blind spot that could lead us to make a wrong choice.

A man shows interest in a woman and because he does not meet her criteria, she rejects him not because he is not worth as a husband, but on her definition of what an ideal husband is. Similarly, if a woman's interest in a man does not meet his requirements, then she is not worthy as a wife.

Marriage today is like a commodity. If you buy a commodity from a shop and you do not like it, the consumer rights laws allow the consumer to take it back for his money within a certain period. Marriage is like that in the eyes of some people. Our reasons for going into a married relationship will determine whether the marriage will hold or break up.

The break up of every marriage lies in the shopping list. Your requirement holds the answer to the success or failure of your marriage. We sit at home, make a shopping list, walk into the supermarket, and pick them up our items. Alternatively, we sit in the comfort of our home and at the touch of a button, we order what we need then it is delivered to our doorstep from the supermarket.

Well, marriage is like that in the eyes of some people. At a touch of a button, an organization can match you with a woman based on the information fed into their system. Organizations both Christians and non-Christians patronise. Whether this system of looking for bride or bridegroom is good I cannot tell. Only those who have passed through this system, if it worked well for them, can speak for the system. So for now let us not be judgemental.

Since the Scripture is silent about where to look for a bride or husband, it is better to keep our drums silent. However, the Scriptures do gives us guidelines on what to look for in a prospective bride or husband. Marriage deals with choosing someone you want to commit the rest of your life to, someone you can love and cherish forever or someone you can say, "This is now bone of my bone and the flesh of my flesh." (Genesis 2:23.)

Have you ever driven a car on a motorway and half way through your journey the car suddenly stops? You open the bonnet of the car engine only to be confronted with complex mechanical components and snaking electrical cables? You become puzzled not knowing what to do.

Moreover, you cannot figure out what to do because you lack the technical knowledge to get the car moving again. You find yourself stranded in the middle of motorway waiting for help to come from where? This is how marriage is. If you find yourself in a married relationship without the basic knowledge of how to get your marriage out of trouble, divorce will be your way out.

We all love to own a car but some drivers do not know how to carry out a basic daily maintenance on the car. Besides, they cannot figure out how to fix simple problems that come with owning a car. Therefore, they are very dependent on the mechanic for simple basic things like topping the engine oil, brake fluid, belt tension and electrolyte level (Battery Water.) Even topping up the radiator water and checking the tyre pressure is a problem for some car owners.

A man who marries without knowing what is really involved in marriage is like a man who before he embarked on a journey, hired a builder to look after his estate. He hired the man without checking his C.V. What the estate owner did not know was that the man he hired was a repairperson not a maintenance man.

When the man returned after some years, he found his estate in a terrible state. He summoned the hired man and asked why he had allowed his estate to deteriorate so badly. The hired man replied,

"Sir, I am only a repair man and not maintenance man. So I was waiting for things to go wrong before I did the repair work."

Many married couples behave like the hired man. They do not know how to maintain their marriage. They wait until problems in the marriage deteriorate badly before they try to repair the damage done. They could have prevented this if they had tried to resolve the problem at the beginning rather than waiting until things got out of hand.

Marriage is about maintenance and not repairs. You do not have to wait until things get out of hand before you try to fix the problem. We need to resolve the problem as soon as we see signs of trouble, rather than waiting until the problems get out of control. The safest rule is to detect, control and stop it.

Marriage maintenance is what is needed in marriage and not the repair method. To wait until the problems in your marriage get out of control should be avoided by married couples. The repair method of fixing problems in marriage should never be an option for married couples.

There are two type of problem solving in every marriage. The first is Marriage Maintenance and the second is Repairs Work. The first option deals with identifying early warning problems in the marriage and dealing with it quickly. The second option deals with a wait-and see attitude. A spouse in this group will do nothing but hope the problems will resolve themselves.

Spouses who want problems to resolve themselves are like an idle man who spends time doing nothing about his or her situation. Word of thought, an idle man is the devil's workshop. Spouses who go for the repair option do not know what marriage is all about. The only thing they know about marriage is how to get out of it when the going gets tough.

There are no get out clauses enshrined in the marriage vows allowing the husband or the wife to walk out of the marriage. This is something couples have to study very carefully before taking the vows. Vows we make are not to be broken because we make the vow before God who instituted the marriage institution.

The story of Lydia is one of the reasons why this book was written. There are many lessons for everyone to learn. Lydia was a very brilliant lawyer and a state's attorney. Her story is worth reading so that we do not repeat her mistakes. Grandmother once said, "Sometimes when we feel we have made the right choice it turns out to be the wrong choice."

The mistake of this young Christian lawyer should serve as a lesson for us. Reading her story does not give you the opportunity to judge her bad decision. You too may have gone down the same road if you were caught in the same trap or found yourself in a similar situation.

Sometimes God cannot give us what we want because we do not know what the future holds. Only God knows the future and what the future holds for us. When God stops us from having what we want, it is for our own good. However, those who find it difficult to accept what God has chosen for them and want to hold on to what they think is best for them will end in muddy waters.

Lydia, a young Christian lawyer, made the biggest mistake of her life, and consequently paid the ultimate price. Grandfather once told me, "Nobody comes to God and walks away disappointed as long as he or she walks in obedience to His word." Walking in obedience to the Word of God is a choice we all have to make.

She met a handsome young man while they were both in secondary school. From there they both went on to university to study Law. After graduating, he set up his own law firm. When the business started expanding, he employed a beautiful young woman as his legal secretary. The employment of this young woman would later become a thorn in Lydia's marriage.

It was during Lydia's first year in the university that she gave her life to Christ. She fought off strong temptations from both her boyfriend and close friends to give up her newfound faith in Jesus Christ. She was not the type of Christian who could easily be persuaded to give up Christ for the world.

Especially knowing what the Lord had done for her. She weighed the options of going back to the world and holding on to her faith in Christ. Then she decided the benefit of holding on to her faith far outweighed what she would benefit from the world. She once remarked that, "My Salvation is non-negotiable and it will never ever come up for negotiation."

Therefore, she kept her faith in the Lord but kept praying for her boyfriend that the Lord would save him just as He had saved her. She kept her faith on one hand and on the other hand kept her boyfriend. Little did she know this arrangement would one day destroy her happiness.

Although she kept her boyfriend there was nothing else that indicates their friendship was immoral. She kept the boyfriend because she did not want to lose him. It is difficult to let go of what we hold dearest to our heart. She had invested eleven years of her life with the boyfriend. Therefore, he was worth holding on to.

Lydia loved this young man very much and looked forward to their engagement and marriage. It is everyone's dream and desire to marry the person of his or her choice. However, in making that choice we must make sure it is the will of God. Against all spiritual advice and revelations, Lydia went ahead and married her unbelieving childhood boyfriend.

Her reason for marrying her unbelieving boyfriend was that she would be able to convert her fiancé after their marriage to the Christian faith. The question we should be asking Lydia is what made her think she could convert her boyfriend after marriage? Word of caution, if you cannot convert the childhood sweetheart during courtship, then do not even think you can do so after you are married.

Lydia gambled with fate and paid a high price. She made the fatal mistake of crossing the Rubicon to marry an unbelieving boyfriend. She willingly ran into a trap set by the devil, by making a costly decision that was totally opposed to God. Here the Scripture is very clear concerning such marriages.

In 2 Corinthians, 6:14-18, Paul spells out the dangers involved in a union between believers and unbelievers. The problem some Christians faces in marriage are due to disobedience. It is said that God has no problem with unbelievers, the problem God has is with Christians. Some Christians are nothing but trouble for God.

Lydia disobeyed the word of God concerning marriages between believers and unbelievers. She broke the commandment of God to enable her to marry her boyfriend. Everybody is free to marry whomever he or she likes. However, what we should bear in mind is what happens when the music stops.

Lydia underestimated the power of Satan by thinking she could convert her fiancé by breaking God's commandments to marry the man she loved. By doing so, she played into the waiting hands of the devil and she only has herself to blame. If you deliberately drink a poison you will die. However, if you drink a poison without knowing the water or food has been poisoned, God may save you from death.

It is not easy to let go what we have invested so much in; this is the problem with so many people. As far as Lydia was concerned, she had invested so much love and attention in this man. However, years of investment are not worth breaking God's commandment for the sake of earthly happiness.

She married her boyfriend for his good looks, personality, his social standing, and success in business. This package blinded Lydia. Many Christian women have gone down the same road. She behaved like a woman with a shopping list. The problem with Lydia's marriage was that they were separated by a distance of about two hundred kilometres.

As a result, they hardly saw each other. The nature of their work dictated their busy schedules. This kept them apart for a long time. Lydia's husband was a very prominent lawyer and was constantly on the move. Thus taking his secretary on business trips, a breeding ground for temptations where the lust of the flesh holds the trump card. This man put himself in the firing line of temptation.

On the other hand, she was a state's attorney with a busy schedule. She hardly had time for herself. Their only form of contact was by telephone. The many visits she made to her matrimonial home were fruitless, because her husband was always on business trips with the secretary.

This scenario was a constant cycle that engulfs the unholy marriage. The question we must ask is; why do some Christians fail to see early warning signs from God? Despite her knowledge of the Scriptures, she failed to see the early warning signs. As a result, it cost her joy, her happiness and finally her marriage.

In many ways some of us are like that, when it comes to making decisions that will affect the rest of our lives. We set our heart on our desire then shut everyone out. We shut others out because of our selfish motives, for fear of having our choice and decisions influenced by those close to us. What we forget is that God would not come down and tell us whom to marry and whom not to marry. He may sometimes use people close to us.

By the time Lydia asked the Church to intercede on her behalf, it was too late. Her husband married his young, attractive secretary. The question we should be asking Lydia is how she got herself into this mess. Like Samson, she stumbled into a doomed relationship that cost her everything she stood for. In the end, she lost everything in the divorce case.

Did she not see it coming? On the other hand, did she think nothing like that would ever happen to her? This young woman was so full of confidence in the man she married. She thought God would protect her marriage. Yes, God protects His children's marriages, but there are conditions to be met before He will protect your marriage. The condition is acceptance of His will for you.

What actually went wrong? Who is to blame in the breakdown of the marriage? The husband or the young attractive secretary who knew her boss was a married man? Is Lydia part of the problem? If the answer is yes, then what role did she play? In our attempt to answer these questions, we must not condemn her.

Lydia's music stopped the day she married the unbelieving man. So what is left for her? Is there any hope left for her? Is divorce the only option left for her? Should she call it the end of her marriage and walk out? Can a Christian be in a bigamous marriage? Should she divorce and remarry? Can she remarry whilst her husband is still alive?

What lesson can be learned from this young woman's story? What can we do to avoid being caught in the same storm? It is sad to say that so many Christians have walked down this path and continue to do so. Our desire to choose what we want is what has spelt disaster in so many Christian marriages.

Let me sound a warning here, we must not blame the devil for some of the problems we encounter in our lives. The Scripture is very clear about this. When we refuse to listen to God and walk away from His plan, He will punish as He sees fit by bringing all sorts of problems into our life. He does this to bring us in line with His will for us.

Disobedience to God does not go without punishment from Him. His punishment is always with love and not anger. After punishing, He restores the erring child so that the enemy becomes ashamed. On the other hand, where there is no restoration after punishment then it is from the devil because he only seeks to destroy and not to restore.

However, if it is from God and there is no restoration then the erring child is refusing to repent. Restoration only comes after repentance. Christians who think they are immune to trouble had better search the Scriptures. The Scripture will expose their over-confidence when they read about men who walked with God, talked with Him, and yet faced trials and difficulties.

The problem with marriage is that when two people make up their mind to get married that is it. Nothing will change their mind until they are confronted with divorce. It is only then that they see their folly. However, for the Christian, the ultimate choice and decision is not in our hands, although God in His infinite Love has granted every person free will to choose.

Nevertheless, our choices and decisions when it comes to marriage are often based on the physical instead of the Spiritual. Our judgements are based on what we see outside, rather than what is inside a person. The problem with some people is that they know where they come from but they do not know where they are going. Marriage is like that with some people.

We know the home we come from, but sometimes we are not well acquainted with the home we are marrying into and we will never know until we are caught between the devil and hell's fire. Knowing the family you are marrying into is very important in marriage. It helps us make very important assessments of our spouse.

Some people are married to family rather than marrying the real person. They marry their spouse because of the family he or she comes from instead of the real person. The status of family should never be the reason we marry. We do not marry a family; rather we marry from a family.

Character, love and submission should be the overriding factors in marriage instead of the status of the family. What we should know is that in marriage it is the man or woman you are marrying and not the family. In marriage, we marry a person from his or her family to start a new family. You may know the man you are marrying but you may not know the REAL man.

The REAL person we will never know until we wake up after the wedding. Then we might have wished we had not said, "I do". Let us marry the real person. The REAL person is who the man really is. Character, behaviour attitude and above all faith in God must play a crucial role in the real man. Faith, in this context, refers to a person who is constantly in touch with God.

Genesis 3:10-11 tells us that Lot made a choice based on what he saw with his eyes. The Bible tells us that, "He lifted his eyes and saw all the plain of Jordan, that it was well watered everywhere. Then he chose for himself all the plain of Jordan." Lot saw the physical Jordan and not the REAL Jordan.

What Lot did not know was that the plain of Jordan, with its rich soil and good water supply that looked good in his sight, was polluted with wickedness. He made a choice based on what he saw with his eyes. He was deceived by what he saw. Thus, he stumbled blindly into heartache and judgement. Like Lot, many Christians stumble foolishly into marital heartache because of poor judgment. Like Lot, our choices are based on what we see.

On the other hand, Abraham was content to let God choose for him. It is always best to let God choose for us because He alone knows the future. Will you today be like Abraham and allow God to choose for you? We must not be like Lot who chose for himself and lost everything, including his family and fortune.

Contentment comes when we want God's will more than our own way. If we allow God to choose for us, it will end well with us. On the other hand, marriage is not like going out in the street and seeing a man or woman for the first time and then and there you make the decision both of you want to get married because it is love at first sight. Oh no! Marriage goes far beyond that.

If we disobey God to satisfy our selfish desires then we should be ready to endure the consequences of our actions. Grandmother once told me, "If the person you love breaks your heart, the consequences can be very destructive. If you are not lucky the wound may never heal and may leave a permanent scar in your life."

Christians finding themselves in this condition allow anger, bitterness and an unforgiving spirit to rule over their lives. Some of them even vow never to marry again because of the hurt and pain they have experienced in their marriage. The scars of painful divorce can cause a man or woman never to marry again.

If you have not read the passage above, then read it now. Paul writes, "Do not be yoked with unbelievers. For what do righteousness and wickedness have in common? On the other hand, what fellowship can light have with darkness? What harmony is there between Christ and Belial? What does a believer have in common with an unbeliever?" (2 Corinthians 6:14-16

The human race is always subject to errors because we are prone to error. The reason we need to submit ourselves to God is to seek his help and guidance in everything we do. God knows and understands our weakness. Therefore, it is folly to pretend we are without weakness.

We always want to hold on tightly to what we think is good for us. As a result, we fail to filter through what we are holding dear to our heart. The question we need to be asking ourselves is, can we look through the mirror of Scripture and say with confidence that the choices we make are what God intended for us?

This reminds me of a pastor who stood on the pulpit and boasted that he was untouchable. He said the mere sight of him would scare witches and demons away. Even Paul, the greatest man after Jesus who walked on this earth, would not make such a boastful statement. As mere mortals, we must learn from other people's mistakes so that we do not go down the same road.

If we deliberately walk into raging storms, we will find marriage wreckers waiting for us. Moreover, do not think you can salvage any mess caused by marriage wreckers. Those who forget history are likely to repeat the mistakes of the past. God in His own goodness has allowed the mistakes, failure and weakness of His chosen men to be written down in the Bible for our own good.

Throughout the ages, men have sought to destroy the Bible. Yet it has survived through raging fires and other destructive elements. It survived through the power of the Holy Spirit who is also the author of the Bible. God preserved the Bible for us to read and learn from the mistakes of the great men who walked and talked with Him.

Our part is observing carefully these mistakes so that we do not end up making the same ones. It is through the love of God that such terrible mistakes committed by great men of God were written down for our own good. God did not try to cover up the mistakes of His devoted men but allowed them to be written down. Therefore, we no longer have any excuse if we use the mistakes of great men of God as an excuse to indulge in the same sin.

8. The Family Relationship

God ordained the family as a basic structure for society. God ordained marriage to provide mutual support, companionship, and unity to the family. This means the institution of marriage is very important because it provides psychological, spiritual and physical welfare for both husband and wife.

The beginning of the relationship of the husband to his wife can be traced to the time when a young man starts to feel special affection towards a woman he admires. However, his affection and admiration towards the opposite sex must never influence his choice of a wife, because these are only emotions.

Knowing what the Bible says about the respective roles of a husband and wife is crucial to the success of the Christian marriage. We must recognise that the Christian marriage must endeavour to create a good home. Not only that, the Christian home should be a place the family can enjoy and be happy. The Christian home should be a home others look to for inspiration.

There must be harmony in the Christian marital relationship and the unity that prevails in the

Christian marriage must serve as a role model to both unmarried Christians and married Christians. On the other hand, a poor Christian marriage can be a reproach to the outside world and rob our ability to be effective witnesses to the LORD.

How the husband treats his wife is the first demonstration of a love-relationship. This can be seen in how passionate the husband is towards his wife, not only that but also his affection towards the wife. A woman can easily tell if she is the object of love and affection of the husband.

A home that is radiant with Christian joy is the perfect home every woman yearns for because it demonstrates the highest priority of unity, trust and faithfulness. A man who truly loves his wife will give her his highest attention. Women are to be treated with love, respect and affection because they are special and precious.

"A man who finds a good woman finds a good thing. She is far more precious than jewels. The heart of her husband trusts in her, and he will have no lack of gain. She does him good, and not harm, all the days of her life." Proverbs 31:10-12. R. S. V. This is true because a prudent wife is from the LORD.

Why is the woman of Proverbs 31 more valuable than rare jewels (31)? It is because of her wisdom, her ability to live life in a responsible, productive, and prosperous way. The woman of Proverbs 31 is a model for women, showing a way of living that brings fulfilment and contentment. She exhibits a lifestyle of work and love, based on godly wisdom.

There many Biblical verses that shows that marriage is very important. However, we will limit ourselves to only two. At a very early point in man's existence, God said, "It is not good for man to live alone. I will make a helper suitable for him" (Genesis 2:18). Jesus Christ said this about marriage.

"The creator 'made them male and female,' and said, 'For this reason a man will leave his father and mother and be united to his wife, and the two will become one flesh.' So they are no longer two, but one" (Matthew 19:4-6).

Scriptures have a great deal to say about marriage, but there are still unanswered questions. We know from Scriptures that Jesus endorsed marriage for He attended a wedding feast, and used illustrations of weddings and marriage to explain the Kingdom of God.

Jesus was asked questions about divorce and in response gave some basic principles regarding marriage and divorce. The Epistles refer to the institution of marriage, the role and attitude of married persons. Married couples need to study these carefully for clearer understanding.

This generation is dealing treacherously in marriage, even worse than the generation before it. This treachery involves a retraction of their marriage vows, but it is also representing treachery against God whom we shall one day stand before and give Him a detailed account of our marriage.

Men and women who cannot break the chains of divorce should not go into marriage. If the desire for marriage cannot retain love in the marriage then we must give up marrying. Those who desire to marry must also desire to honour the marriage vows. They also must be committed to the marriage institution and work towards its success.

On the wedding day couples say the following words, "I do" and again, "Till death do us part." Yet it is not death, which separates married couples, it is greed, selfishness and self-centeredness. When people take marriage vows as a piece of recitation to enable them to be pronounced husband and wife then, they will find no need to uphold the marriage vows.

What is provoking these skyrocketing divorce rates? This is what a friend once said, "Our court have made it too easy to get divorce." The danger is that people are taking it lightly. Nevertheless, God never takes divorce lightly. God makes Himself extremely clear through Malachi: "I hate divorce." (2:16). See also (Deut 24:1-4.)

The institution of marriage is becoming endangered, evidenced by high divorce rates throughout the world. The kingdom community of believers are not excluded from this unfortunate situation. Every broken marriage is influenced by the devil. Therefore, it is the responsibility of married couples to work towards the success of their marriage by keeping the devil out of their marriage.

In marriage, we must know where we are going. This is all-important. It is essential that in marriage we have a definite goal, and aim to reach that goal. To go into marriage and not knowing where we are going is altogether too vague and indefinite.

It is like a man or woman who starts out on a journey and does not have a destination in view. It is important that in marriage we not lose sight of the starting point. The starting point is all full of joy and must never be lost.

It is necessary we keep in mind that every marriage has its own problems. In addition, this must be kept in view and steps necessary to reach a happy resolution are kept in mind. A married couple's ability to read the warning signs gives them a head start to stop problems before they gain roots.

A man going into marriage is like an architect who sets out to draw a building plan. It takes time, planning, thinking and hard work for an architect to come out with a master plan that will make the building able to withstand adverse weather conditions. Before an architect draws up plan for a building, he considers several factors.

First, the area where the building is to be built: is it prone to earthquakes? If it is, then he has to design a building that can withstand earthquakes. Secondly, the soil condition: e.g. is the land waterlogged, clay soil or sandy soil? Not only that, he must also know the history of the land: for example, was the area once a river. Knowing the land on which he plans to put up a building is very important to an architect.

Similarly, a farmer who sets out to cultivate land must know the soil condition. Knowing the soil condition allows the farmer to use the right type of ploughs on the field. Using the wrong plough on soil will not yield the right results. The soil condition tells the farmer which type of wheels to use on his tractor to prevent wheel slip. Wheel slipping of a tractor's drive wheels always wastes power and fuel. This wastage may be serious, even if the wheel does not spin.

From these two examples, we can learn a lot about marriage. First, we know why an architect must know the area where to site the building. Similarly, knowing the woman or man you are going to marry will play a crucial role in whether the marriage can withstand storms.

In the second example, we learnt why the farmer has to know the soil condition before choosing the right plough for the field. Knowing the man or woman you plan to marry will make the fruits of your marriage yield an abundant blessing.

Again, we saw why the farmer must know the soil conditions to prevent wheel spin that leads to waste of power and fuel. Knowing the person you are marrying will prevent uncontrolled finance that can sometimes lead to quarrels in marriages.

In the institution of marriage, Power and Fuel have to do with Control and Decision on Finances. This involves who takes the major decisions when it comes to how money is to be used in the family.

Who takes the blame when things go wrong? Being observant will enable you to notice whether your spouse will be careful when it comes to money.

A man or woman going into marriage without knowing much about the person he or she is going to marry is like a driver who does not know his blind spot. The beauty of women blinds most men when it comes to marriage. Marriage has little to do with outside appearance.

A woman's beauty is not her character. This we cannot see, for it is every man's blind spot. Beauty can be seen in the open but character can only be seen from within. Sorry, character is not something we can easily spot. On the other hand, women can also be blinded by wealth. Nevertheless, wealth has nothing to do with a man's character.

Grandmother once told me that women are drawn to money the way fresh meat draws flies. A woman with an uncontrollable taste for luxury will marry a man for his money rather than for good character. The causes of marriage troubles are buried in these two and the troubles start here.

Appearances can be very deceptive, besides it does not give the true picture of the character of a person. Because we are human, we cannot know who a person really is. A person's true nature is obscured from us. These are what newly married couples will be confronted with in marriage and therefore have to be prepared.

9. Sex outside Marriage

"You have heard that it was said, 'Do not commit adultery.' But I tell you that anyone who looks at a woman lustfully has already committed adultery with her in his heart." (Matthew 5:27-28)

One thing must be made clear from the Scripture verse above: it is aimed at both men and women. As it says, "anyone who looks at a woman lustfully has already committed adultery with her in his heart." Therefore, a woman must refrain from putting a man in a situation that will make him lust after her.

For example, if you give vital information to a thief that enabled the thief to break into a building and steal, although you may not have taken part in the robbery, the information given makes you an accomplice to the crime. In legal terms, it called aiding and abetting. You do not have to take part in a crime to make you guilty. The part you played leading to the crime makes you guilty.

Similarly, a woman who dresses seductively to make a man lust after her is equally guilty of adultery. A world in which women dress to expose about sixty percent of their body in the name of fashion is a breeding ground for men who are morally weak to lust after their flesh. Women have no excuse whatsoever to dress to make men lust after them.

What is the Scripture's view about sex outside marriage? Does Scripture seek to impose its view on sex outside marriage on us? On the other hand, does Scripture seek to appeal to men and women to engage in sex as God intended? We must allow the Scriptures to speak to us concerning the issues of sex before marriage.

Sex, the ability to produce life, has become an all-consuming interest of British society. Children become involved in sexual activities even before adolescence. Unmarried young men and women have moved from bed to bed, from one flat to another, changing sexual partners as simply as they might trade in a used car, but with no guarantee attached.

The cheapest and the easiest thing to do today is changing sexual partners, it is free for all without any restrictions or guarantees. Pornography is a hot cake that has raked in millions of pounds into the bank accounts of its producers. It has hooked children, young people and old men and women, but the disturbing thing is that even some men of God are in bondage of this evil pornography.

Pornography has corrupted the minds of the youth, which has proved to be the by-product and the breeding ground for crime in our society. Compounding this problem is the wretchedly low moral standards of the film and television industries that are helping to pollute the minds of the average British family right in their own living rooms.

In our cities, pornography is often linked to organized crime; murderers and rapists have testified that they began with pornography. This evidence proves what this evil and shameful product has done to our young men and young women. Because pornography is such a big money making industry, greediness has prevented governments from putting them out of business.

The revenues and taxes the government rakes back from this evil industry, its source of lucrative employment for desperate innocent young women and men looking for gainful employment to get out of the dole: are these the very reasons why the government has turned a blind eye?

We must continue to fight against sexual perversion and acceptance of sex outside marriage, which have tragically affected such a large segment of British society. Poor moral conduct by well-known public figures in sports, music, entertainment, and government, and sad to say from religious leaders has not been a good example to the youth

The Scripture places a clear ban on sexual intercourse for the unmarried. There is no point trying to get around it. Do you know Scripture's ban on sexual intercourse for the unmarried is based on profound insight? See 1 Corinthians 6:12-19 and Colossians 3:5. There is nothing sinful about any of man's basic physical desires. It is how man misuses them that makes it sin. Hunger is not a sin, but gluttony is. To desire a wife (or husband) is not a sin, but sexual immorality is.

Man is a sexual being with sexual desires or sexual drive. How man channels these desires and drive will determine whether he values and cherishes this gift from God. Sexual desires and drive are part of human nature, which needs to be satisfied. Against this, the Scriptures have laid out guidelines on how this need can be satisfied.

Sexual desires can only be satisfied within the context of marriage. Sex is part of the joy of marriage and it is only within marriage that it can be satisfied and enjoyed. Beyond this is a deliberate violation of God's intended purpose. A thief may well enjoy his booty, but not as a person who has earned his wealth legally.

A student may cheat to gain his degree. Nevertheless, the thought of it will always come to haunt him. Any time he or she looks at the certificate, it reminds him he never worked for it. There is no joy, no happiness and no satisfaction in something we never earned by merit. Cheating does not bring inner satisfaction; whatever joy we derive from it is temporary.

If we really want to enjoy something then we must obtain it legally. The legality of sex is only through marriage and marriage alone. Sex outside marriage is like a man or woman who sets out to feast on or taste what does not belong to him or her. There is no natural pleasure in what we have not obtained legally.

Sex is great and a wonderful gift from God to a married spouse to enjoy and be satisfied within marriage. Those who engage in sex outside marriage are cheating themselves. Just as a thief may not find anything morally wrong in stealing, similarly a man or woman who has no respect for the institution of marriage will find nothing morally wrong in sex outside marriage.

People who see sex as pleasure or as a desire to be satisfied will treat sex as food or drink. We eat and drink to live. Sex on the other hand is not like food and drink that satisfies our hunger and quenches our thirst. Man cannot live without food and water, but we can certainly live without sex.

Sex is for married people only (between a man and a woman who have been legally married in a court of law or in Church by an ordained pastor) and that is the bottom line. This is the way God wants His children to satisfy sexual desires. Sex is very good medicine for a man and a woman only if used as prescribed. God's prescription of sex is for married couples only.

If we are to experience the healing that comes from sex and enjoy its benefits then we must adhere to its requirements. Marriage is the only requirement for sex. That is only with the person to whom are married. The moment we challenge the legality of sex outside marriage we show intent to violate God's command on sex.

Whilst sex can be good medicine for married couples, it can turn out to be deadly poison that can lead to all sorts of problems for the unmarried. It is evident that sex can lead to death through abortion; sex can lead to all sorts of health problems, for example through HIV, gonorrhoea, syphilis and other sexually transmitted diseases.

We live in a society where sex has turned teenagers into parents. As a result, it has created many problems for families through teenage pregnancy. Teenage pregnancy is one of the breeding grounds for the high rate of crime in our society. These are facts that we cannot dispute.

What we have in our society is a scenario where sex has turned teenagers into instant adults. Outwardly, these teenagers talk and behave like adults. However, inwardly they are nothing but children who should be under the control of their parents. Today boys as young as sixteen are parents and girls as young fourteen and fifteen become mothers.

What do teenagers at this age know about parenthood? These teenagers who do not know the a-b-c of parenthood are bringing children into the world they cannot discipline. A dangerous situation that will eventually turn their homes into breeding grounds for crimes, which neither parents, nor can the state have control over. This is what sex has turned our children into.

The ugly side of sex is the way it has created monsters out of our children. In addition, society is powerless to do anything about it. We are reaping the evil we have sown in our children. Parents are powerless to do anything about it because the law has their hands tied. In some homes parents appear to play the role of children when it comes to the sexual activities of their children. Is this a no-go area for parents?

The following extract is taken from an article in the METRO, sub-titled 'Teenagers not ready to have babies'. "The reason Britain is the teenage pregnancy capital of Europe is because youngsters have an unrealistic idea of what it means to be a parent. That is the view of 72 per cent of people interviewed by the Harris Poll.

Some 56 per cent believe the government makes it financially attractive by offering benefits. Whilst 44 per cent believe that high teenage pregnancy rates are a symptom of our broken society. Ignorance about birth control is seen by 37 per cent, as the reason and 32 per cent believe sex education in schools is out of touch but 16 per cent think that sex education encourages promiscuity.

Of those polled, 42 per cent think parents are unwilling to talk to their children about sex. In addition, 29 per cent cite the availability of pornography as the reason. Britain has one of the highest rates of teenage pregnancies, accounting for seven per cent of births compared with an average of three per cent in Western Europe."

From the above statistic it is evident that the blame lies with our lawmakers who make laws that create the impression that having sex outside marriage is fine. The lawmakers do not understand what pre-marital sex has turned our teenagers into, if they did, they would cry out to the Creator who alone has the answer to teenage problems.

On Friday the 13th of February 2009, the front page of the Sun Newspaper carried a shocking state of teenage pregnancy in our society. The headline reads, "**EXCLUSIVE: Baby-faced father of little Maisie." DAD AT 13. A BABY-faced boy cuddles a newborn girl- and incredibly, he is the tot's DAD.**

Four –foot Alfie Patten is just 13. He was 12 when his 15-year old girlfriend Chantelle Steadman conceived after just one night of unprotected sex. They decided to go ahead with having baby Maisie after Chantelle found she was pregnant. Alfie, of Eastbourne, East Sussex, told The Sun: "I did not know what it would be like to be a dad. I will be good, though, and care for it." The young pair are being backed by their parents. Chantelle said, "I was on the Pill but missed one."

The youth of today need all the help they can get from the state and non-governmental organizations in education about premarital sex. On the other hand, the church that should play greater role in instilling moral discipline in these teenagers, is failing the youth. Sex outside marriage is a deliberate violation of God's natural law regarding sex.

We must subject all of our physical drives to the Holy Spirit. We live in an age where unmarried couples living together call themselves "partners." This deliberately sinful arrangement between men and women accepted by society as the norm is very wrong. Society should not accept cohabitation as the norm because it violates the basic principles of the institution of marriage.

Societal changes in the past 50 years included a shift in the attitudes towards co-habitation and having children out of wedlock, which could be the result of the high moral degeneration of our society. Moreover, it is the cause of the crime wave in our society today. What we are experiencing in our society is an uncontrolled cultural revolution in sexual morality and sexual behaviour.

Created by the wave of co-habitation, we know where this will go. Nevertheless, what we do not know is when it is going to end. Men and women who respect the institution of marriage should distance themselves from cohabitation. Those who sign up to this unholy ideology are provoking God's anger.

When we deliberately violate God's natural law on sex, we show utter contempt for His word. Cohabitation is an institution created by Satan in opposition to the marriage institution God designed for sex. Therefore, those who cohabit are singing praises to Satan. Is there anything to gain by teaming up with the devil to destroy an institution God ordained?

Cohabitation is nothing but open marriage systems where no vows are taken so are no binding rules. No witnesses, so no witnesses can be produced to testify or prove they are married. No one joined them together so there is no blessing. They are nothing but business partners who seek to protect their investments.

This joint business venture hangs on a thin thread and is crowded with suspicions and mistrust, so battles fought in this kind of relationship can be fierce. It leaves those involved wounded with bitterness because of wasted years.

This reminds me of my next-door neighbours. They lived together as if they were married. One cold winter night Natasha knocked on our door and asked "How long does the recording on the C.C.T.V video recorder stay before it is wiped out?" When I asked her why, she answered:

"I suspect my boyfriend is cheating on me." I told her the information she was requesting was on the digital video recorder, but I could not release it. I told her to go and come back after I had discussed it with my wife. Ten minutes after walking away, there was a second knock on the door. When I opened the door, Dean greeted me.

When I asked what I could do for him, this was his reply: "Please, if Natasha asks for a copy of the video tape recording do not give it to her because she is mentally unstable." Oh! So Natasha has suddenly become mentally unstable because he was caught cheating on camera. What a strange world we live in. A faithful woman catches her partner cheating on her. In his defence, he accuses her of being mentally unstable.

For all the years they have lived together, she was mentally sane. Did he ever love Natasha? Society should not recognize cohabitation as an alternative form of marriage. Marriage is a wonderful gift from God to the human race. Because it is a gift of

God, it should be sacred without defilement. When the marriage bed is without defilement, there is abundant blessing.

Lawmakers are busy drafting laws that will recognize cohabitation. They aim to protect cohabitation against separation or death. The enactment of such a law will put marriage and cohabitation on an equal level. In the eyes of such a law, marriage will no longer be relevant. What they are telling the teenagers is that cohabitation is perfectly normal without having to go through a marriage ceremony.

This kind of law if ratified will downgrade the institution of marriage. Marriage is about love, while cohabitation is about the lust of the flesh. Cohabitation satisfies the craving for sex. Marriage is about fulfilling God's plan. People who love each other can wait until they are married, whilst people who cannot wait cohabitate.

The following extracts are taken from the **METRO** Newspaper. It says, "YOUNG couples are increasingly choosing to skip marriage and move in with each other. Husbands and wives made up just 48 per cent of the population of England and Wales in 2010, while one person in six was cohabiting.

Britons were also being hitched latter, according to the Home of National statistics, with the average age of a first-time bride at 30, compared with 32 for the groom. The report said: One of the main reasons for the decrease in the marriage population is the growth of cohabitation by unmarried couples.

"In the early 1960s in Britain, less than one in 100 adults under 50 are estimated to have been cohabiting at any one time," said the report, adding that **living with a partner is seen as an alternative to marriage,** which has steadily fallen since the 1970s. In 2010, the number of divorces in Britain increase by a whole percentage point of 9.3.

The misconception of sex is when it is expressed as love. Sex has nothing to do with love. Sex has to do with satisfying the natural desires of the flesh. Love on the other hand has to do with our relationship with each other. Love seeks the other person's highest interest. Sex outside marriage satisfies selfish interest.

Sex and cohabitation are not birds of the same feather and can never be. On the other hand marriage and sex are birds of the same feather, they flock together to fulfil the will of God. Only in marriage is the joy of sex consummated. The unity of love and marriage is in the spirit, soul and body. Cohabitating couples live in sexual sin.

Married couples engaged in sex within the context of marriage are doing the right thing because it is legitimate. Therefore, they have the blessing of God. If two consenting adult think they love each other then they must do what is right in the sight of God. That right thing is marriage. We must give marriage its due respect. This changing society must understand the values of marriage, what it stands for and learn how to give marriage a good name.

We live in a world where powerful people are working around the clock to dismantle the institution of marriage. In addition, these powerful people are the lawmakers. Behind the scene are the real people who propel the lawmakers. The reason for this is that they see the institution of marriage as old-fashioned institution that no longer has any value in modern society.

Lawmakers who cohabitate will protect the common-law husband or common-law wife system. This changing world will always find a means of accommodating our disobedience to God by inventing or creating suitable phrases that match our lifestyles. "Having an affair" is a phrase that describes a person who commits adultery.

A man lusts after his own daughter and then marries her. Then each of them claims to be suffering from the psychological condition called Genetic Sexual Attraction or GSA. Instead of society frowning at them they choose to sympathize. Society speaks in their defence by claiming it is possible for this to affect siblings or blood relations who first meet as adults.

I think we must call a spade a spade and call this relationship sinful and not Genetic Sexual Attraction. A man deliberately kills his wife and admits the crime in a court of law, but denies murder claiming he was suffering from mental illness. This was after the wife's parents hired a bodyguard to protect her.

Today people have a way of escaping justice by justifying their actions. A man deliberately kills his wife at the slightest provocation and the law says, "He did not intend to kill her but he committed an unlawful act." Fine words indeed. Nevertheless, such fine words will only fuel the unending circle of evil in this generation.

Sexual sin has a devastating effect on our spiritual and physical life. Sexual sin not only harms us but also controls our bodies. Sexual sin has a powerful control over us by weakening our resistance, and makes us its slave. You must have the courage to say no to someone that you are not married to, who invites you to have sex.

You must say no because you have the will to say no. Do not allow peer groups to influence you into having sex: you cannot cope with its aftermath. Let us look at the following examples: the first example is that of a medical student from South East Asia. She is a very good friend of mine. Whilst she was in medical school, she lived in a posh flat bought by her rich father.

She shared the flat with her boyfriend as if they were married. The irony of all this is that in most cases once they leave University, couples go their separate ways never to see each other again. Is there any gain in exposing your nakedness to a man who may never marry you? What pride will a woman have left if before her marriage she slept with so many men?

Any time her parents were on visits the boyfriend disappeared and resurfaced when the parents were gone. The young man was nothing but a parasite feasting and enjoying what he had not earned legally. His disappearance and resurfacing clearly show his guilt. The ability for a man or woman to preserve his or her body until after their wedding makes sex the most enjoyable thing ever.

It is the day God rejoices over His children preserving their bodies in honouring the institution of marriage. This young medical student knew what she was doing was morally wrong, that was why she was playing cat and mouse games with her parents. The world sees nothing morally wrong with this kind of lifestyle.

When I tried to talk her out of it, this is what she said: "If I stop having sex with my boyfriend there are so many women out there who are more than willing to take my place and offer him what you are asking me to give up." This remark reveals three things. First the fear of losing her boyfriend to someone else; secondly she was powerless to stop what she knew was morally wrong; thirdly she had no control of an illicit relationship she knew would one day destroy her sexual happiness.

This woman is not alone in this method of satisfying sexual desires. Even some lawmakers who should show a good example are involved in cohabitation. This changing world appears not to place any moral value on the institution of marriage. Lust produces bad sex because it denies the true marriage relationship.

Lust turns a person into a sex object because it is not enjoyed legally. Lust is all about gratification of the flesh and nothing else. Jesus condemned lust because it cheapened sex. It makes sex less than the reason for which God designed it. Society today thinks it is best to cohabitate rather than marry.

The second example is a young man called Stanley. When asked why he chose to cohabitate, this is what he said: "I don't want to make a mistake. I want to be convinced this is the woman I want to spend the rest of my life with." Should we trust this statement or give him the benefit of the doubt?

If one studies the content of this statement, you will notice that it shrouded in secrecy. He has carefully chosen his words to hide his real intentions. This man is nothing but a testing officer sitting at the end of a sex production line. Testing wine for its good quality is not the same as sex.

You cannot start having sex with the view of sampling different women until you find the right sexual partner. Quality control is something you find in the food and drink industry and not with sex. After fathering two children with his partner, he is still not sure whether this is the woman, he wants to spend the rest his life with.

Is there any wisdom in this kind of arrangement? The truth is that this young man does not intend to marry his partner. People like these are interested in relations without formal marriage commitment. A relationship where there are no commitments. Each of them could choose to walk out of the relationship without having to go through a divorce court.

Those involved in this type of relationship walk out with whatever they came with. Therefore, there are no disputes over who takes what. It is sad to see someone you cherish and adore walk out of your life not wanting to see you again. Conversely, he or she has erased you from his or her memory.

What if after ten years they realised they cannot live together, who loses out in this illicit relationship? Surely, the woman who wasted ten years of her life with a man who never intended to marry her in the first place.

The phrases common-law husband or common-law wife are defined by the Oxford Advanced Learner's Dictionary as, "a person that a woman or man has lived with for a long time and is recognized as a husband or wife without a formal marriage ceremony."

This reminds me of a story of a young beautiful estate agent I met through Business links (name withheld). Having lived with a divorce lawyer for six years the man never showed any sign or mentioned anything about marriage. So one beautiful hot summer afternoon she took the man out for lunch in a posh restaurant.

They sat outside under the blue sky and rapped in glorious sunshine, they enjoyed the afternoon with unfettered enthusiasm. After lunch, she posed the question of marriage to the man. The man simply brushed the topic aside and told her "it is time to leave." Has the cat been let out of the bag? Oh, yes! The statement shocked her.

She could hardly believe what she was hearing. The writing was clearly on the wall. When it comes to marriage, she is not the right type. A smart and intelligent woman would not need a code breaker to decode this message. Concisely, she is only good as a girlfriend. She walked out of the doomed relationship before it sunk her.

Six months after leaving her boyfriend, she met a young man at a friend's birthday party. A year after meeting, the young man proposed to her. This woman was smart to have walked out of a shameful relationship that had no future. Today they are happily married with two children.

Some people are not smart enough to read the writing on the wall. People like this wait and wait hoping the waiting will be worth it, and could result into marriage. This is dreaming. The devious thing about some men is that they do not want to be married and they will never tell their partners. If the partner brings up the issue of marriage, they show them the way out of the relationship.

Paul, a lawyer friend of mine, is a typical example. He has broken the hearts of about three beautiful young women. Each time any of them raises the question of marriage he walks out of the relationship. I remember one of his victims invited her parents all the way from Australia for them to meet their future son in-law.

He read a different meaning into that visit. As soon as her parents were gone, he told the young woman, "It is over between us." Heartbroken and not knowing how to tell her parents their future son-in-law has broken up with her, she walked out of a relationship that held no future for her.

In another case, a Brazilian woman named Sara walked into my office one cold winter afternoon in a joyous mood. When asked, "How is your boyfriend?" tears started flowing from her eyes. She started sobbing uncontrollably. I felt very sorry for playing "Mr. Kill Joy."

This woman had spent fifteen years cohabitating with her boyfriend. Out of this relationship came two lovely children: one eleven-year-old boy and a six-year-old girl. The children and their mother adored this man very much. Did this man also adore his wife and children? This we will discover as the story unfolds. This couple met and fell in love and decided to cohabitate. To consummate their love they decided to live together as a "married couple" in the eyes of a sinful world.

Harry Stock Sullivan gave the definition of love as "a condition that exists when another person's well-being and security are as important to you as your own." It is a condition, not just an emotion or a feeling. I am convinced that if you have the condition, you will have the feeling.

Imagine what feelings you would have if you were in a situation where somebody cared as much about you as you cared about yourself. Nevertheless, in the mindset of this man I doubt if he has any feeling for his live-in lover. The fact of the matter is if the person you are living with has no feelings for you, then ask yourself if it is worth staying in the relationship.

One day Sarah took the children to an amusement park. At the park, she realized she had left her purse home so she left the children with a friend.

When she got to the front door, she heard noises coming from the house. Human instinct told her listen to the conversation going on in the house.

When she heard the voice of their family friend, she stood still. What she heard was shocking; overwhelmed and unprepared for it, she was taken by surprise. When the family friend asked Sarah's partner when he was going to marry Sarah, his answer to the question almost froze her to death. She stood outside the door gasping for breath. "Is this real or am I daydreaming?" she asked.

She sat outside the door with her head buried in her palms until she heard the voices of her children. The thought of her children gave her the strength to withstand the shock. This was the question. "I have married my partner after five years. When are you going to marry Sarah?"

Then the bombshell, "If you are stupid enough to marry your partner, I am not stupid enough to marry Sarah." Does this answer sound like a man who had any feelings for Sarah? Like Sarah, many young women are going through similar problems. Some of them are suffering in silence because they have chosen to remain quiet.

Does this man care for Sarah? No, he does not care for her; Sarah was nothing but a sex slave to satisfy his lust. We need to understand that sex is not the same as love. Those who think it is the same will mistake sex for love. This is the reason why people having sex usually say, we are making love or we made love together.

Sarah wept and wept saying, "I love him, and I really love him. I cannot live without him. I will kill myself if he leaves me." It is not about you loving someone and be willing to die for the sake of love. The question you should be asking yourself is, does he love me? You may love someone and be prepared to die for him but will he be prepared to die for you?

It is not worth being in relationship when the person does not love you. This relationship calls for defining the difference between love and sex. The most demeaning thing about sex is living with a partner who exploits your body as a means of sexual gain. Sarah fell in love with a man she thought had feelings and desire for her.

After he fathered her two children, she felt the children were a wonderful gift to seal their relationship and lead into marriage. But, this man never once showed any feelings or affection for her. What hurt Sarah was that she had to hear the way her partner felt about her from a family friend.

For Sarah it was like piercing her heart with hot metal. Unfortunately, we live in a world where people are not honest with each other. The most dangerous situation in any relationship is living with a person who pretends to love you when in fact he has not the slightest feeling for you.

The only time you realise your partner does not love you is when you are told the door is not locked; you are free to walk out. You came into this relationship of your own free will and you are free to leave if things are not going the way you expected. This statement is what you may one day hear from someone who claimed you are the best thing that ever happened to him.

The society we live in has made cohabitation very attractive to our young men and women. The sad thing is parents give their consent. A friend once remarked, "I don't know whether I am doing the right thing by consenting to this system and not knowing whether this man will one day marry my daughter."

Cohabitation attracts the youth as a magnet attracts iron filings. It has taken our youth by storm, a storm that has overwhelmed and blinded our youth about God's intended purpose for sex. Let us give marriage a chance. Grandmother once said, "There are people who love to have children but do not want to marry." Having children out of wedlock desecrates the spirit of marriage.

Cohabitation is the evil in our society that seeks to destroy the institution of marriage. When we refuse to change our lifestyle toward sex, then we leave God no option but to judge us according to the way we live our lives. We need to change our attitude to sex while there is time for us to do so.

A generation bent on disobeying God's intended purpose for sex will continue cohabitating; nothing short of this will satisfy them. The worst scenario in this evil is that some Christians who should speak in defence of marriage are themselves cohabitating.

10. Children

"Sons are a heritage from the LORD; children a reward from him." (Psalm 127:3)

Today about 3.8 million children are caught up in the family justice system in the U.K with no sign of that number dropping. Every indication shows that it is rising. Everyone in society is affected: the rich and poor, the haves and have-nots are now affected by family breakdown.

Before you start contemplating how to get out of an irreconcilable marriage, you need to weigh the options very carefully, especially where children are involved. You need to ask yourself questions that will produce answers to guarantee the children's spiritual and physical welfare.

How will the children cope without a father figure in the house? Will the children be willing to accept a replacement father or mother? Will this new replacement parent be able to instil discipline in the home? Will the children accept his or her discipline? Are you sure this new replacement parent can effectively take over the absentee father or mother's role?

Can you look into the future and say the children will have the same love for the replacement father as they had for their biological father or mother? Can this replacement father be entrusted with the children in your absence? Have you thought about the children's feelings and interest?

How would this divorce affect the children's relations with their friends in school and outside school? What good reasons are you going to give to the children for the break-up of the marriage? Did you go the extra mile to save the marriage? Children asking such questions would demand more than a yes or no answer.

Be sure you are not going to have things easy; some children can be very problematic. When it comes to the issue of a replacement father or mother, you must be prepared for the worst. Some children cannot guarantee you a peaceful home with people they do not consider as members of the family.

Who stands to gain in the divorce settlement: you or the children? In whose interest are you divorcing your spouse? Yours or the children, in most cases, the children come out worst-off in divorce cases. Emotionally they are very much affected because the once happy home no longer exists. The love and affection which once existed between the parents and which the children saw and admired is no longer there.

Why should married spouses ever fight one another before their children? In a marriage with children in the family, a married couple should demonstrate the power of love in the marriage and not fight each other for their own selfish interest. Married couples must never show their selfish differences before their children. The married home must be a home where children can see love being demonstrated practically.

Children do not need to see their parents fighting each other in the home or outside the home for any reason. What children want to see is a strong, loving relationship, love that binds the family together with an unbreakable cord of love. Children want to see how affectionate the parents are to each other.

11. Unfaithfulness in Marriage

"I made a covenant with my eyes not to look lustfully at a girl" (Job 31:1). "Should you not fear me?" declares the LORD. Should you tremble in my presence? I made the sand a boundary for the sea, an everlasting barrier it cannot cross. The waves may roll, but they cannot prevail; they may roar, but they cannot cross it." (Jeremiah 5:22).

Yet people are defiant and rebellious in their hearts. Defiant in their marriage vows because they have no fear of God. Their hearts are filled with deceit. Because of wrongdoing, our sins have deprived us of good and happy marriage. Those who have turned aside and gone away from their marriage vows will have no peace in their marriage.

The book of the Song of Songs gives us a clear indication that romantic love within the bonds of matrimony is desirable and is endorsed by God. God has given us the capacity to enjoy the sexual relationship with our spouse, but the couple who wish to keep the flame of romance burning brightly must at all costs maintain the mutual respect and love from the beginning of the marriage.

After marriage we are no longer our own, no longer free to choose and act as we please. We are tied down with our marriage vows. When you both said, "I do" this is what you both got yourselves into, there is no turning back. You now belong to your wife alone or you belong to your husband alone. From now onwards you will only enjoy sex with your spouse.

Although God instituted marriage and gave man and woman the capacity for lovemaking, He leaves every couple the responsibility of keeping the glow in their marriage. The mutual love and respect that brought the couple together in the first place must remain in place if the marriage is to succeed. However, should the ardour and passion begin to lessen, then we must look for what went wrong and then fix it.

God has given moral boundaries in His Word for us to live within. He gave them not to frustrate us, rather as a guide to keep us within the boundaries of marriage so that we may enjoy His blessing. However, those who deliberately flout these boundaries will be doing so at their own peril.

We must recognize the fact that moral failure takes place in the heart long before the act is committed. With evil seed, evil desires lodged deep in the human spirit, circumstances such as fatigue or an unhappy marital relationship provide all that is needed to bring about the fall from grace that often proves to be a death-dealing or seriously crippling blow to a marriage.

Be warned that with sexual immorality the body becomes a rot. The devil always works around our weaknesses. Yes, we all do have weaknesses but the will to say yes or no to someone who invites you to have sex with him or her whom you are not married to depends on you and not the devil.

Temptation is only a bargain price used by the tempter to entice his customers towards what the Scriptures forbid them. What he offers in the form of a bargain is so attractive and irresistible that you want to have it. Sometimes the offer is too enticing to refuse. The tempter can only tempt and entice your human weakness and this is how far he can go.

Beyond that, he has no power to force you to go along with his suggestions. You have the power to turn your heart away from the bargain before you. When we are faced with temptation, we have only two options: either accept the offer on the table and go along with temptation or simply reject the irresistible offer from the tempter and walk away in victory.

The tempter can only suggest and appeal to your sexual emotions. The tempter is only allowed to operate within these limits. His next strategy is to make the suggestions very appealing and something to be desired. Lust hidden in the heart is as destructive as the act of adultery.

Although he makes the bargain something desirable, you still have the spirit of Christ in you to walk away from it. Desiring the bargain itself is no sin. It is only becomes a sin when you decide to have a piece of it. The thought to have what does not belong to you and the decision to accept and go along with the thought is what will lead you into committing the act.

Something to be desired is the key phrase and it becomes his tool, which will lure you to accomplishing his purpose. That purpose is to make you disobey God. There is nothing to be gained by disobeying God. Rather we have more to gain by being obedient to God because an obedient child receives the best from his father.

The Scriptures makes it clear that "the soul that sinned will die." It is clear from the verse that it is not the devil who tempts you who will die, but you who was carried away by your lust. Remember the aim of the tempter is to disgrace you, render your testimony and witnessing ineffective. This is what you have to give careful thought to before you decide to act.

Married people who respect marriage will never engage in sexual relations outside of their matrimonial home, no matter how strong the temptation. However, those who have no regard and respect for marriage deliberately engage in sexual relationships outside their matrimonial home.

A spouse who engages in extra-marital relationships should examine himself to see if he is being controlled by the spirit of lust. Because there are some married Christians who are possessed by lustful spirits. For a married Christian to engage in extra-marital relationships goes beyond the norm of Christian ethics.

It will take a married Christian possessed by the spirit of lust to commit adultery. Such a Christian needs help and not condemnation and crucifixion. Some Christians lack the will to resist the lust of the flesh; Christians who fall in this group should seek spiritual help.

If such a Christian does not seek help, he will destroy his own marriage. Hence, one of the causes of high divorce rates in our society today. Spouses with sexual weakness must discuss this weakness between themselves to avoid infidelity.

A wise preacher once stood in his pulpit and sounded the following warning to all married couples. "Drink water from your own cistern, running water from your own well. May your fountain be blessed, and may you rejoice in the wife of your youth. And may her breast satisfy you always. May you ever be captivated by her love." (Proverbs 5:15, 16, & 17).

Every man must let the breast of his wife satisfy him. After all, whatever this other woman has, your wife has the same thing if not better. A wise preacher once penned down the following words to his lover, "I am a rose of Sharon, a lily of the valleys." In respond, the lover said, "Like a lily among thorns is my darling among the maidens." (Song of Songs 2:1-2).

Let this passionate words be engraved in your marital home to remind you of the strong bond of love that exit between both of you. Then, burn it in your memory so that when you are faced with temptations tell the tempter, "I will not betray the lily of the valley," It takes the power of a seductive spirit to cause a married person to commit adultery.

Satan always tries to identify our weakness and builds a stronghold around it. Satan has only one aim as far as sex is concerned, to make us slaves to sexual sin. Remember: a slave has no control over his master. Therefore, your weakness becomes your master. We must stay away from anything that will enslave us.

In 1 Thessalonians 4:3-5 the Apostle Paul wrote in response to what was going on in the Church. Paul told them, "It is God's will that you should be sanctified: that you should avoid sexual immorality; that each of you should learn to control his own body in a way that is holy and honourable, not in passionate lust like the heathen, who do not know God."

A Christian who engages in sexual immorality opens the floodgates to all kinds of demonic activities that will destroy his spiritual life and ruin any possible ministerial career. Such a Christian is heading into very dangerous territory that may result in him being held captive. For a married Christian to be unfaithful in his marriage shows there are forces involved in his spiritual life of which he or she may not be aware.

Some Christians may be aware but are powerless to resist the spirit that is controlling them. It is morally wrong for a married Christian to engage in extra-marital affairs; not only that, it is also against the ethics of Christian marriage. When the soul of a married Christian is not submitted through his spirit to God, he becomes a channel through which every kind of unfaithfulness and mistrust can infiltrate the marriage and lead to divorce.

What you do not know is that beneath the enticing bargain of the tempter is his desire to publicly disgrace and humiliate you. Once you succumb to his offer, he walks away, leaving you to pick up the pieces. Do not walk with him, do not talk with him and do not buy what he has to offer.

Satan, our spiritual enemy, uses our desire to tempt us into sinning. A man's spiritual weakness can be linked to his desires, and once a man loses control over his desires Satan takes control over him and makes him his slave. The key word in temptation is desire, which is our Achilles heel.

However, if a man can conquer his desire then he can prevail over the tempter. Our real enemy is our desire. This the devil knows very well and he works through our desire to lead us into sin. The only weapons available at our disposal are the spiritual weapons Paul listed in Galatians.

Our relationship with God, Jesus Christ and the Holy Spirit should be what should stop us from sinning. The Holy Spirit is a restraining Spirit that prevents us from sinning but if we deliberately break free from Him then we are on our own. The Holy Spirit is the only person who can prevent us from sinning.

The power of prayer is what can set a Christian free from the spirit of lust. As a Christian walks in the spirit he or she walks into freedom from the lustful desires of this world, but Christians who pray less or have no desire to pray will have no weapon with which to fight against the spirit of lust.

Watch out for loose men and women who are always willing and ready to have sex with anybody. The reason for this is that they have no control of their sexual drive. People who fall in this group cannot stay a day without having sex.

There is nothing morally wrong with it, as long as it is done within the confines of marriage. On the other hand, uncontrolled sexual appeal outside marriage is a mark of a demonic influence. The joy of sex can only be experienced within marriage. Outside marriage, it is nothing but lust of the flesh.

A married Christian who wilfully engages in a sexual relationship outside his matrimonial home is in violation of the Holy institution God ordained. A married Christian caught in this trap brings upon him the following.

The anger of a Holy God: for the defilement of the very temple in which the Spirit of God dwells, that temple is your body. Sexual immorality renders the body of a Christian unfit for the indwelling of the Holy Spirit. This is the reason why we must obey Paul's words in Galatians.

Destroys the joy of marriage: Marriage is a covenant between a man and a woman who have taken a vow before a priest or a pastor who is God's representative and a witness to that marriage, therefore, if any of them does anything that will break the peace of the marriage God will hold them accountable.

A marriage vow is more than a contract that we can break by paying damages. A unique vow is explicitly intended to be binding until death separates the husband and wife. The marriage ring is to remind couples that they must remain faithful until death separates them.

Opens the door of his heart for the invasion of a demonic spirit: Do you know that a husband who engages in sexual immorality turns his home into a spiritual battleground? A battle he cannot win, because he has been spiritually stripped naked and bound. Hence, his family become defenceless against evil spiritual forces.

Spiritual wilting point: At this stage, a Christian no longer feels the presence of the Holy Spirit. As a result, the restraining work of the Holy Spirit does not operate in his life. This leaves him with no spiritual defences against the enemy. It will take the grace of God to revive him, if only he is willing.

He puts his loyal spouse at risk of contacting sexually transmitted disease. He may lose the trust of his spouse because of his immoral behaviour. When a husband loses the trust of his wife, it will be very difficult to regain it. For a marriage to work there has to be trust.

His life is filled with spiritual emptiness: The void left by the Holy Spirit can never be filled by anything else. This is dangerous for any Christian; a Christian without fellowship with God is a dead Christian. See Psalm 51:11&12.

Unless the natural desires that attract us to members of the opposite sex are channelled exclusively towards marriage, the temptation to engage in sexual immorality can easily overpower our self-control and destroy a happy marriage. With sexual sin, the body is affected, because that body is the temple of God.

Sexual sin breaks the unity of marriage and sometimes leaves both partners unable to pray together. It takes unity, faith and the Holy Spirit to experience the power of God. Every Christian husband is the priest in his home. It is his responsibility to intercede for the family. People who intercede for others must live a life of purity that is constantly in tune with the Holy Spirit. Therefore, it is imperative spouses live by the Spirit and walk in the Spirit.

The Apostle Paul told the Galatians, "Since we live by the Spirit, let us keep in step with the Spirit." If a Christian husband who is supposed to be the intercessor for his family is living in sexual immorality, how can he intercede for the family in times of spiritual warfare? This is why the Christian husband must keep himself pure for God and his family.

Purity is a mark of the Christian marriage and should be our coat of arms, which we must proudly wear and display for all to see the beauty of Jesus Christ in our marriage. Spirit-filled Christians must be on the lookout, for there are men and women dressed in Scriptures in the Church who are nothing but Satan's agents.

They prowl on unsuspecting Christians with the aim of tricking them into marriage. These agents can sweet-talk their way into a woman's heart and trick her into marriage. These kinds of people have Scriptures readily available to support their actions. They use knowledge of the Scriptures as bait to trap unsuspecting Christians.

The sad story here is that unsuspecting men and women become sitting ducks. It is only when you are married to them that they unleash their ugly side. The reasons for Christians going through divorce could be many. The unity of prayer of husband and wife can render the power of Satan ineffective, so that his evil plots will not affect our spiritual and physical lives.

Do you know that the unity of prayer holds the key to a loving married relationship? The unity of prayer is what will move God to punish speedily those who try to break up the marriages of His children. The unity of husband and wife in prayer keeps storms out of their marriage and brings calmness. So build your marriage on love and unity.

The blessing of marriage is through the unity of prayer. Whether a marriage will fail or succeed depends upon love and unity of prayer. The power of God's presence can be experienced in every marriage through the unity of prayer.

Christian husband and wife, hear the WORD of the LORD. "In that day you will no longer ask me anything. I tell the truth, my father will give you whatever you ask in my name. Until now, you have not asked for anything in my name. Ask and you will receive, and your joy will be complete." (John 16:23-24.)

Are you standing on the promises of God, which cannot fail? Take God at His Word and hold on to His Word. Now hear the WORD of God again, you Christian husband and wife: "So shall my word that goes out from mouth: It will not return to me empty, but will accomplish what I desire and achieve the purpose for which I sent it." (Isaiah 55:11)

Grandfather once told me that, "the idea of men and women being thrust together in close proximity for weeks and months at a time is a recipe for disaster." This is where courting couples should be very careful and not play into the hands of the tempter.

Temptation is stronger when courting couples put themselves in environments that make it easy for the tempter to tempt them. We must not underestimate the power of the tempter. Even the Scriptures say, "So, if you think you are standing firm, be careful that you don't fall." (1Corinthians 10:12)

There are no strict rules in the way courting couples should conduct themselves when they are together. However, the safest rule is to avoid close bodily contact if it is possible. Not only that, they should avoid being alone in a room for a long time. Being alone in a room for a long time can create some sexual feeling between courting couples if care is not taken.

We all know where our weak point is; therefore, we should not put ourselves beyond our limits where our resistance cannot sustain us. The desire to keep ourselves pure until our wedding day should inspire us to avoid any situation that will otherwise make us sin and lose the joy of the first night of the wedding.

The joy of the first night of marriage is the cream on the cake. If you lose out you have lost it for good. The guilt will haunt both of you for the rest of your lives. The first night after your wedding is the most important day of your lives. It is a special day you will both remember. Therefore, you must resist the temptation of being denied this particular day.

Remember what the Scriptures say in 1 Corinthians 10:13: "And God is faithful; he will not let you be tempted beyond what you can bear." Paul's warning to "take heed lest you fall" (1 Corinthians 10:12) is as necessary today as it has ever been.

It is evident that some courting couples have problems holding themselves together when they find themselves in compromising situations. When courting couples are together, they should avoid contact that could transmit sexual feelings. To have any lustful thought of sexual feeling is to commit adultery in the heart.

Unfortunately some courting couples knowingly or unknowing put themselves in a tempting position that can trigger desire; for example hugging and kissing for quite a considerable time can trigger sexual feeling. This should be avoided. Our ability to resist such feelings differs from one person to another.

What may tempt you may not tempt someone else. This is where courting couples must be very careful. You may see it as funny and playful; the other person may not see it that way. It is the duty of Christian couples not to spoil the party before the big night. The advice is to keep yourself clean by resisting.

Some courting couples think: after all we are getting married so what prevents us from sleeping together? Such thoughts weaken one's moral resistance. It is a situation courting couples should avoid for the sake of good testimony. It will take the grace of God for a spirit-filled Christian to come out of such close proximity with a clean body.

Can gunpowder and fire live together? This question is for you, the reader, to answer. Joseph was an example of a man who came out with a clean body after his close proximity to Potiphar's wife. Joseph's victory is a classical example of how to overcome temptations. Run, baby, run and do not look back is the command.

His reply to Potiphar's wife gives us three reasons why he would not have sexual relations with her. First, he refused to betray the unlimited confidence that Potiphar had placed in him. Second, he told the temptress clearly that she was Potiphar's wife. Even though she did not respect marriage, Joseph did. He saw the violation of marriage as something evil.

Third, he saw that adultery was a sin against God: How then could I do such a wicked thing and sin against God? Joseph's behaviour toward the woman matched his words: "He refused to go to bed with her or even be with her." When she seized him, he left his cloak in her hands and ran out of the house.

It was better for Joseph to lose his cloak than to lose his reputation. Similarly, it is better preserving your pride than losing it for nothing. In today's world where sex is regarded as a hobby, it is absolutely certain many men and women will find temptation difficult to resist. It is a world in which sexual conquests has become something people boast of and take delight in.

We have become sex slaves. Instead of being ashamed of it, we become boastful of our sexual conquests. Sex has become a household word, which some people see as part of everyday life. We must try to avoid what will one day kill off our testimonies.

12. When the Wife Becomes the Second Wife

"He who finds a wife finds what is good and receives favour from the LORD." (Proverbs 18:22).

Do you know that some men are married to two women? The first wife is the mother and the second wife is the woman he married. This situation arises when a man takes his mother with him into the matrimonial home.

The role of the second wife is to warm his bed, childbearing, cooking and housekeeping and to contribute financially towards the household, whilst the role of the first wife is to interfere and make decisions without consulting the REAL woman of the house. The first wives are nothing but troublemakers in the home.

Decisions in the home, what goes on in the house and the management of the house is the second wife's business and not for the first wife. Therefore, the first wife must keep her nose out of it. The moment the first wife starts interfering in the marriage she is sending a signal to the second wife that she is in charge.

If a man goes into marriage with his mother, he makes the marriage crowded. If a man really loves his wife, he will not take his mother into his marriage. A man who takes his mother into his marriage is looking for trouble. Marriage is a bond between husband and wife to the exclusion of all others.

Therefore, the marital home is out of bounds to troublemakers; the marital home has no room for troublemakers and troublemakers are not welcomed in the marital home. It does not matter if these troublemakers are members of the immediate family. Troublemakers will always be troublemakers: keep them out of your marriage before they spell disaster in your home.

Women do not like rivalry and if you create it in your marriage, you will never know peace. **A man who loves his wife will never provoke her to jealousy.** Moreover, **a man who provokes his wife to jealousy does not seek her highest interest.** A husband who really respects and loves his wife will not entertain troublemakers in his home.

If a man is married to his mother, he will run to her for advice on how to fix his marriage problems. He will run up to her because he does not know how to carry out basic maintenance work in the marriage. Men like this must grow up and detach themselves from their mother. Only then can he take control of his marriage.

I remember on one of my visits to mother for advice, she told me, "Son, if you are not mature enough to handle your marital problems send your wife to her parents for safe keeping until such a time as you are spiritually and physically matured." Marriage is a learning process, therefore we do not give up when things are not working as we expected.

Mother wanted me to be independent because she would not be around for me always. She wanted me to be able to handle my own affairs when she is no longer around to help. She told me, marriage is not for the novices but for those mature enough to handle marriage problems.

Again, she told me marriage is full of pitfalls. When we fall, we get up and find out what caused the fall, so that it does not happen again. Sometimes the fall is a testing time for us, it is not meant for us to quit, rather staying focused and learning what caused the fall. We fall to gain experience and not to run away from the fall.

Some mothers-in-law are happy playing the leading role in their son's marriage. They are always first to know what is going on in the house because their son relays information to them. Because they keep the lines of communication open at all times for their son. Besides, she is the first person the son runs to in times of crisis in the marriage.

They run to the arms of their mother like a frightened schoolchild. Every man loves his mother, which is a good thing. In marriage a husband's love and attention is for the wife alone. Women by nature hate competition; the slightest signs of competition will provoke them to jealousy.

If a husband shifts his love and affection from the wife to his mother then he is married to two women. Avoid situations in your marriage that can cause serious problems for the sake of peace in the home. Men who become very attached to their mother whilst growing are likely to take their mother into their marriage.

A smart woman should easily spot this during courtship and start working on it before marriage. Once you notice the strong bond between mother and son you should be bold enough to make your feelings known to your fiancé, and tell him he must know where to draw the line when you both say, "I do," to each other.

The wife will need to approach this with extreme caution and not show any signs of frustration. If you give away the slightest sign of frustration, your mother-in-law will read a different meaning into it, and take pre-emptive action to secure her unrestricted asses to your marital home. This is where self-control comes into play.

A doctor friend from Malta became too attached to his mother while he was growing up and took her into his marriage. His attractive mother lives in Malta whilst he lives in London with his wife in a one-bed room apartment to save money so that they can purchase a house. When his mother came to visit, it was time to catch up.

The mother hugging of her son with kisses on the cheek and mouth became a constant sight in the matrimonial home. The mother became the centre of affection and love. This young woman became so consumed with jealousy that she forgot the woman kissing her husband was her mother-in-law. Her husband's affection was something she felt was exclusively for her.

Things grew worse when the mother started fixing her son breakfast because he had to leave in the early morning for work. When she tried to talk her mother-in-law out of the breakfast fixing, this is what she said, "I hope I am not making trouble for you." Well she has just let the cat out of the bag.

The last straw was when the mother decided to extend her stay. She came for only five days and then decided to stay for an additional five days. By now, the wife could not hold herself together. Her frustrations were all over her face with no one to turn to and not wishing to come between her mother-in-law and her husband.

She walked into my office and told me she had had enough and was going to tell her mother-in-law she had outstayed her welcome. I told her that would be like going on a suicide mission and she must be prepared for the consequences. I told her to do nothing and say nothing for the sake of peace. Sometimes one can use this method to frustrate troublemakers.

It is very difficult to break a bond that has existed between mother and son for years. What we have here are two jealous women vying for the attention of one man. The odds are stacked against the wife. It takes prayer and prayer alone for the husband to break free from a mother who sees the son as her centre of love and affection.

The husband is responsible for his wife's happiness in the marriage. Therefore anything that will take away this happiness must be stopped. The husband's centre of love, joy, happiness and affection is the wife. The wife must also respond with submission to make the marriage complete.

Marriage makes a man mature and responsible enough to stand on his own two feet. Therefore, problems in marriage must be confined to the matrimonial home. The wife must be the number one person in the husband's life. This goes for the wife as well. Ignore this rule and be sure to have trouble in marriage.

The prophet Amos shared light on the walk that involves two people, which is worth memorising. "Do two walk together unless they have agreed to do so?" (Amos 3:3). It takes two to tie the knot and it takes two to untie the knot. The marriage knot you tied with so much love must remain tied until death undoes it.

People who want to get married must be ready to break with their past lives completely; otherwise, they are bound to break the heart of their spouse. We cannot bring into marriage the kind of life we led when we were single. This one of the problems most young marriages face. In most cases it is the men who are found wanting because they cannot make up their mind where to draw the line.

Although some people are married, they behave as if they are still single. I once met a young woman at a gym flirting with a married man who used to be her boyfriend. When the receptionist called her by her married name, she did not respond because she was so lost in a passionate conversation with the married man.

When the receptionist walked to her and asked, what her name was she gave her maiden name. When the receptionist asked her why, she said "Oh! I forgot I am married." She has since divorced her husband, the man also divorced his wife, and they are now married.

Grandmother once likened a heart breaker to a man who bought a roasted whole chicken from the supermarket and kept it in the fridge. Everyday he took a portion and kept the rest in the fridge. As the days went by, he lost the appetite through eating the same chicken everyday.

Therefore, he gave the rest of the chicken to a neighbour and got himself a fish. Marriage is like that for some people. But marriage is not like a piece of chicken we buy from the supermarket and discard it after the sell-by date or pass it to someone else when we have had enough of it.

Marriage's journey is without end. Those who embark on it must never look back. Along the journey, we are bound to encounter difficulties and temptations. As we journey, age will have its effect on us, and as a result, we will experience changes in our bodies. These changes are the result of nature taking its rightful course.

In this journey, we will come across youthfulness and its beauty advertising itself. We must resist the temptation to get rid of the old for new. We must resist the temptation to exchange what we hold dear for a temporal pleasure that will bring us nothing but trouble. In fact, the beauties we see along the journey have been garnished to tempt us.

If we fall prey to the bait, we will never complete the journey with the person we started with. Never give up your marriage for another relationship, no matter the temptation. Marriage is a lifetime relationship with the exclusion of all others. It is a life commitment with only one person, and that person is the person to whom you are married.

God who created marriage intended it to bring joy and happiness to the union of man and woman. Yet what we see is constant raging battle in marriages. Man's quest to live a life of self-centeredness could be the root cause of these raging battles. Women by their nature need attention and it must come from the husband.

If a man really loves his wife, he will be very attentive to whatever his wife is saying and try to meet her needs. Needs in this context have nothing to do with material needs, rather it has to do with attention and affection towards your wife. For example, your wife is talking to you about a pressing issue in the marriage and you do not seem to be concerned about her plight. Instead, you are more concerned about what is irrelevant to her.

Things are going wrong and she wants them sorted out quickly and all she gets from you is, "Don't you know others don't have what you have." Well you have just screwed things up. The last thing you need is to come home to an angry wife, a situation every husband must avoid.

A friend once remarked, "When Imogene is happy, I am happy." I hope every husband would be like Charlie. Charlie understands he is the initiator of love and not Imogene. It is the responsibility of every husband to make sure his wife is happy. There is more to marriage than we think, if only we are willing to explore the world of marriage.

Husbands must love their wives enough to give them their attention. The husband should fulfil his marital role as the Scriptures demand and not try to run away from his responsibilities. Just as we fulfil our responsibilities at work, so we must fulfil marriage responsibilities.

A happy wife is an indication of a happy marriage. A loving husband is a blessing to the family. A husband who makes his marital home a home of joy and happiness will find he is at the very centre of his wife's heart. Such a husband will never lack the warmth of his wife and her marriage becomes her pride and joy.

An unhappy wife points to an unhappy married relationship. The reason is simple: every woman's joy is to be in a happy married relationship. She goes the extra mile to keep her marriage working because she values the joy of marriage. Usually the wife is the one who protects the marriage with jealousy.

A happy home is every woman's pride and joy. The home is the only place a woman can run for protection, shelter, comfort, and love. A happy family home is what every woman cherishes. It is something she will guard with jealousy. Therefore, the husband must do everything possible to make the marital home a pleasant place for the wife to live.

Women have been involved in battles fought all over the world. Nevertheless, the last thing a woman will want is for her home to be turned into a battleground. A woman will go the extra mile to stop battles being fought in her home. Women do not normally start marriage battles; neither are they the causes of marriage battles. Rather, they stop it before it happens.

Christians should not see raging battles as sign of a doomed marriage, although such unpleasant situations or difficult circumstances could be due to external intrusion by those who do not want the marriage to work. Battles we try to avoid in our marriages will surely show up someday. When they come, we must remain steadfast because the power of prayer can calm the raging storms in the marriage and make things turn round in your favour.

The weapons to calm the raging storm in our marriages are the word of God, faith and the power of prayer. With these mighty weapons, we can surmount the insurmountable storms in marriage. We Christians have indeed mighty weapons in our hands, but the devil will make us believe that we lack the ability to use such weapons.

To achieve this, the devil uses his own weapons of fear and doubt to paralyse our faith in God, thereby preventing us from using the only weapon that can defeat him. Be steadfast and take hold of the sword of the spirit, which is the word of God. Remember the battle with the devil is not a physical battle but a spiritual one.

Christian wife, have you suddenly forgotten you have a mighty weapon in your hand? Do you lack the ability and skills to use it? If you fail to do something about the spiritual battle that is taking place in your marriage then you are giving your enemies the opportunity to hold on tightly to what they have stolen from you.

As children of God, we must not accept defeat in marriage. Accepting defeat simply means you have publicly acknowledged to those who played a part in bringing your marriage down that they have won both the spiritual and physical a battle in your marriage. When the Christian goes to battle with Jesus Christ, he or she wins. With Jesus Christ, we do not lose but we win.

Again, you have also relinquished to your enemy that which God has given you. Is this what you want? You surrendered the gift of God cheaply to your enemies. From the day you got married, your enemies have been plotting to bring down your marriage. Against this, be very careful you do not walk out of your marriage for your enemy to walk in rejoicing.

Should a Christian accept that his or her marriage is over and walk out of the holy institution God ordained? Before you decide enough is enough, ask yourself these questions. Did I really love this person? Am I part of the problem or can I be part of the solution? Get on your knees before Jesus and you will be a winner.

Satan fears nothing like a Christian on his or her knees praying. Tell God, "I want my spouse back, he belongs to me and me alone and no one else." Just as God will never give up on you so you must never give up on your husband or wife who has just walked out of the marriage. Instead, tell the LORD, "I have suffered much; preserve my life, O LORD, according to your word. (Psalm 119:107).

If we yield to the Holy Spirit through prayer and fasting and work with God in our marriage, then our marriage will rest on solid rock. Not only that, but it will become unmovable, unshakable and safe from influence by outside forces. If we hold on to God's written law in the Scriptures, and be sincere, honest and loyal to each other, then the LORD will protect our marriage from the invasion of devouring locusts. If we hold on to the marriage vows that joined two hearts together then no one can separate us.

12. Divorce: Who Is To Blame

"For this reason a man will leave his father and mother and be united to his wife, and the two become one flesh? So they are no longer two, but one flesh. Therefore what God has joined together, let no man separate." (Matthew 19:5-6) "Come to me, all you who are weary and burdened, and I will give you rest." (Matthew 11:28).

It is quite common to hear some business people say, "Contracts were meant to be broken." Tragically, that is all too often true. People today make and break commitments with seeming abandon. On paper, they may agree to certain terms. However, when the terms are no longer convenient, they break the promise on their commitments. Alternatively, they end the relationship when their interest in the other person no longer exists.

The story of the Parable of the Lost Coin speaks of perseverance. The woman in Luke 15:8-10 teachers us something about dedication to our marriage. You will notice that she did not just sit down and cry because her coin was lost. She decided to do something about it and went to work according to a definite plan of action.

She could have crawled through the house feeling with her hand for the coin. Instead, she made use of what she had in order to do the best job possible. With the lighted lamp, she could see well. With her broom, she could reach farther under the furniture and into the corners.

Her zest to fine the lost coin prompted her quick action in making use of what was available in the house. The earnestness with which she looked for the coin led her to where the coin was hidden. She made very good use of the only tools available to her, which were the light and the broom.

Moses had a shepherd's staff; with the staff, he led a nation from slavery into freedom. Samson with a donkey's jawbone killed a thousand men. David, with just a sling in his hand slew Goliath. What can we say about Gideon? With just three hundred men, he defeated an entire army. In addition, the woman in Luke 15 only had a lamp and a broom and she found the coin. What do you have in your hand to stop divorce?

God expects us to use the natural talents that He has given us in solving our marital problems. In addition, He wants us to work with the Holy Spirit in resolving our marital problems. You would notice that the woman's hard work and persistency paid off. Our dedication to our marriage and the desire to make it work it what can make our marriage a success and keep divorce out of the marriage.

"Getting a divorce is now easier than obtaining a driving licence; this is the decision of a senior family judge." People need to re-educate themselves about the importance of stable marriage relationships for the good of society because of the huge problem of family breakdown.

Today the stigma of divorce has disappeared and been replaced the fashionable term "EX", a term that suits our society yet makes the institution of marriage a mockery. The church and the secular world must tackle the high rate of family breakdown.

Cohabitation is the reason why the stigma attached to divorce has disappeared in our society today. However, the rate at which cohabiting couples break up is higher than with married couples. This is good news for the marriage institution. If this continues, it will make people who opt for cohabitation consider a U-turn.

Beautiful marriages are marred by the ugly lifestyles of married couples. Every marriage suffers because of the bad living of the husband or wife. Bad living leads to bad divorce where spouses vow never to talk to each other. This is the problem married couples must wake up to before things get out of hand.

Every married couple ought to be charged to live by the marriage vows. Those who cannot live by the marriage vows should not be married. Our obedience to the marriage vows advances love for each other. Christians will be missing the joy of marriage if virtue and love do not rectify their conduct.

It is the very nature of the marriage vows that should make us quit bad conduct and live until "death do us part." Cold and dead marriage exists with bad conduct and we must work to change our bad conduct. **Seeking each other's highest interest advances love in marriage and changes bad lifestyles.**

Our life must give colour to our marriage and make others want to be married. Bad living makes a bad marriage. We cannot talk to God about our marriage problems when we have not lived our life to honour God. Again, we cannot expect God to help us overcome our marital problems when we deliberately walk away from His counsel.

If the unmarried look at married life and say, "if this is all that marriage is about, then I don't want to be part of that institution," then you have shamed the institution of marriage. The Christian marriage is a lamp that should give light to a marriage in darkness. However, if the lamp goes off because it has no oil (love) then it seizes to be a light to the world.

Love is the firm foundation of the Christian marriage and this must be demonstrated practically for all to see. The unbelieving world would want to see this before they can accept our message. However, if this is the reverse then how can we expect them to accept our message? Christian marriage must be an example to the world. The Christian marriage must be unique in its entirety.

Marriage is a covenant institution ordained by God. Marriage is a holy institution ordained by Holy God. Therefore, the Christian marriage must begin with holiness and end with holiness when we stand before the Holy God. **A good Christian marriage is an effective channel of communicating the message of Salvation.**

Despite this, recent years have seen skyrocketing divorce rates. Yet divorce is nothing new. It was common throughout the ancient world, usually favouring men. Thus, the law did not establish divorce, but brought justice to an existing practice. Moses spoke of a certificate of divorce (Deut, 24: 1-4). Apparently, the husband was to initiate the preparation of the official document dissolving the marriage.

He could have it written if he found any "uncleanness" in his wife. No one knows exactly what "uncleanness" was supposed to mean, but it was sufficient grounds for divorce. Yet the law spoke not so much to the subject of divorce in general as to the question of whether a previously divorced couple could remarry after the wife had been through a second marriage.

The statute seemed to aim at preventing people from moving in and out of marriage in a way that trivialized the institution of marriage. Marriage should not be like a house you can move in and out of at any time you like. Marriage is not like a car you can change anytime you feel like replacing it with a new one.

If you see a beautiful house you like, you simply get rid of your old house and buy the new one that suits your taste. Nobody can question you for that.

Well, marriage is not like that. In marriage, we are dealing with flesh and blood and not bricks and mortar. Marriage deals with human feelings whilst buildings have no feelings.

How should believers today regard divorce? Is it prohibited in the Bible? This is a very complex issue, and various traditions hold different points of view. Biblical principles suggest that settling questions about divorce should start with a proper understanding of marriage.

Marriage is a Holy Institution established by GOD. When God created the world, He made male and female and established that they be united in marriage (Gen. 1:27, 2:24). The marital union should be characterized by singular faithfulness; indeed, God considers the marriage bond sacred.

Marriage is based on Trust and Faithfulness. Cultures may vary in how they form marriages. In some the partners marry for love, in others the marriage is arranged. However, it comes about, once established God considers marriage a sacred bond and expects the partners to honour that union with exclusive, lasting commitment. (Matt 19:16)

GOD hates unfaithfulness. Just as people marry for various reasons, they divorce for various reasons. The primary reason for divorce is unfaithfulness, not only sexual infidelity, but emotional unfaithfulness, allowing one's affections and commitments to wander away from one's mate so that trust, commitment, and communication break down.

Through Malachi God declared that He hates divorce. (Malachi 2:16). However, the context makes it clear that God hates divorce because He hates unfaithfulness, the cause of divorce. God's intended purpose for marriage was that married couples be faithful to each other.

Divorce is a Concession by God. God hates divorce, but He permits it as a concession to the fallen nature of humanity. (Matt. 19:8). Easy divorces were the standard of the day in the cultures surrounding ancient Israel. The law established guidelines to limit the Hebrews from abusing each other through divorce.

Grounds for divorce are few. Today, a marriage can be dissolved easily. However, if one considers the Bible, there are few reasons why divorce is permissible. (It was never mandated, except when Ezra commanded certain Jews returning from Exile to dissolve their marriage to pagans, Ezra 9-10.)

The New Testament appears to allow two reasons for divorce: adultery (Matt 5:32; 19:9) and the desertion of a Christian by an unbelieving spouse (one Corinthians 7:12-16). There could be other valid circumstances the Scripture does not address, such as persistent physical or emotional abuse.

There is a place for compassion for divorce. As much as God hates unfaithfulness and divorce, He shows compassion for divorced people and is ready to forgive and to restore any who have come short of His expectations when they seek His pardon.

Divorce, whatever the grounds, is not a sin that cannot be forgiven. Yet neither is it something to be taken lightly. Marriage is a solemn commitment that should be entered into carefully and with a view towards permanence. On the other hand, what we see today is the reverse order.

Divorce is an acknowledgement that sin wreaks havoc on God's design. Yet it need not be the only response to a troubled relationship. Marriage is important enough for partners to try all available means to preserve it when they face obstacles. The obstacles we face in marriage can easily be pushed aside with love, through prayer.

Has divorce anything to do with age? At what age should a man marry? In addition, what age should a woman marry? Are men and women who marry later in life better able to hold marriage together than men and women who marry early in life? Today, some men marry at the early age of eighteen or nineteen, while some women marry as young as sixteen or seventeen.

I think people at this age should be in a higher institution or in college learning a trade that will prepare them for the future. Even in some cultures, girls marry at the tender ages of twelve to fifteen. Girls at this age enter an arranged marriage, frequently against their will and often with a man they have never previously met. There is little communication, cooperation or affection.

Arranged marriages are not based on love, rather people are compelled to marry because it is the family's wish. Women who find themselves in this kind of marriage expect to develop love for the husband as the years goes by. Family who are involved in this system of marriage do not regard love as an essential prerequisite for marriage. In most cases, the marriage is based on what both families can gain.

By comparison, for the Christian, new life in Christ calls for a new pattern in marriage

(Ephesians 5:21-19). Paul instructed the husband to love his wife and seek her personal development. The wife is to respond with commitment and loyalty. Her submission is not subordination but a wholehearted response to her husband.

So what is the ideal age for marriage? This is the opinion of a cross-section of people spoken to. For women the majority of people think the ideal age should be twenty-five. For men the accepted ideal age is thirty. The assumption is that physically, mentally and spiritually, men and women at this age are well prepared for marriage.

Can this assumption be true? The question we should be asking is what makes men and women at that age well prepared for marriage? The shocking news is that divorce is rampant among the so-called "ideal age for marriage." Statistics shows that the divorce rate among those who marry below the ages stated above is spiralling out of control.

However, it should be noted that this is not always the case. It is evident that marriages among some men and women below the ideal age are doing far better than marriages among the supposed ideal age. What a contrast. What are the causes of the rampant divorce in our society?

Until the problems are addressed by Church leaders and community leaders, we will continue to see the downward spiral of divorce among Christians and non-Christians. Some Church leaders are insensitive about the issue of divorce. Therefore, it does not form part of the sermon coming from the pulpit. Jesus Christ spoke about the issue of divorce to His generation. The apostle Paul also emphasised the question of divorce.

The worst thing about divorce is watching married couples who were once passionately in love suddenly become sworn enemies. Our society is faced with this grim picture of a failing marriage institution. This pathetic situation makes a mockery of marriage. This trend can only be reversed if we work hard toward it.

Some of the causes of the skyrocketing divorce rates could be linked to impatience between married couples. **Lack of forgiveness in marriage is the worm that will eventually destroy the marriage vine.** It starts by eating its way from the roots of the marriage until it reaches the head by which time the situation becomes hopeless.

Once the supporting roots have been destroyed by an unforgiving spirit the marriage has nothing else to stand on. It is only a matter of time until the next storm blows over and sends the marriage tumbling down. You will only have yourself to blame if you allow an unforgiving spirit to destroy your marriage.

People who think they are perfect and without fault should not go into marriage because they will not find a perfect man or woman in this world to marry. Perfection in marriage is something you will never find because perfection does not exist in marriage. However if you should find a perfect man or woman do not join in holy matrimony with the person because you will ruin it with your imperfection.

God who instituted marriage knew from the beginning that this fallen race could not make marriage perfect. Every marriage has its problems. The problem is the person you are married to and yourself. Marriage has no problem; the only problems in the marriage are the two people in the marriage.

In every marriage, it is the responsibility of the married couple to make it work. Depending on outsiders to fix your marriage problems will not work. So do not take your marriage problem outside your matrimonial home. Marriage is about teamwork and spouses must cooperate fully for its success.

Love can be defined as "a condition that exists when another person's well-being and security are as important to you as your own." This definition can be used as a decisive test to test the sincerity of love in every marriage. Before you tie the knot, ask yourself this question: Among all the women in the world, why did I choose to walk with this particular woman down the aisle?

Among all the men in the world, why did I choose to live the rest of my life with this particular man by saying "I do"? The answers to these questions will unearth the reasons why divorce is so rampant in this generation. The reason why some people marry is what will eventually lead to divorce. Marriage is one of God's wonderful gifts to humanity.

God wants us enjoying it with the same person "till death do us part." Only God alone can safeguard marriage and hold it together because he ordained the marriage institution. Well if this statement is true, then why are Christian marriages breaking up? The rate at which Christian marriages are breaking up is alarming.

Are Christians whose marriages are breaking up really Christians? Alternatively, are they merely churchgoers? Are couples who wed in churches Christians? This question may hold the answer to the reasons why Christian marriages often end in divorce. To be fair to the Christian faith, we need to be sure couples who are married in the Church are Christians.

The reason for these questions is that when it comes to Christian marriages statistics shows that far more marriages that are Christian are breaking down. Moreover, we need urgent solutions to curb this high rate of divorce and restore sanity to the Christian marriage. We need to approach this problem with earnestness.

The problem we face in our society is that once two people make up their minds to marry nothing can stop them. They want it done and done quickly. Even if during counselling sessions they are cautioned not to rush into marriage they will not listen. Situations like this call for pastors to exercise their authority.

From the beginning, God never intended marriages to end in divorce. It was man's lustful desires that made God lay down the condition for divorce. Despite this, man has consistently violated these conditions. See Mark 10:1-12, Matthew 5:31-32, and Matthew 19:3-9.

The problems Christians face in marriage have absolutely nothing to do with God. Marriage is a divine institution and God who instituted it is the same yesterday and today. He has not changed. The human race keeps breaking marriage vows to suit their lustful desires. As a result, we pay the high price of divorce.

Has God failed us? Is God tired of holding Christian marriage together? Has God who created the institution of marriage decided He has had enough of human weakness and failure? God never fails and He will never fail the institution He established. We fail because we choose to walk away from His good counsels.

The question we should be asking concerning the high divorce rate is: who has failed whom? What must God be thinking of today's skyrocketing divorce? Who is to be blamed? Should God and the Bible be blamed? Who then should we blame, the two imperfect couple who decided to come together as man and wife without the blessing of God?

Someone must take the blame, if someone must take it, then who should it be? If you examine the Scriptures very carefully, you will know where the buck stops. We do not need to look beyond human frailty to find whom to blame. The frailties of human nature are what will draw us towards divorce.

As for God, He is perfect; His written Word, the Bible, is infallible. That leaves the two imperfect people as the most likely culprit. We must agree that the cause of every broken marriage lies with man. In addition, both spouses should be held accountable. Marriage does not just break up suddenly; it starts with little problems that build up to become a mountain.

We are nothing but mere mortals subject to human weakness and failures. However, should human weakness and failures be good reasons to continue violating marriage vows? The answer is no. God has given everyone the will to say yes or no. The fear of standing before a Holy God should be what must make us honour our marriage vows.

This reminds me of Paul's words in Romans 6:1-2. "What shall we say, then? Shall we go on sinning, so that grace may increase?" In verse 2, Paul gives a negative answer. In reply, he says "By no means! We died to sin; how can we live in it any longer"?

Marriage is like a triangle (God, the husband and the wife) where the man and the woman are under oath, or takes a solemn vow to adhere to all the requirements of the marriage vows. The oath is based on trust that each of them will faithfully obey and seek each other's highest interest.

Are there any get-out clauses in a marriage vow? Well let us examine the following marriage vows from the Church of England. This vow reads, "I---- take thee ----to be my lawful wife, to have and to hold from this day forward, for better for worse, for richer for poorer, in sickness and in health to love and to cherish, **till death do us part,** according to God's holy ordinance, and thereto I plight thee my troth."

The Bride: "I --take thee --- to be my lawful wedded husband, to have and to hold from this day forward, for better for worse, for richer for poorer, in sickness and in health, to love cherish, and to obey, **till death do us part,** according to God's holy ordinance; and thereto I give thee my troth."

A traditional Roman Catholic vow reads: "I ---take you---to be my lawful (husband/wife). I promise to be true to you in good times and in bad, in sickness and in health. **I will love you and honour you all the days of my life."** There are no differences in the two vows. Neither of the two vows allows an exit clause.

Both vows view the institution of marriage as an institution ordained by God. Both agree that only in death can the couples be separated. Both vows agree with the Apostle Paul's words in Ephesians. "Husbands love your wives. Wives must submit to their husbands (respect their husbands)." The husband vows to love and cherish the wife. The wife vows to obey the husband.

The marriage vow is a unique vow that is intended to bind both halves of a couple together until death separates them. The words "for better for worse; for richer for poorer; in sickness and in health" as they stand will demand absolute commitment to each other without any preconditions attached.

The marriage certificate is like a contract and it includes blanks for the principals making the contract to sign. Their signatures attest that they agree to the terms of the contract, and by signing on the dotted lines, they confirm the agreement that only **natural death can separate them.**

It is not going to be easy to keep the vows, for circumstances do change with passing time. Spouses may change. There may be disagreements, difficulties and disappointment. Nevertheless, in all this, we must remember that love is more than a feeling; it is a commitment.

Seeking each other's highest interest in marriage is the mark of fulfilling the marriage vows and the sign of a happy marriage. We seek each other's highest interest because we want the marriage to work. We seek each other's highest interest because we love the other person in the marriage and will not to do anything that will hurt our wife or husband.

We seek the other person's highest interest in marriage because we are ready to accept and accommodate the other person's faults and failings, knowing neither of us can be perfect. It is only when spouses seek each other's interest that there can be peace and harmony in the marriage.

If a man seeks his wife's highest interest, he will never do anything to provoke her to jealousy. Provoking your spouse to jealousy will be the last straw that will destroy a happy marriage. A man who provokes his wife to jealousy married her for other reasons and not because of love.

There is no provocation in love. Love stirs up happiness and not jealousy. Love does not provoke jealousy. Transparency is the only antidote for jealousy in marriage. Where there is transparency in marriage, there is no room for jealousy to thrive. The bachelor life stops from the day a man says, "I do." The same goes for the married woman, her days of unmarried life end from the day she said, "I do."

Sometime some married couples forget they are married and as a result carry their bachelor lives into the marriage. God has laid a perfect, solid foundation for the marriage institution by giving us the guiding principles. Therefore, those who want to build on them must be very careful to build with the correct building materials, which are love and submission.

Those who have said, "I do" to each other have agreed in principle that they will obey every word enshrined in the marriage vow. In addition, husband and wife must be faithful to each other. Do they really obey the vows they publicly declare before God, the officiating priest and witnesses present?

In a marriage where spouses are committed to each other to obey the marriage vows, divorce will have no resting place. Have these vows simply become lip service? God is the chief witness in every marriage vow since He created that institution. Therefore, the marriage vows taken in the presence of God must be seen to be active and working.

The word commitment is in jeopardy these days. Some people even call it the "C" word, as if to shame it as something we would not even acknowledge. After all, the demands and costs are too great. Today, convenience usually wins out over the sacrifice involved in being committed to someone. It rather unfortunate that some people are not prepared to make sacrifices in their marriage, it is only when it is convenient to them.

God's anger will be on marriage vow breakers for He will hold them accountable. Some day when we stand before God, every married person will give an account of what part he or she played in making the marriage work or what part we played in destroying the marriage. This includes in-laws and those close to married couples.

In addition, those whose conduct contribute directly or indirectly to the break-up of every marriage, beware the anger of God will surely will be on those who make a marriage crowded. On this note, do not think you can get away without paying for the consequences of your actions that led to the wrecking of someone else's marriage.

Therefore, avoid every appearance of temptation that will lead to breaking someone else's marriage. Remember temptation itself is not a sin, it is only when you allow the desire of someone else wife or husband lead you into fulfilling that desire that makes it a sin. Grandfather once said, "Desiring someone else wife is as dangerous as lying in bed with the most poisonous snake."

People who are looking for husbands or wives should not look for one from the marriage pasture.

It is a no-go area for the unmarried. If you are looking for a husband, do not go for someone else's husband. That goes for the men as well. A man or woman looking for a wife or husband should look for one from pastures confined to single people and not from pastures reserved for married people.

Do not be tempted by someone else's wife or husband, no matter how strong the temptation. If you do, and the wife or husband cries out to God for vengeance then be sure you will see the wrath of God as you have never seen it before. If you want to see the anger of God, then try snatching someone else's spouse for yourself. Do not try it. It is the quickest path to an early death.

Malachi 2:16 records God saying, "I hate divorce" The Church finds itself in an unenviable position of being almost the only agency or institution that can and will stand for the sanctity of marriage and family. We must provide support and counsel for those with troubled marriages and work earnestly to bring separated couples back together when it is feasible to do so.

We must search the Scriptures for the teaching of Christ and the men of God who have dealt with this difficult subject. Nevertheless, should divorce occur, and continues to occur with increasing frequency, we must reach out to the victims of broken homes with a non-judgemental love like that of Christ, who came not to condemn but to redeem.

13. Remarriage: What Does The Bible Say?

"Now to the unmarried and the widows I say: It is good for them to stay unmarried, as I am. But if they cannot control themselves, they should marry, for it is better to marry than burn with passion." (1 Corinthians 7:8-9)

Do you not know, brothers—for I am speaking to men who know the law—that the law has authority over a man only as long as he lives? For example, by law a married woman is bound to her husband as long as he is alive, but if her husband dies, she is released from the law of marriage. So then, if she remarries another man while her husband is still alive, she is called an adulteress. But if her husband dies, she is released from that law and is not an adulteress, even though she marries another man. (Romans 7:1-3)

THE CHRISTIAN MARRIAGE IS NOT LIKE A GARMENT TO BE TAKEN ON AND OFF WHEN IT SUITS US. IT IS A LOFTY CHALLENGE ABOUT HOW WE LIVE THE

MARRIAGE LIFE BEFORE A HOLY GOD AND THE WORLD, WHO ARE WATCHING US.

Under a marriage contract, a husband and wife are legally bound to each other for life. When one partner dies, however, the other is released from his or her marriage vows and is free to remarry. It is very true that a woman is bound to her husband as long as he lives, likewise is the man bound to his wife as long as she lives.

Grandmother once said of remarriage, "You get rid of one demon and a worse demon sets in. You dispatch one oppressive husband and another oppressive, ugly man appears. You never know where the next demon is coming from." Again, grandfather once said, "A successful marriage is not a gift but an achievement.

It is an achievement because we incorporate love, submission, prayer and the desire to make the marriage work for the glory of God who created the institution of marriage." We marry because we want to mirror the image of God. For man is the image of God. We marry because we want to create something that never existed before (children).

We marry for good reasons and not for selfish reasons. We marry because we want to be married and not to be single. We marry because we want to honour and fulfil God's intended purpose for marriage. Are we willing to go the extra mile in our marriage to shame the word DIVORCE?

What do the Scriptures say about remarriage? Does it encourage remarriage or does it discourage it? What guidelines do the Scriptures lay down for remarriage? Are these guidelines open to individual interpretations? If the answer is yes, then do we interpret Scripture to suit our selfish interest?

In matters of remarriage, whom should we obey: the Church doctrines or the Scriptures? In the question of remarriage, whose word should be the final authoritative word? Is the Church the sole custodian of the Scriptures and its final interpretations? These and other questions need to be addressed.

Remarriage is a subject that has left a bitter taste in some Christians' mouths. The subject of remarriage is one of the reasons some people leave the Church and never return. When it comes to remarriage, care must be taken for those who want to remarry to understand what the Scriptures say.

We need to search the Scriptures to find out what God says about divorce. Jesus Christ, Paul, Luke, Moses and some of the Old Testament prophets spoke concerning divorce. It is worth studying carefully to find out what each of them had to say.

A pastor once said, "For the Christian marriage happens once, only death can bring about a second marriage." Once you tie the knot that is it. This means there is no turning back. Except you know you can stay single for the rest of your life. Is this pastor right in making this statement?

For the Christian, there is no second marriage as long as the other person in the marriage is still alive. We live in a world where some Christians do not care what the Scriptures say about remarriage. Their self-centeredness seems to have blinded them to what the Bible says about remarriage.

At this, let me reiterate that the demon in divorce is remarriage. This evil has plagued the world of marriage for centuries. When a man or woman remarries while the other spouse is still alive, that is what is called the demon in remarriage. Remarriage is the major cause of divorce in our society today.

A young woman once remarked, "If the marriage is not working get rid of him and look for another husband." This kind of language should not play any role in what Scriptures say about marriage and remarriage. The author of the Scriptures never intended marriage to end in divorce. From the beginning, God's plan was for marriage to be a life commitment.

Man's selfish nature made God lay down the rules on divorce. The Scriptures make it clear that a person can only remarry after the other person in the marriage has died. It is so sad that many Christians openly flout the rules concerning marriage and remarriage. Their desire to remarry appears to override Biblical principles.

As a result, many Christians have joined the bandwagon of "marry today, divorce tomorrow when the marriage isn't working." This may be why some Christians do not attach much emphasis on working to save their marriages. Instead, they fuel the flame of divorce. In matters of remarriage we must be very careful be obey what the Scriptures say.

A West African proverb says, "If you are afraid of divorce you will never get a good marriage." This is satanically inspired proverb, which, can fuel the circle of divorce in society and create a breeding ground for single parenthood. I think the proverb should read as follows, "If you love marriage you will be afraid of divorce."

This kind of language should not play any role in what Scriptures say about marriage and remarriage. The author of the Scriptures never intended marriage to end in divorce. From the beginning, God's plan was for marriage to be a life commitment. Man's selfish nature made God lay down the rules on divorce and remarriage.

The Scriptures leave us with no alternative to what God has spoken regarding remarriage. We only have two choices, obey what the Scripture says or ignore it. The Scripture will never lead us astray because the Word of God is perfect and without error. Luke makes very crystal clear that, "Anyone who divorces his wife and marries another woman commits adultery, and the man who marries a divorced woman commits adultery." (Luke 16:18).

Ponder over the verse carefully and let God speak to you before making a decision. Again, Paul in his first letter to the Corinthians concerning marriage stated that, "To the married I give this command (not I, but the Lord): A wife must not separate from her husband. But if she does, she must remain unmarried or else be reconciled to her husband.

And a husband must not divorce his wife." (7:10-11). It is worth studying the whole of chapter seven. Read carefully the teachings of Jesus on divorce and remarriage as recorded in Matthew 5:31-32 (paralleled in Luke 16:18) and Matthew 19:3-9 (paralleled in Mark 10:1-12). Then examine the similarities of Jesus and the writings of Paul.

You would have noticed that both forbid divorce and both forbid remarriage. You will also observe that while Matthew wrote within the context of a Jewish culture, Mark wrote for the gentile Church. See Mark 10:1-12 in comparison with Matthew. The point here is that Jesus spoke within a culture where women simply did not have the option to divorce; whereas in Mark and Paul that is not true.

In both cases, therefore, the teaching of Jesus is applied to women as well as to men. Against this, is there any hope for a young woman whose husband walked out of the marriage? Let us take for example a situation where the woman is young, beautiful and sexually active. The woman is in her thirties and divorced.

Alternatively, a young man whose wife has walked out, telling him, "I'm not coming back." Are we going tell them to remain unmarried for the rest of their lives because the ex-husband is still alive? Let us be honest, can a young person in his or her late twenties or early thirties who is divorced remain unmarried until the time her husband dies?

Let us take this case study. I know of a young man called Turner whose wife died through natural causes. He met and married a woman who had divorced her husband. This is a complicated case because both of them are in the same Church.

The problem in this marriage is that the woman's husband is still alive. To make matters worse and complicated for the woman she had turned down any form of reconciliation initiated by her pastor. This put them in the hot spot for scrutiny, making their situation even more difficult to comprehend.

During counselling, their pastor told them in plain words that their decision to get married broke every command of God. Therefore, he cannot join them together as husband and wife, but they are free to get married elsewhere. They found a Church whose pastor thought otherwise and willingly married them.

When they came back as a married couple, they found that the holy men and women in the Church would not tolerate their presence. In the eyes of the congregation, this newly married couple were sinners. When the church becomes a house of judgement instead of house of worship, then it ceases to be what it has been commissioned to be.

When the Church is turned into a place of judgement instead of a place where sinners can find love and forgiveness, then it loses its divine purpose. The newly married couple never stood a chance in the Church. The knives were out for them. The hostility towards the newly married couple was shameful and bizarre. The couple met a stony faced and uncaring congregation.

The reaction of some of the congregation members will make one wonder if such an attitude is in line with Jesus' teachings. When Jesus was once confronted by the likes of these holy men and women He told them, "Those without sin should cast the first stone." When a Church loses its caring flavour, it behaves in this manner.

The pastor did not publicly condemn them, but his body language did. Egged on by the holy men and women in the Church, the pastor spearheaded the popular slogan, "Pull them down and drive them out of the Church." It rather unfortunate that the Church that is supposed to be identifying itself with sinners is instead shutting its doors to those they consider sinners.

Is this what has become of the Church Jesus built and left behind? It is a shame that we cannot make room for each other's faults. Instead of helping a falling brother up to his feet, we humiliate him. This attitude of the Church towards those they consider sinners give the sinner no option other than to leave the Church.

Before the married couple could settle down, the pastor and his associates succeeded in exiling them to a spiritual wilderness. Their exit was so quick they could not say goodbye to their few friends because they could not withstand the barrage of condemnation. Sometimes I wonder whether pastors who preach from the pulpit have been called by God.

The second case is that of a young, beautiful Brazilian woman called Edilene. She walked out of a marriage she thought was the best thing that ever happened to her. Whilst she married because of love, her husband married her because of his feeling. The two words are quite different and have different meanings in marriage.

This is the sad story of a very attractive young woman who leaped without looking; if she had looked very carefully, she would not have been in her present situation. She rushed into the marriage because she was in love, without finding out if the other person loved her. As a result, she came out of the marriage worse-off with a burden of two children.

The question she wants to know is what options are there for her if she wants to remarry? Would the Scriptures condemn her, or would the Church? To make matters worse, the husband has found himself a new wife. Can anything be salvaged? What would you tell a young, beautiful woman like Edilene asking such questions?

The dreadful thing in marriage is when a person marries his spouse on the basis on his feeling towards her instead of love. Feelings can be defined as an emotion distinct from reason. It can also be defined as sensation or emotion. If a person marries you because of his or her emotion towards you, then that is not love.

Do not mistake passion for love or lust for love. Both lust and passion are part of emotional rage. What appears to be love at first sight could in fact be lust at first sight. When feeling has burnt itself out, it turns into divorce. Therefore, we must understand the difference between feeling and love.

So many people marry because of feeling and not for love. It is true that there is some element of love in feeling but the overriding part of it remains lust. You will not realize this until that small element of love has burnt itself out. Only then would your understand the true motive of his or her love.

The most dreadful scenario in marriage is when one of the spouses married because of feelings while the other person in the marriage married because of love. The problem here is that the one who married because of feeling never makes his or her intentions known. This makes marriage a thing of uncertainty.

Marrying because of feelings is one of the major causes of divorce in our society today. He who marries for love will never divorce. The reason for this is simple, love keeps him or her loving the other person "till death do they part." Love is like a magnet constantly attracting husband and wife to each other.

Marrying because of feelings is something one cannot hide forever. Eventually it will be exposed because feelings fade with time but love never fades. Love lives on forever. When feelings have lost their flavour the only escape route is divorce and the speed at which they push for divorce betrays the reason for the marriage.

You may love someone enough to marry him or her; however are you sure the person is in love with you? If your answer is yes and your marriage ends in divorce then the other person never loved you, rather his love was based on his feelings toward you. Where there is love, divorce is toothless, so it cannot bite. True love conquers divorce. Divorce has no place in a marriage where the love of God reigns.

The sad state of this young Brazilian woman reminds me of a friend in Nigeria. We both come from the same country but we met in Nigeria through work. It was in Nigeria he gave his life to Jesus Christ and from there he never looked back.

Whilst in Nigeria he met and married a young, beautiful woman. They were blessed with three children. This was before they both became Christians. The couple are a living example of the joy of Christian marriage. The joy of Salvation brought the brightness of Christ into their marriage.

When the Church decided to appoint the young man as an elder because of his dedication and commitment to the work of God, the troublemakers in the Church quickly seized the initiative to dig out his past life. A word of caution: never discuss your past life with anybody other than your spouse. If you do, then be sure those who know of it will use it against you someday.

The fact that they have not used it does not mean they will not, they are only waiting for the right moment to strike, when a higher position in the Church becomes available which interests them. You will never know the person you are talking with is a sworn enemy until it is too late.

This young man became entangled in two marriages that gave him six children during the time of his ignorance. It was an unfortunate situation he never thought would become a subject of scrutiny in deciding his suitability for an eldership in the Church.

It is obvious the troublemakers in the Church were envious of his promotion to a position of authority in the Church. Therefore, they set out to destroy his happiness. The devil did this by resurrecting the buried past life of this young man. The reason for this is simple; one of the devil's schemes in marriage break-up is to pour cold water on any marriage that glorifies God, thereby quenching the love in the marriage.

Do not be surprised at this because it is his nature. Remember the devil cannot act alone; he will need people to use. He operates through those with whom we pray, with whom we sing hymns and songs of praise. Finally, the very people we study the Bible with and the very people with whom we share Christian love.

Your past life should not be an issue you should discuss with people who cannot be trusted. Even the Scriptures tell us to trust no one except God. Be warned: envy and jealousy is what will make your natural born enemies use your past life to pull you down. Be warned do not trust a person because he or she is a Christian.

This is what happened to this young man. He spoke to Christians he thought he could trust about his past life. When the time came for a decision to be made for a high office in the Church, the demons in the Church were out in full force with sharpened axes. They had nursed this moment for years and the time had come. Why the sudden change in the attitude of these friends?

These Christians calling for his head had been in the Church for years and they had not been considered for a deacon's position let alone the position of an elder. During the interview, it emerged that he was once married and divorced after having fathered three children with his ex-wife, before coming to Nigeria. This revelation infuriated the Pharisees in the Church.

Therefore, the knives were out on an issue that was between God and the young man. His past life was nobody's business. The demons in the Church would have none of it. This unfortunate young man had come face-to-face with hungry troublemakers in the Church who would not take no for an answer.

The unfortunate situation for this young man was that some of the troublemakers were members of the Church council. Therefore, he was not surprised at the verdict. When the council meeting ended, the final judgement was pronounced. This was their final judgement on the helpless Christian. "Divorce your second wife and go and be reconciled with your first wife."

The scenario here is that they are asking the man who had divorced his first wife to divorce his second wife with whom he has three children and go and be reconciled with his first wife. Is this what the Bible teaches? Certainly not, there is not a single verse in the whole Scripture that can support this unfortunate decision.

To make this young man's situation even worse, his first wife had remarried. Yet the troublemakers were holding their ground, insisting he go back to his first wife, even though they knew the young man's ex-wife was married to someone else. How do we reconcile the decision of the Church's council?

In an issue where the Scripture is silent, it is better to be quiet, say nothing, and let God deal with the issue. The problem some Churches face is the issue of Biblical interpretation. The rule is that if we are not sure of the intended meaning of the text, we must seek advice from someone who is an authority on Scripture.

The verdict handed to the young man was rather unfortunate, it clearly shows the Church had lost track of its commission. Christians like these read the Bible and apply it without finding out the actual intended meaning of the text. In the interpretation of Scripture, we must be very careful we do not try to answer every question.

When expounding on the Scriptures, we are well advised to follow this rule: where Scripture has not spoken it will be good to remain silent. We will never understand some things while on this side of eternity. While not everything we may want to know is in the Scripture, everything we need to know is there.

The most important thing in Bible interpretation is that: The text cannot mean what it never meant. The intended meaning of a text is what should be the guideline for Scriptural interpretations. Poor Biblical interpretation is as deadly as words coming from the mouth of demons.

It is so sad that Christians fail to see how Satan uses inferiority, inadequacy, self-belittlement and our past life to defeat us. Thereby he prevents us from realising our potential, as God would want us to. The devil will always resurrect our past life and use it as his trump card to bring us down. However, he cannot accomplish this task alone; he will need a helping hand.

This is the reason why he always extends a hand of friendship to Christians. If you find yourself in a similar situation, take heart and agree with the apostle Paul in his words to the Philippians, "But one thing I do: Forgetting what is behind and straining towards what is ahead." (See Philippians 3:12-14). We must refuse to let past guilt pull us down.

The attitude of the Church council members should remind us of the Pharisees in the days of Jesus Christ. He encountered similar problems with the Pharisees who had a critical attitude towards people they considered sinners. The

Pharisees raised the bar of the code of conduct for the Jews through their traditions.

Nevertheless, when Jesus came, He raised the bar above the Pharisees and this created a confrontation between them. The Pharisees would rather die defending the Temple and its traditions than die for God. Similarly, there are Christians who are willing to die for the Church and its teachings than die for Christ.

Whatever we were in the past is nobody's business. It is between God and us alone. He alone will judge us for the things done in the flesh. God knows our past lives yet He has called us to be partakers in the joy of Salvation. God knows we are nothing but rotten fruits and rotten fruits are no good for His kingdom. Yet He loves us. God does not look at us as we are; rather He looks at us through the blood of Jesus Christ that was shed for us. When God sees the blood He forgives and we are accepted.

14. The Power of Love in Marriage

"Love is patient, love is kind. It does not envy, it does not boast, it is not proud. It is not rude, it is not self-seeking, it is not easily angered, it keeps no record of wrong. Love does not delight in evil but rejoices with truth. It always protects, always trusts, always hopes, and always perseveres. (1 Corinthians 13:4-7)

This is how someone described marriage. "Marriage is the process of blending together two different things. To illustrate this, let us take copper. Copper is still copper. However, there is a process of taking two metals that are different and blending them together into a new metal.

A more dramatic example is to add zinc to copper to make brass. This is the marrying of metals. The two that are different together can become something new. This is the way marriage is. We are different yet when we come together as husband and wife we become new."

Love is the most powerful motivating force in marriage. Love for our marriage helps us to reject conflicts that would destroy our marriage. For a successful marriage, we must get rid of the tattered old clothes of bad habit, bad attitude, indifference towards our spouse and the habit of criticizing everything our spouse does.

Anyone's success or failure in marriage depends to a large degree on his or her attitudes and motives. This is certainly true in marriage. Attitudes can either drive a wedge between spouses or bring spouses to a loving marriage relationship. Sincere love is more important than buying your spouse gifts. **"Love has an eloquence all its own. It speaks more forcefully and persuasively than words."**

Our attitude towards marriage reveals the love (or lack of it) that is so effective in marriage. The deeper your love for your spouse the more dynamic it will be in whatever mood we are in. Love for your spouse is the key to a successful marriage. If you let love dominate your marriage you will chose the right attitude towards your wife and children.

The attitude of glad response to your wife clears the line of communication between you and your wife. Love makes it easier to communicate with your spouse. The spirit of marriage is love. Love that comes from the heart makes us concerned for the needs of our spouse. Not only that it also makes us miss our spouse when they are out of sight.

We are all familiar with the phrase "the honeymoon is over." You are aware that we know that the honeymoon is over with the first conflict. When this happens, most people feel cheated, defeated, inadequate, and in doubt as to who they married. The first conflict after the honeymoon is the real test of the marriage and the time when spouses who are not prepared are confronted with the reality of marriage.

A goal in marriage is to learn how not to enter into conflict. The reason some leave home is to get away from constant quarrelling and fighting, only to find out they are repeating history over again. Conflicts are part of the human race. Nevertheless, let us, "Make every effort to live in peace with all men." (Hebrews 12:14). Even in the Church, conflicts are fiercely fought with double-edged swords. If the Church cannot avoid conflicts then who can?

In marriage, the battle is difficult for three reasons. The first reason is conflict is generally unexpected. When a bride gets married, she does not walk down the aisle saying, "For the rest of my life I am going to be happy because I am marrying the man I love."

Marrying the man you love is not a guarantee that you are going to have a happy marriage. Yes, we all marry the woman we love or we want to marry the man we love. Nevertheless, marrying the person we love is not a precondition for marriage. Marriage has nothing to do with the person you love, for the following reasons.

The word love appears to have lost its meaning in marriage; love is used to represent sex, because making love is regarded as having sex. The word love has nothing to do with the person you want to marry. Unless you can prove beyond reasonable doubt that the person you claim you love **seeks your highest interest.**

Seeking a person's highest interest is what is called love. It does not change with passing time. Loving a person without seeking the person's highest interest is not genuine love; rather it is love with a hidden motive. Because a person's love may change as the years pass, you have to make sure your fiancés feeling towards you is sincere.

Man's love changes but the word love does not change. Man's love is selfish, but love is not selfish. Man's love is self-centred, but love is not self-centred. Man's love is self-seeking but the word love is not self-seeking. Man's love can turn to hatred, but the word love does not hate.

Love is the primary condition for marriage. Love purifies the heart of married couples from all elements of divorce. Marriages that are built on the foundation of love have no room for divorce because divorce does not form part of the marriage building blocks. Divorce is part of the winds of adversity that blow over marriage.

Love is the supreme condition for marriage and marriage inspired by love can weather through the storms of divorce. When a man loves a woman he is not blinded by love, rather his heart and mind are open to the reasons for love. Love is the reason we marry and not just because of companionship.

Without love, the Christian marriage is robbed of its sweetness and its beauty. The Christian marriage is rooted in love where it grows in the soil of trust, faithfulness and truthfulness. Its fruit are without blemish, transparency is its trademark. The binding cord of the Christian marriage is the love of Christ.

The Christian marriage is influenced by 'agape love' that is divine love. When the Christian marriage is built on it, it becomes rock solid, unmovable and unbreakable. Anybody who encounters it can feel its strength and comfort. There are no limits to the power of Christian love, especially in marriage. Come, taste divine love, and see that it is sweeter than honey.

Everyone is free to marry the person he or she loves. The biggest question is, can you look into the future and confidently say, "I am glad I married the person I love? Therefore, all shall be well with my marriage." What you must understand is that some people's love fade with time, this is the reason you have to look before you leap.

Many people live with the fantasy that, "Prince Charming came out of the forest on his horse, and swooped up the princess, and he took her off to the castle where they lived happily ever after." Do not forget that this is only a fairytale. Moreover, fairytale marriages are not like real life marriages.

The marriage battle is unexpected, so we are unprepared. Lack of preparation is the second reason that marriage is difficult. There is an old saying, "To be forewarned is to be forearmed." If we see a thief coming in the night, we lock our door and hire a watchdog, and stand behind the window with a weapon. The weapon is intended to stop the thief from breaking into our home.

We take some action to prepare ourselves. However, most of us, because we do not really expect battles in the marriage, do nothing. The second step is to be prepared. If we go into marriage thinking all will be well then we are deceiving ourselves because there is no perfection in marriage.

Married couples fight over so many things. One of the major things couples fight about is the rule of their relationship as they define roles. For example who keeps the chequebook, what are the priorities in the home and who decides what to buy and what not to buy. Again, the role of decision-making must be defined in the marriage.

Battles often occur when people are trying to set rules for the defining roles. For example, Diana is spending deep into the family's accounts, bringing them near bankruptcy. David finally snapped! "We must live within our income."

What do you think was the cause of the problem between David and Diana? I think the problem could be on the issue of who plays the leading role in the marriage. On the other hand, who plays the driving role in the marriage? I would like to use an illustration of a gear train to explain this.

In a train of gears, we have the driver gear and the driven gear. The driver gear is the main source of power transmission, whilst the driven gears just follow. The driven gear plays no part in the transmission of power; it is there to complete the transmission.

Marriage is like that in the minds of some men. They play the leading role whilst the women just follow. This system is bad for marriage and diminishes the role of women in marriage. The wife is part of the decision-making and not a listener; she is equal partner and not a subordinate.

The problem with this system is that the person responsible for the entire decision-making is also responsible for anything that goes wrong in the marriage. Sometimes decision-makers are very good in shifting blame onto someone else. This is called the blame game, often played by husbands who do not accept the responsibility of their mistakes.

Steve and Susan are at each other's throats and all you hear from Steve is, "If it were not for you, I would have been better off, but because I am married to you, I am not." This is how husbands who take all the decisions or take the leading role in marriage get out of being held responsible for problems in the marriage.

In some families the husbands prefer to concentrate on achieving goals, they become task-oriented. They are more concerned about results than about interpersonal relationships. A husband in that position takes the role of giving orders, persuasive, initiatory and making decisions.

A task-oriented husband will end up driving a wedge in his marriage because he has no time to take stock of the marriage. The drive to succeed makes the husband work and work. This makes him forget he has a wife waiting at home. This is one of the reasons for infidelity in marriage.

Men can become more concerned about success than the interpersonal relations of the family. This is dangerous and bad for marriage. When work keeps married couples apart, frustrations set in due to loneliness. This situation can tempt some spouses to seek what is missing in their home elsewhere.

I know of a friend through a business link whose fiancé was a professional. She travelled all over the world making money for her financial company. They hardly saw each other. Sometimes she would be gone for months. On one of such trips, she was away for two months and when she returned there was another woman.

She tried to work her way back but to no avail. The relationship was doomed before she even took her flight. She never for once thought her fiancé could end the relationship. She was badly affected by the break-up of the relationship that she became withdrawn. Puzzled by her unusual behaviour I tried to discern what was going on.

When I asked her why, she said, "Your friend has got himself a new woman." That was the end of that relationship. In another example, an Ivorian woman's husband worked fifteen hours a day, seven days a week. His two jobs meant getting up at 04:00 and leaving the house at 05:00 whilst his three children aged twelve, ten and seven were still in bed.

He comes home after mid-night when his family were in bed. This man hardly saw his children. The wife was desperate and wanted to talk, but the man would not talk because he was too busy to talk about issues he considered unnecessary.

This man had a catchphrase sticker on his door that read, "We do what is important before what is desirable." He expected his wife to read the catchphrase and stop nagging. He considered his work very important and his wife's constant nagging as something desirable. This man's misplaced priority is what would one day destroy his marriage.

This man's schedule was overloaded with long hours and gruelling commuting which left the household responsibilities and the children's increasing weekend activities to his wife. As a result, the wife had to work herself to breaking point, just to keep up with the children's academic work.

When letters started coming from their school demanding why the children's homework was not being done, the wife gave the husband an ultimatum. Yet, the work alcoholic husband ignored the warning because she was nothing but an attention seeker. A work alcoholic husband has no social life because it means nothing to him.

The following day when the husband came from work, the catchphrase was replaced with another catchphrase that read, "Show this family some love and respect by fulfilling your marital responsibilities." She hoped the husband would read the catchphrase and heed to the family's demand.

When the husband ignored the warning, a second catchphrase appeared on the bedroom door that read, "What the family needs is love and affection." This woman was pushed beyond her breaking point. If a person is pushed beyond his limits, he or she will fight back. In this case that is what this neglected family did.

The alarm bells were ringing by now, but the husband stubbornly ignored the warning. The drive to succeed rendered him deaf and blind to the plight of the family. In desperation, his wife took pre-emptive action to teach the husband a lesson. When we shut our ears to the plight of those close to us, we pay for it.

She and the children needed love and that can be provided by no one else than the husband. Besides, the children needed their father to play with. Yet, the task-orientated father valued money over his children. A workaholic husband will certainly lose control over his family.

When the wife's pleas were ignored, she took matters into her own hands by having the locks to the house changed. When the husband came home at 00:00, he found the lock to the house had been changed. When he called the house phone line, this was the response: "Sorry, this number is no longer in use."

When he tried calling the mobile phone the response was: "This number is no longer available." A broken workaholic finally realized his folly. If you keep your nose to grindstone, this is what you get out of your marriage. We all work to put food on the table, but having food on the table without the breadwinner at the head of the table is of no use.

Grandfather once said, "In our quest to scoop handfuls of honey from the honeycomb we forget that the makers of the honey are not friendly. But those who think the custodians of the honeycomb are friendly will retreat hastily with swollen eyes." Stubbornness will only lead us to our own peril.

A task-oriented husband will dismantle his own marriage brick by brick without realising his self-made target is what will take the final brick from the marriage foundation. A victim of his own self-destruction, he has only himself to blame.

The rising cost of living, mounting credit card debt and worry about making ends meet are some of the causes of stress in marriages. These can make a target-related husband use his work as his second home. This can take a terrible toll on the marriage and lead to a breakdown in communications.

Self–denial and sacrifice are the bright colouring that relieves the dullness in marriage and turns a marital home into a happy home. Salt is like love, which penetrates marriage to season it, and preserve it. Similarly, love is like sugar that sweetens marriage. Different ingredients come together to make a cake, but the dominant ingredient is flour. So is love, the dominant force in marriage.

Love dispels and drives out misunderstanding in marriage. Where there is love there is no coldness in marriage. Where there is love there is no dullness in marriage. Where there is love, sadness turns into joy. Love is the only thing that can make a task-orientated man give up his busy life.

The sun is a star that shines in the sky during the day and gives the earth heat and light without which there would not be life. Similarly, love is like the sun's rays that keep marriage alive, without which divorce would ravage marriage. Love is what promptly scotches divorce in marriage. Just as the sun is very important to human life, so is love very important to marriage.

This reminds me of Diogenes the Greek philosopher who was visited by Alexander the Great in Corinth. While Diogenes was relaxing in the morning, Alexander the Great, thrilled to meet the famous philosopher, asked if there was any favour he might do for him. Diogenes replied, "Yes, stand out of my sunlight."

Watch out for people who pretend to be your great admires who hang around your marriage, and ask you if there is any favour they can do for you. In fact, there are the very people standing in the light of your marriage. Therefore, tell them to stay out of the sunlight of your marriage.

Marriage without love is like the earth without sun to give light and heat. Marriage without love is like a flower without beauty. Marriage without affection is like a flower without fragrance. The spirit of love is the aroma of marriage. Love strengthens marriage. Love in marriage is irreplaceable.

Those who think money can replace love will end up building their marriage foundation with straws. Love is irreplaceable in marriage because a marriage foundation is built on love and not with money. Money does not form part of the marriage building blocks. Although money beautifies marriage, it is not the source of happiness in marriage.

Women who think money beautifies marriage had better think twice. What happens if the money runs out? Will they walk out or stay? In his sermon on money, the great wise preacher said the following: "Money is the answer for everything."

(Ecclesiastes 10:19c.) Again, in another sermon he said, "Money is a shelter" (Ecclesiastes 7:12).

Nevertheless, so many people place their marriage under the shelter of money. In concluding, the great wise preacher said, "Whoever loves money never has money enough; whoever loves wealth is never satisfied with his income." (5:10). Perhaps reading the sermon titled 'The Wife of Noble Character,' by the great wise preacher will open our eyes.

Money may make a woman feel secure in her marriage but it cannot guarantee the marriage. Money can buy so many things for married people but it cannot buy love. Money can add a spark to marriage but it cannot keep the flame of love burning forever. What keeps the flame of marriage burning is love.

Money is like fire, it is a good master and a bad master. It cooks our food and warms your home. On the other hand, it is the root cause of many divorces in marriage. Money can do so many things in marriage, but it cannot stop divorce. Love is the ultimate power that can stand in the way of divorce and stop it from happening.

The marriage race is won not by money but by love. He who loves takes the bride home and not the one with money. Love alone can empower spouses to complete the marriage journey. It is the oil of love that keeps the flame of marriage burning and never runs out. Although money can take marriage to a great height, it cannot prevent it from falling. It is only love that can take marriage to the highest level and stop it from falling.

Money is like a sweetener in marriage, which is a good thing. Love on the other hand acts as a preservative, which is far better. A loving and caring husband is like a preservationist who works to prevent his marriage from decaying. Whatever money offers in marriage is temporal, but whatever love offers in marriage will last forever. Love in marriage guarantees perfect peace; love in marriage offers ultimate happiness. This is something money cannot offer.

Where there is love, there is self-control. If a person cannot control his or her temper then marriage is not an option for him or her. People with a temper should deal with it before thinking of marriage or else they are bound to destroy someone else's happiness. Bad temper can only be tamed by love.

Quarrels are unavoidable in marriage; however, they should not be turned into a battleground. Some quarrels do spice up marriages, so they must be treated as such. Never allow quarrels to turn your home into a war zone. Love turns quarrels in marriage into laughter.

A husband has no good reason to beat his wife because of anything said or done. God who instituted marriage did not give any legal rights to the husband to beat his wife up whenever she provokes him. Love diffuses and dispels provocation. Wife beating is not part of the marriage vows.

It is no good being spiritual and holy when you are with Christians, however, when you come home you are nothing but terror to your own family. When you are out of the house, there is peace and joy. However, the sight of you outside the door sends panic and fear through the family.

Women are to be loved and cherished and not to be used as punching bags. A husband must never show his strength and courage on his defenceless wife. Men who genuinely love their wives will never lay a finger on them. This reminds me of how our mother instilled self-control in us.

When we were growing up, any time we fought with any of our sisters, mother stepped in to protect the girls even when they were in the wrong. When ask why she was siding with the girls, this is what she told us: "To teach you it is morally wrong for a man to hit a woman and that is the only way to prevent you from beating your wives when you get married." As far as mother was concerned, beating a woman is a taboo.

I remember one day when our elder brother wanted to beat one of our sisters because she tripped him. This is what mother told him: "Son, it is better to cast out the demon which makes you beat your sister at the slightest provocation than allow that demon to control your life and destroy your marriage someday."

We saw it otherwise, as a mother being over-protective of the girls. At that time, we thought she never liked us. Now when we look back we realise it was her love for us that made her try to correct our bad tempers. In Proverbs 22:6 King Solomon says, "Train a child the way he should go, and when he is old he will not turn from it."

Women are the weaker sex and all they need from their husbands is love. Love stops whatever starts fights in marriage. Mother once told us that a man who respects his wife would never fight her, no matter the provocation. The husband is the initiator of love and not the wife. This is what the Bible says. It is a command and not advice.

The context of the verse is not appealing to you but rather commanding you to love your wife. Husband and wife love each other. Loving your wife means obeying the LORD. This is the reason why every man must love his wife so much so that nothing done by the wife can provoke him to raise his hand against her.

No matter what your wife has done, raising your hand against her is against the ethics of marriage. Marriage is not about fighting each other but about loving each other affectionately. Men who have a problem with this should stay away from marriage. Real love makes a husband adore his wife rather than raising his fist against her.

Men with very bad tempers should deal with that canker before even thinking of marriage. God never intended the matrimonial home to be turned into a war zone. Men who turn their homes into a battle zone do not really understand what marriage is all about.

I know of a man who once flew into a rage and attacked his wife just because she had put too many Brussels sprouts on his plate. In his fit of rage, he threw the plate across the room, and then beat his wife until she ran of the house with a swollen eye. For one whole week, he kept ranting about the sprouts.

She then went to stay with friends. When his wife returned, he revived the argument. He then hit her in the left eye, knocking off her glasses, and threw a remote control across the room. Is this a good reason for this man to beat his wife? Something is not right here. Sometimes it is difficult to tell what goes in the minds of some married men.

This man chose his wife above all the women who caught his attention. From the very first day he saw her he fell in love with her. So why is he now treating her this way? Something has definitely gone wrong with this man. Why did he marry his wife when he knew he had a problem with his temper?

A husband who respects the institution of marriage will never lay a finger on his wife, no matter how many sprouts he finds on his plate. The behaviour of this man is shameful, disgraceful and unacceptable in marriage. This kind of behaviour desecrates the spirit of love and fellowship that exists between husband and wife.

Again, it breaks the bond that unites a man with his wife. After thirty years of marriage, the ugly temper that lay dormant in this man finally surfaced. The volcanic temper lay dormant on the surface but beneath it was active. This is something we cannot see until it starts spewing poisonous gas.

Its eruption can be deadly. This is how this man's dormant temper erupted. The wife did well by running away from the path of the explosive temper to a safe place. We do not stand in the path of volcanic eruption, we run for our life. Temper is something we cannot suppress forever if we fail to control it from childhood.

The human temper is like a seedling; to prevent it from becoming a bent tree you straighten it while it is growing. However, if you allow it grow to become a full tree you cannot straighten it. God wants every matrimonial home to be peaceful and loving, where joy and happiness abounds. Love turns bad tempers into good tempers.

There is not one Scriptural verse in the Bible that gives the husband the right to beat his wife. A husband must adore his wife enough to resist the temptation of raising his fist against her. No matter how strong the provocation is. Remember the day you saw her and chose her above all the other women around you.

A wife is the joy and pride of every husband. The wife always initiates any feeling of joy in the home. A wife's joy springs from sincere love and feelings she wants to share with her husband and children. The wife initiates every feeling of pleasure and satisfaction. A wife gives pleasure and satisfaction to her husband.

When she is out of the house, the house becomes very cold and when she is in the house, the husband can always feel her lovely warmth. A wife is the apple of her husband's eye, any man who touches her touches the apple of his eye. This is the reason why a husband should seek to protect his wife in the home and outside the home.

The reason a man walks with a strong arm around his wife is to reassure her that she is in safe hands. A wife is a perfect gift from God: any man who finds her finds comfort in her arms. Every husband must guide and protect his marriage. For every one will give account of how they conducted their marriage.

A person's nature is shown by the way he reacts in a given situations. A temperamental husband can turn his wife into a punching bag. A husband with temper is nothing but a death trap in the home. No woman must live in an abusive and dangerous marriage. An abusive home is the wrong place for children to grow.

For a Christian husband to abuse his wife raises questions about the genuineness of his conversion. Besides, a he can never be a good ambassador for Christ. With some people, marriage can be very hard, difficult and painful. However where such things abound we need to ask the LORD for help.

A marriage vow is a binding obligation to love, honour and cherish your wife as long as you live. A husband who loves and cherishes his wife will never abuse her no matter what she might have done. Women need a loving home and not an abusive home. An abusive home is the devil's paradise. A husband's reaction to extreme provocation will tell the wife the kind of person she has married.

Love makes women talk. If this is a problem for you then you had better start learning now. Talking is part of women's nature and men cannot stop them from talking. It will be futile to try stopping your wife from talking. While women express their emotions by talking, men keep their tongue tightly glued to the roof of their mouth or use their fist.

A husband must never insult his wife or use offensive language to belittle her. Neither should a husband compare his wife to any other woman. The wife is the queen of the house and she should be treated as a queen. She is a queen above all queens. A wife is a companion of love. The best thing to happen to a man is the woman he married.

You cannot beat your wife, insult her, belittle her, and then expect her to make you happy by warming the matrimonial bed. A decent and respected woman will make a point by making her bed in the living room and leaving the cold bedroom for the husband. A husband who respects himself will do nothing to make his wife cry.

I have watched countless men reduce their wives to mere punching bags at the slightest provocation. How can you reconcile loving your wife and beating her at the slightest provocation? Can a person love his wife and beat her at the same time? Do you want your wife to respect you? Then be affectionate towards her by making her feel happy in her matrimonial home.

The statement "I love you" is probably the most seductive used in this world. People who beat their wives do not understand the word love. A woman once told her pastor how her husband dragged her down the stairs because she put two sugars instead of one in his tea. After he had blackened her eyes, he still wanted to make love to her that night.

She told the pastor, "I am so puzzled. Does he love me?" No! This man does not love his wife. It is only a man who marries his wife because of sex who will behave in this manner. If this man really loves his wife then he should put his love for her into action. Sex with your wife stops from the very day you start abusing her.

A husband in his right mind will never lay his hand on his wife for whatever reason. Husbands who beat their wives may have serious mental problems and should seek psychiatric help. Wife beating is not enshrined in the marriage vows. Violent men should stay away from marriage.

If we are to take a bride from her family only to turn her into punching bag, then no father will give away her daughter in marriage. Wives are to be loved, cherished and showered with gifts and not fists. The two key words in the marriage vow are LOVE and OBEY; the rest of the vows hang on these two words.

Love is practical, not theoretical. You must express love practically for your wife to see it at work. Married men who express their love for their wives in theory do not love their wives. Husbands put your love into ACTION and express love practically. To buy a beautiful bunch of flowers for your wife and then turn her into a punching bag the following day is never a sign of love.

Do not turn your wife into a punching bag only to buy her flowers the next day. Buying flowers for your wife after turning her into a punching bag is an insult to a woman's dignity. Wife beating is bad for marriage and bad for children. This is every woman's nightmare. A wife is a gift from God to be a helpmate and to be loved. It takes love to bring a man and woman into a matrimonial relationship, and that flame of love must never be quenched by fits of rage.

The beauty of marriage is love. So men who are quicker in using their fist than expressing their love practically should consider staying away from marriage altogether. You will be doing yourself a favour if you take your temperamental behaviour to God in prayer. Only a shameless husband will buy gifts for his wife after beating her. What a wife need is love and affection and not flowers after turning her into a punching bag.

The wife is part of the decision-making in the home and not a listener. Whatever goes on in the house and outside the matrimonial home is her business and she has every right to know and demand answers from the husband. That includes whatever goes on in her husband's life outside the home.

If a man loves his wife, he will keep nothing from her. Marriage problems begin when spouses try to hide what goes on in their private lives. Then the hiding turns to lies, lies then opens the door to mistrust in the marriage that can create a breeding ground where divorce can thrive.

In marriage one plus one equals one. This is what we call God's mathematics. Spiritually and physically, you and your wife are one flesh and no longer two. The union of two becoming one starts from the day you said, "I do." Spouses who are united in spirit and flesh do not lie to each other.

Marriage is a spiritual and holy institution and must be held sacred. Because the one who instituted the marriage institution is Holy and demands holiness in marriage, and nothing short of that. All those who walk along this path should respect and honour that institution. Marriage is both spiritual and physical.

Therefore, for a marriage to work for us we would need all the marriage building blocks in their proper places. Not only in their proper places but active and working. Some of the building blocks in marriage are faithfulness, patience, gentleness, honesty, loyalty and sincerity. Without these, there is no marriage. A marriage without these qualities is like trying to make an empty sack stand upright. Only love can meet these requirements.

Only a wife can tell whether her husband meets the above criteria and similarly only the husband can tell if his wife has the above qualities. It is quite natural for married couples to appear in public as the perfect couple without faults. Publicly they give the impression that they meet all of the building block criteria.

Behind the façade of unity and happiness, all is not as it appears to be in the marriage. We call this a deceptive show of public unity. One look in their faces will reveal the cracks in the false public display of unity. It will not be long before you see that all is not well in the marriage. Nevertheless, there is still hope for a failing marriage if spouses can work toward it.

Married couples must incorporate the marriage building blocks in their marriage and these virtues should be seen working in the lives of husband and wife. They must be active and not dormant. Both spouses must work hard towards the marriage building blocks. Married couples who hold the marriage institution in high esteem will surely work together in achieving the objective of the building blocks.

Although we cannot be perfect, we must work towards achieving the objectives of the building blocks. The main objectives of the marriage building blocks are to act as a protective covering, which allows the marriage to weather storms. Some people respond differently. Therefore, it necessary for the active one in the marriage to stir up what is dormant in the other person.

This does not mean the active person in the marriage is better than the dormant one. Trustworthiness must be the guiding principle in every marriage. Good marriages are based on trust and marriage without trust is shrouded in suspicion. Can two walk together except they agree? Married couples must love each other enough to live by trust.

The institution of marriage must have transparency as its trademark. Grandmother once said, "In a marriage where spouses have something to hide there is no transparency, and that is what can ruin the marriage. As married couples, we owe the institution of marriage transparency."

15. Forgiveness in an Imperfect Marriage

"A new command I give you: Love one another. As I have loved you, so you must love one another. By this all men may know that you are my disciples, if you love one another." (John 13:34-35.)

Paul in his letter to the Romans chapter 12:17-21 summarises the core of Christian living: if we love someone the way Christ loves us we will be willing to forgive. If we have experienced God's grace, we will want to pass it on to others. By forgiving your husband or wife for whatever he or she has done, you have recognized that he or she deserves forgiveness. In addition, you love him or her in spite of what he or she has done.

Forgiveness can break a negative cycle and lead to mutual reconciliation. By forgiving your husband, you will make him ashamed and change his way of living. By contrast, if you fail to forgive your husband or wife and drag he or she to the divorce court to seek justice because what he did still hurts you punish yourself also.

Forgiving your husband or wife whom you love so dearly will make you free of a heavy load of bitterness. Breaking the trust of the marriage can be very painful because it hurts to see the person closest to your heart breaking your heart. The forgiveness in such a situation must be whole because forgiveness involves both attitude and action.

In Matthew 5:32 Jesus said, "But I tell you that anyone who divorces his wife, except for marital unfaithfulness, causes her to become an adulteress, and anyone who marries the divorced woman commits adultery." This does not mean divorce should automatically occur when a spouse commits adultery.

The word unfaithful implies a sexually immoral lifestyle not a confession or repented act of adultery. Those who discover that their spouse has been unfaithful should make every effort to forgive and reconcile to restore the marriage relationship. As a Christian wife or husband, we must cultivate the attitude of forgiveness and reconciliation in our marriage.

A wife who is unwilling to forgive her husband has not become one with Christ. In the same way, a husband who is unwilling to forgive his wife has not become one with Christ. Spouses who fail to forgive become a channel through which bitterness, anger and hatred can set in and lead to divorce.

The golden rule in marriage can be found in Ephesians 5:22-33: **Wives, submit to your husbands as to the Lord. For the husband is the head of the wife as Christ is the head of the Church, his body, of which he is the Saviour. Now as the Church submits to Christ, so also wives should submit to their husbands in everything.**

Husbands, love your wives, just as Christ loved the Church and gave himself up for her to make her holy, cleansing her by the washing with water through the word, and to present her to himself as a radiant church, without stain or wrinkle or any blemish, but holy and blameless.

In the same way, husbands ought to love their wives as their own bodies. He who loves his wife loves himself. After all, no one ever hated his own body, but feeds and cares for it, just as Christ does the church- for we are members of his body. For this reason a man will leave his father and mother and be united to his wife, and the two will become one flesh.

If we glean through these verses thoroughly we will discover the golden nuggets hidden there. For a marriage to work according to the golden rules, we need to tap into these two words: submission and love. The Christian marriage hangs on these two words.

The first word "submission" is a command from God. In verse 21, it says, "submit to one another out of reverence for Christ." What we need to know here is that submission in this context has nothing to do with status, one person being above another person; rather it has to do with role and function.

Where the wife is to submit herself to the husband, submission simply means identifying the role or responsibility or function of the person in your life and then releasing him to fulfil that function. It is allowing the person to be what God intends him to be in his relationship to you. When we do this then we are obeying God's command.

Here the couple must identify the unique roles in the marriage as dictated, first, by the fact that they are male and female, and second, by the fact that they are husband and wife. In Ephesians chapter 5, the husband is the initiator of love and the one who provides for and cherishes his wife.

The husband is the one that gives time and attention to his wife. The wife, on the other hand, is the responder and the one who gives reverence or submission to the husband. Conversely, the wife must submit to her husband and the husband must love his wife. Let us not run from the responsibilities God has commanded us to keep.

Now let us take a look of the theme of submission, mentioned in verse 21, "as unto the Lord:" This is a comparative clause. However, in Greek there are two different types of comparative clauses. (1) Elucidation, which means that the wives are to give their husbands the same unquestioned, absolute submission they give Christ. Would this apostle expect wives to render the same submission to imperfect husbands they give to their Christ?

(2) Emphasis, which means that wives are to submit to their husbands, as submission rendered by them truly is submission rendered to Christ Himself. When the wife yields her will to that of her husband, she yields to the Lord provided the husband's direction is made "in the fear of God" (v.21) or in line with God's will. Love and submission in marriage is a fertile ground for forgiveness to bear fruit.

Grandmother once said, "Do not let an unforgiving spirit hold you captive." Lack of forgiveness is the main root cause of divorce that is ravaging the

Christian marriage. The "I do not care attitude," is eating deep into the fabric of the institution of the Christian marriage, and it has affected our heart, soul and mind and nothing is being done about it.

The attitude, "I will rather walk out of the marriage than forgive" is nothing but a satanic attitude. It is bitterness at its most extreme. As Christians, we have no excuse not to forgive because we are the custodians of the Bible, the written Word of God. Forgiveness is one of the ethics of the Christian faith.

Jesus Christ spoke extensively on this issue by making it clear that unless we forgive those who offend us, God will not forgive us. What has your spouse done which is unacceptable that you cannot forgive him or her? What has your husband done that is unpleasant and making it difficult for you to forgive?

The Christian husband has no reason not to forgive his wife, likewise the Christian wife no excuse not to forgive her husband. The Christian wife has no moral justification for throwing her unfaithful husband out of the matrimonial house. In the same way, the Christian husband has no authority to kick an unfaithful wife out of her matrimonial house. In times of crises, forgiveness is a word we should not lose sight of, so that we do not listen to the devil.

Yes, he or she may have broken the trust of the marriage; yes, he or she may have been unfaithful. However, if it is possible, forgive and stay with him or her. Love in marriage can defuse anger due to unfaithfulness. By doing this you will be shaming the devil and his associates who have been working to break up your marriage. Giving marching orders to a spouse for unfaithfulness may be right, but it is never a good option. Love can overrule.

Yes, we know it hurts to see your spouse break the trust of the marriage. Yes we know it will break your heart to find out your spouse has been seeing someone else behind your back. Yes, your husband has been cheating on you. But the question you should be asking yourself is: do you sincerely think divorcing your spouse on these grounds is the right thing to do?

Yes, your spouse may not have been loyal, but what does the word loyalty mean, does it mean to be committed to another person's well-being as much as you are committed to your own? This is what I think it means. Well, your spouse has been disloyal therefore; the first word that comes out of your mouth is divorce.

Have you thought about the implications involved? Are you acting on impulse? On the other hand, has God asked you to divorce your unfaithful spouse? Well, God would never ask a husband to divorce his wife, likewise the wife to divorce her husband. This is what most married couples do not want to hear in times of unfaithfulness in marriage because it angers them.

If you refuse to listen to what the Holy Spirit is saying to you, then the devil will tell you what you want to hear. In all cases of adultery, most Christians turn to listen to the devil rather than listen to God. This is because they like what Satan is whispering in their ears more than what the Holy Spirit is saying to them.

There are no records in the Bible of God asking anyone to divorce their wife or husband. The Christian God is a God who hates divorce. When you begin to hear the word divorce in your ears at the time when your spouse has been unfaithful to you, beware of who is behind that inner voice.

Such words are definitely not coming from God, rather from the devil because the word divorce is the devil's marriage trademark. God will never suggest to anyone to divorce because it is not part of His nature. What the Holy Spirit will suggest to you is the word forgiveness. When God asks you to forgive your unfaithful spouse, then it is for your own good.

We must recognise that in all cases of infidelity human weakness plays a greater role because of our shortcomings. The problems are that most people's lives comprise a lifestyle that leads them to fall into sexual sin. This can be true in our own lives as well as others; our walk with the spirit can help us overcome this pitfall.

However, when we fall we should not be discouraged, it is part of the learning process. We must summon the courage to get up and shake off that which caused the fall, then get up in the name of Jesus Christ. Then move forward without looking back, but we must be aware of the pitfall ahead of us.

In Proverbs, King Solomon says, "For though a righteous man falls seven times, he rises again." There are many snares and temptations on our way; however, we must endeavour to push them aside for the sake of faith in Christ and our marriage. When the Christian falls, he brings shame to the very gospel we proclaim. The love for the message of Salvation should keep us from falling.

Are you well acquainted with what the Scriptures demand of a person who is contemplating divorce? Do you think divorce is the only way out? Think about these two words, Love and Forgiveness. A woman who really loves her husband will forgive his infidelity to shame the woman who committed the act with her husband.

Do you know that forgiveness mends a broken heart? A husband who has the highest interest of his wife at heart will forgive her no matter what she has done. Think about this very carefully and allow forgiveness to rule in your marriage. Adultery is bad for marriage and demeans the institution of marriage. Besides, it breaks the seventh commandment.

Your husband commits adultery, so you walk out of the marriage because you can no longer put up with an adulterous man. Good for you if you think you are doing the right thing by putting your husband away. But what guarantees do you have the next person you will be marrying will be an angel? Take note of this: marrying a Christian does not mean you are married to an angel.

It is said, "The devil you know is better than the angel you don't know." You must know that the other woman who made your marriage crowded may have deliberately set out to seduce your husband, hoping that you would walk out of the marriage so she can walk in. Do not walk out of your marriage so that the person who seduced your husband can walk in and take control of your matrimonial home.

A seductive woman who catches the attention of your husband will stop at nothing until she has your husband in her lap. Unless your husband has what Joseph had that made him run away from the temptress. Sorry, we do not have many Christians like Joseph these days. Nevertheless, God is able to empower us to resist sexual temptation if only we draw near to him in earnest prayer.

Seductive women are like charging bulls. They are shameless and without conscience because they have no respect for the institution of marriage. They have only one aim in life, to destroy marriages by seducing married men and thereby inflicting pain on their wives. Men who seduce married women are worse than animals.

Never entertain seductive woman in your matrimonial home, no matter the relationship. She could be your sister, mother, cousin or friend. Do not waste time in showing her the way out before it is too late. You have nothing to lose by kicking them out of your matrimonial home. There is more blessing in kicking a seductive woman out of your matrimonial home than having her stay.

For example, a friend's babysitter once made the following remark when she saw him swap his shirt for a T-shirt. When she saw his well-built broad, hairy chest, she said. "Wow! You have wonderful body and you are fit, this is what every woman will desire." This shameless babysitter appears not to have any regard for the institution of marriage.

The shell-shocked wife interrupted and said "Thank you for the comment about my husband's chest. But sorry, you no longer have a job." What a lustful comment about someone else's husband! The wife was smart to discern the lustful thought of the babysitter and terminated her appointment immediately. The wife acted quickly to stop the babysitter from destroying the peace in her marriage.

Do not underestimate the power of a seductive woman. They are like the worms that destroy the vine. They are canny and deceptive. One can hardly tell what they are up to until it is too late. You can never compete with them. Only by being vigilant and prayerful can you become aware of their presence.

Seductive women have an angelic appearance; this makes it difficult to suspect them. They prey on unsuspecting wives by using different devices to get to what they want. Once they find their way into your home, they temporarily lie dormant making it difficult to unmask them. This is the dangerous part of their schemes. During this time, they work hard to gain your trust, so you do not suspect them.

This gives them ample time to asses the weakness of your husband. Again, they find out his favourite food, drink, colour and type of dress. They strike when they have the situation in the house under their control. Watch out when they start interfering with your husband's dressing.

For example, when you hear comments like "Please can I straighten your tie for you? Can I do the collar of you shirt for you? "Can I fix your buttons for you?" When you hear these words and see these things happening, then the days of your marriage are numbered. Throw them out before they create problems in your marriage.

You will be looking for trouble when you ask a relative or friend to cook for your husband. It is said, "A way to a man's heart is through the mouth." This is the quickest way for a seductive woman to snatch your husband from right under your nose. You are better off ordering a take-away than asking a seductive woman to cook for your husband.

A seductive woman knows very well that a man will always compliment delicious food served him. Watch out how she reacts to these compliments and what she says in return. A married wife's ability to read the early warning signs can save her marriage from the clutches of a seductive woman.

Seductive women are troublemakers therefore throw them out of your matrimonial home before they make trouble for you. They do not deserve mercy or a second chance. The only thing they are good at is destroying the peace in the marriage by creating a fertile environment for divorce.

A seductive woman will always wear a see-through nightie in the home to attract attention. As the woman of the house, you must summon courage to tell your guest, whether she is your sister or friend, that such inappropriate dressing should be confined to the guest room. If she ignores your warning and persists, throw her out of the house. You are better off without her presence in your matrimonial home.

Grandfather once told me that, "The practice of hugging and kissing the opposite sex creates lustful feelings and should be avoided because it is a goldmine for seductive women." It is very risky for men who have a moral weakness because a seductive woman can easily tell from such an encounter that the man she is hugging has a moral problem.

This reminds me of a close family friend we once offered temporary accommodation to. She was in the shower when I pressed the doorbell. She looked through the bathroom window, and saw me standing outside. She shouted through the bathroom window, "Please wait. I'm coming down."

What happened next was unbelievable. I never for once thought I would come face-to-face with a temptress. When she opened the door, she was completely naked and drenched in soapy water. She smiled and said, "Come in." Following her would have been like walking into the arms of the devil. She was stunning, with a beautiful smile on her face that would make a man lust after her.

I declined the offer and told her I will be waiting in the car. I was there to help her pack her belongings because she cleverly asked my wife if I could come and help her. She looked very innocent but very dangerous. By asking permission from my wife, she had cleverly killed off any suspicion and gained her trust.

She was stunning, with an irresistible body; beautiful yet very dangerous. Two weeks after moving into our home my wife was admitted into hospital. It was a time of foreboding. For the two months my wife was in the hospital, this woman virtually took control of the house. She did what was good in her eyes.

Coming home from work was so frightening because I did not know what I would be exposed to. I opened the front door gently without making any noise. Once inside, I had to tiptoe from the living room to the bedroom and then tiptoe from bedroom to either the kitchen or the bathroom in order not to alert her to my presence in the house.

For the two months, I slept on the sofa in the living room. This means I had to overstay each visit to the hospital to make sure she was asleep in the guest room before I got home. This was what I had to endure in our home for that terrifying two months. I had to tread carefully with this temptress woman because one false move or wrong word would create a scene.

If you ask such a woman to leave your house, she may turn around to accuse you of making advances towards her or trying to seduce her, knowing very well that your wife is in the hospital and there are no witnesses, just the two of you so outsiders will believe her side of story without verifying. Remember women know how to cut and paste stories to make them stick. Every decent man should avoid this kind of situation.

When my wife was discharged from the hospital, she told her: "Could you believe that your husband slept on the sofa throughout your stay in the hospital? Your husband is a coward because he was scared of me. Maybe he thought I would seduce him." I think she wanted to come clean. Seductive women always have an alibi to serve as a safety net.

However, my wife told the temptress she had overstayed the temporary arrangement. Then she gave her a week's grace within which she must leave the house. She moved out of the house before the time given her. Wives must summon the courage to tell people who could pose a problem in their marriage to leave their home.

My grandmother once told us that to avoid temptation we should never look a seductive woman twice in the face because the second look usually arouses sexual feeling in the heart, which then transmits this feeling to the mind.

She said the first look is not a sin, but the second look is a sin because lustful look can arouse desire. Once desire sets in, it arouses sexual feelings. This sexual excitement if not resisted could lead to sexual sin. The only way out of it is to run and never look back. You will remember that when Joseph ran from the temptress he never looked back.

This reminds me of what grandmother told us. She said, "The safest way to avoid seductive women is by running away from them and never looking back." That was exactly what I did. She told us the reason for refusing the advances of a seductive woman is not to sin against God. This happened to be the words of Joseph to the temptress woman.

Seductive women can work their way into a married man's heart without raising suspicion. Like a chameleon, they camouflage themselves to their surrounding to hide their evil intentions. The safest rule is that by being smart and vigilant you can recognise them by sight.

Sin is ugly and Satan sometimes disguises it to make it appear more attractive. However, when we see it as it really is, as God sees it, it is repulsive and vile. When we see our actions and attitudes as God sees them, we will not behave like the evil one who still opposes God. Friendship with the devil is what will make us sin against God.

Do you know that God condemns divorce? If you do not know, then read what God says in Malachi 2:16, "I hate divorce," says the LORD God of Israel. Therefore, a Christian contemplating divorce should examine all Scriptural passages concerning divorce. Before you take the final decision, pause for a moment and read carefully what God is saying to you.

Divorce is one thing that unites both Christians and non-Christians. The behaviour of Christians and non-Christians in all divorce cases is the same. It is difficult to tell who is a Christian when it comes to the issue of divorce, because they fight each other all the way to divorce court and after the court ruling.

The only time some people forget they are Christians is on the issue of divorce. The behaviour of some Christians during divorce cases is worse than that of unbelievers. The only time they will ever talk to each other is when they stand before God. Married couples can save themselves from this situation by allowing forgiveness to fix the problem in the marriage.

In a marriage where reconciliation appears impossible and divorce is the only way out, both people must be sure a third party does not influence their decision. The most dangerous situation in marriage is to have the flame of divorce being fanned by outsiders. Those who toe this line usually work with the devil to break their marriage.

To those of you who are contemplating divorce: are you sure it is the will of God for you? Are you sure is the Holy Spirit asking you to divorce your spouse? Do you think God will contradict Himself on the question of divorce? How sure you are that God will agree with you in your decision to divorce your spouse. Does forgiveness mean anything to you?

Married couples who cannot forgive will surely have difficulties in making their marriage work. The answer for a spouse going through marital problems is FORGIVENESS. Forgiveness can calm the raging storms in your marriage. Where there is love, there is forgiveness.

If you give forgiveness a chance in your marriage, it will strip the powers of anger and bitterness and turn them into joy. If you give forgiveness a chance in your marriage, it will mend the broken marriage. Give this careful thought. It is the only remedy for a marriage going through difficulties.

Forgiveness has formidable power to silence divorce, not only that, it has the power to kill off divorce forever in your marriage. If you invite forgiveness into your marriage, it expels and erases divorce from your marriage. Forgiveness is like fire extinguisher, which can quench the burning fire of divorce in your marriage.

Therefore, it is in the interest of all married couples that the arteries of marriage are kept free, opening and running from clots such as unfaithfulness, unforgiving, bitterness, anger and lies that will abstract the continuous flow of love in the marriage; that can result in divorce.

Spouses who cannot forgive are nursing bitterness in their heart and this bitterness is like a raging fire that destroys anything in its path. The only thing that can stop a raging fire is to starve the fire of oxygen, fuel and heat. Similarly, the only thing that can stop divorce is **forgiveness, love and self-control.**

Most Christians think adultery is only a sexual sin. Do you know that it is not? It is a problem of loyalty. When a husband or wife at work is found to be unfaithful, the first thing that comes out of our mouth is, "Oh what a dirty thing he has done. He is a dirty person. How can I trust him? All he deserves is divorce and that he will have? Have you thought about the power of forgiveness? Forgiveness is the absolute power that can stop divorce

Once a Christian gets married, he is declaring to the whole world, "apart from this woman I am married to, no other woman will see my nakedness and neither will I see the nakedness of any woman apart from my wife." The wife is no exception; they are both in this vow together. Each of them must resist any appearance of temptation that will result in infidelity.

Reconciliation must be the key word in marriages going through difficulties. Married couples who have no place in their heart for reconciliation will surely have the devil as their mediator. Behind every infidelity in marriage is the devil. The devil hates marriage because it is an institution ordained by God.

When divorce stirs up trouble in your marriage tell him, I will never seek to do anything that will harm my husband or wife. Tell the devil, I will never seek out revenge because it is written, "It is mine to revenge" (Deuteronomy 32:35a). We must love our spouse enough to forgive them and say no to divorce.

Tell the devil that even though your husband or wife has betrayed your trust you will forgive him and seek nothing but his highest interest. By this action, you have silenced the spirit behind the word divorce. This leaves you the victor. Those who say yes to forgiveness will live to enjoy a happy marriage.

Divorce is like a double-edge sword that wounds the intended victim and hurts those who wield it. We have nothing to gain my using this dangerous weapon except sorrow, misery, resentment and bitterness. On the other hand, we stand to gain if we use the weapon of peace, which is forgiveness.

The Holy institution of marriage is being threatened, evidenced by the high divorce rates throughout the world. The Christian community is not excluded from this madness. Even some Christians view the marriage institution as a commodity. As a result, they shop for a prospective spouse the way people shop around for commodities.

Therefore, they walk into a shopping mall and pick up what attracts their eyes from the shelves. However, as soon as it reaches the sell-by date, he or she starts contemplating what to do with the beautiful commodity he once picked from the shop. A friend once said, "In marriage, divorce is the sell-by date."

Then after some years, the beautiful commodity begins to fade. It fades because it is part of human nature, which we have no control over. Things fade with time, however, if what you have is good, hold on to it. Someday it could turn out to be a lifesaver. If it is good, hold on to it. It will never let you down.

Instead, what some people do when they notice the commodity is outdated and out of fashion is to start planning how to replace it. Although the commodity in their possession is good and performs its task in the house, yet because they have seen something more beautiful than what they have, they want to replace it.

Marriage is like that in the eyes of some people. They marry today and divorce tomorrow as soon as the youthfulness of the wife begins to give way to ageing. A person who finds himself in this situation forgets that nature must take its course and allow the new to give way to the old.

People like these forget that even the world is changing as the years go by. We must hold on to what is dear to our heart irrespective of the changes taking place. Marriage is not about beauty but rather about true love. Marriage has to do with what is in the heart, not outside appearances.

A good wife is worth more than the most beautiful woman under the sun. The worthiness of a wife is based on character rather than beauty. If the beauty of Christ cannot be seen in a woman then she is not worthy to be wife, no matter how beautiful she is. Beauty makes a woman proud but good character makes a woman humble. See (Esther 1:11&12).

This is what grandmother once told me: "Marriage is a like a fruit. It is the sweetness that counts, not its attractiveness. Outward attractiveness," she said "can be very deceptive." She also said, "With time a woman's beauty may fade but her sweetness remains as sweet as ever."

Marriage is a process of blending two things together, and these two things are a man and a woman. However, we need another two ingredients that will hold them together to make the marriage an ongoing process. Without these ingredients, marriages will not hold together. These two ingredients are love and submission.

Love alone will not hold a marriage together, for there must also be an understanding of who is responsible for what in the marital relationship that calls for structured authority, (see Ephesians 5:22-33). Most divorce is based on this selfish idea: What have I gained from this marriage? All there is in this marriage is trouble. Moreover, things are not getting better.

How can I get out of this unpleasant situation? Oh! How I wished I had listened. I made the biggest mistake of my life by marrying you. This man tricked me into marrying him. Love is blind is a common phrase. Therefore, I was blind in marrying this man. The question we should all be asking is, is divorce the ultimate way out?

You may have come into this marriage with high hopes, but now everything has turned against you. What you once held dearest to your heart is now detestable. The once-solid foundation of the marriage is now so pulverized that even the slightest wind of adversity will send it tumbling down.

On the other hand, the believer should want to know, "How can I best love this other person? How can I best be redemptive? Oh! God, what must I do to place this sinking marriage back onto that solid rock?" That rock is Jesus Christ. Christ is the anchor to rest upon during marriage storms.

To survive the storms of marriage, marriage must be anchored in the rock of ages. Divorce is not ordinarily going to be an option for a person asking these kinds of questions! We live in a world where marriage has become like a commodity people can pick up and dump whenever they no longer need its services.

This leaves the spouse with bitterness in their heart. In addition, this bitterness can turn to hatred and hatred can develop into murder. I will use a young, Brazilian woman's experience of bitterness to illustrate how it can develop into murder. A person who is nursing bitterness in his heart will seek revenge instead of allowing God to avenge him.

Nadia is a Brazilian friend of mine; we met through another Brazilian friend. Although she was not a Christian before coming to London, the good news is that she found Christ in London and she now lives for Christ. Her story which we are about to read is a classic example of how bitterness can make some people seek vengeance.

She once remarked, "I came to seek greener pastures, but Christ has changed my reasons for coming to London. So my reason for coming to London no longer means anything to me." It is true that when we meet Christ, our perspective changes. However if we allow the troubles of this world to change our perspective we are bound to go down the wrong road.

This is exactly what happened to this young woman. She met and married a young Brazilian man. After a year, they were blessed with a baby boy. Two years after the birth of their first son, she became pregnant with their second baby. They were so happy about the second baby that they thanked God for His blessing and mercies.

Then tragedy struck. One cold winter morning her husband went to work, never to return. She and her son waited patiently for the head of the family to return home but he never did. What had happened to her husband? She was caught in a dilemma, not knowing what to do; she sat and pondered over the disappearance of her husband.

Her two-year-old boy was crying on a cold winter's night for his father and his mother could not explain why Daddy is not at home. The little boy kept asking for daddy and his mother could not come up with a convincing explanation as to why his father had not returned home. They waited and waited and he was nowhere to be seen.

The following day, through the help of some friend, she was able to track down the husband. She found out he had set up a second home with a mystery woman. The missing jigsaw piece in this whole drama was that this new woman had not the slightest idea her new Mr Wonderful was a married man.

Her whole world fell apart. How is she going to tell this story and where does she start? How does she explain to a two-year-old his daddy may not be coming home for a long time? It is a tragic story that would haunt her for the rest of her life and may leave a lasting scar in her heart.

This is the story of woman whose husband abandoned her and her two-year-old son for another woman without caring that his wife was seven months pregnant with her second baby. This heartless husband deliberately set out to destroy a happy home he built with his wife. The behaviour of this man makes me wonder whether some people really understand what marriage stands for.

We live in a world where some people do not care about the way others are suffering as a direct result of their behaviour and actions. Sometimes it is worth examining our behaviour and attitude, and see if others are being hurt because of our irresponsible behaviour. Jesus Christ spoke about the **Golden rule**; I think it will be worth looking at it.

Did this man think about his little boy? Did he not know his boy would be looking for him? Only a heartless and a self-centred man would go down this road. Without even thinking his two-year-old son will be crying day and night for him to come home. Self-centred husbands have no feeling for their family.

When the new woman finally found out about his treachery, instead of kicking him out, she decided to hold on firmly to him. In her own words, she said, "I have invested so much time, money and love in this man I cannot let him go back to his wife." In Jeremiah 17:9 the prophet writes, "The heart is deceitful above all things and beyond cure. Who can understand it?"

There are no words to describe the behaviour of this unrepentant woman, who is responsible for the infidelity in someone else's marriage and yet she is unrepentant. Claiming she is entitled to hold on to the man because she has invested love and money in him, makes one believe she comes from a culture where such behaviours are accepted.

Marriage is not an investment and has nothing to with investment. The word investment is defined as a thing that is worth buying because it will be useful or helpful. People who see marriage as an investment will kill for the sake of love. This is the reason why some people kill their spouse when their investment is being threatened by a third party. Those who do not understand what marriage is all about will regard marriage as an investment.

People who invest in marriages will not let the other person in the marriage go without a fight. Such fights usually result in death; this is because their whole life investment in the marriage is sinking. They will rather sink it than let the other person walk away with the investment.

As for this man's accomplice in this disgraceful act, Mother Nature has no words to describe her evil and callous actions. For a woman to take someone else's husband in and pretend as if the other woman never existed, or as if the wife has no feeling, is a terrible crime against the institution of marriage.

It's institution she herself will one day swear loyalty to and make a vow before God, the officiating priest and other witnesses that she will uphold and keep the marriage vow sacred. Sometimes it is worth reading the golden rule repeatedly to refresh our memories. The attitude of this woman reminds me of what grandmother once said, "If we unknowingly take what does not belong to us, and realise our mistake, then human instinct or our conscience should make us return what does not belong to us."

This young woman was like a wounded lioness. She found herself in a strange country with no relatives and no trusted friends she could confide her problems to. Besides, she was seven months pregnant with no one to turn to. However, she found help and comfort in a young Nigerian woman who supported her financially throughout her ordeal.

In her desperation, she vowed that her husband would not live to see his next birthday. She contacted people she knew with ties to an underworld criminal who could kill her husband. Her only problem was money to pay the hired killers. The only friend who could help financially refused, and tried to talk her out of her evil plan.

She turned to banks to raise a loan, but the banks refused her application for the loan. For some unknown reason no bank would loan her the money she needed to pay the hit men, although she was credit-worthy. She tried raising a loan from friends and other sources but this was also to no avail.

As a result, she took on part-time work to raise the required money demanded by the hit men. In her quest to get the money demanded by the hit men, her son was caught in the crossfire. She worked and worked, and in the process neglected the young boy. Sometimes in our attempt to seek revenge by taking matters into our own hand, people close to us can be hurt in the process.

The reason for this was simple; her attention had shifted from caring for her son and herself to killing her husband. This is the ugly road bitterness can take us down. Bitterness is like a two-edged sword, it wounds the intended victim and wounds the one who wields it. With hindsight, no one would want to go through life on a selfish and heartless road.

When she finally made the amount of money required to pay the hit men, she told her son daddy would be home today. Little did she realise she was prophesising when she said it. The statement was a prophecy, and it was fulfilled that very day. From the first day she hatched the plan to kill her husband; God was working behind the scene to stop her from shedding blood.

When the hit men failed to turn up at the appointed time, a faint voice within her told her to go and look for her husband. At first, she resisted the faint voice. Nevertheless, the voice would not leave her. The more she resisted the voice, the more the voice kept reminding her to go to the house where her husband was staying.

Finally when it became apparent that the voice was the voice of the Holy Spirit, she got up, went to the home of the woman with whom her husband was staying. When she entered the house, she saw her husband and his girlfriend having dinner. They were both amazed to see her and her son. For a moment, they all stood still without uttering a word.

Against this, she looked straight into the woman's face, with her left hand pointing at her and said, "Look, woman, this man belongs to me and whether you like it or not he is coming home with me now." Her simple statement resonated with complex themes and emotions that baffled her husband.

There was a stunned silence while they considered the bold statement. Then she turned to her husband, this time with her right hand pointing to him, and said, "Are you coming home with us or not?" This was a wife determined to disarm a marriage wrecker before her activities led to divorce.

The shameless husband got up without uttering a word to the girlfriend and without finishing his food and followed his family home. When they got home, she told him, "You have betrayed my trust and brought shame to this marriage, but from the bottom of my heart I forgive you." This Christian wife demonstrated the power of forgiveness.

This woman is a genuine Christian who understood the Biblical meaning of forgiveness as defined by Jesus Christ. Today they are bound together by an unbreakable cord of love, which cannot be broken by the likes of that shameless husband-snatcher. Never leave your husband for a shameless woman who is determining to take him away from you.

In another example, A JEALOUS wife who suspected her estranged husband was seeing other women bludgeoned him to death with a hammer. She sneaked up on her husband as he sat eating his lunch, after she had earlier discovered he had phoned another woman. This was while trying to resurrect their fifteen-year marriage.

She later remarked, "If I can't have him, no one can." This kind of statement is satanically inspired and can lead a person to kill. This woman sees forgiveness as a taboo. People who have no place in their heart for forgiveness will react before thinking. Grandmother once said, "The most dangerous thing in this world is to step on the toes of people who regard forgiveness as a sin."

Harbouring this deadly statement in her heart developed into anger and boiled into a fit of rage, which led a mother of five to deprive her children of their father. Is this a good reason for a woman to kill her husband? Definitely not, because no one has the right to another person's life, no matter the reason.

The callousness with which this woman carried out the murder of her husband stemmed from years of harbouring bitterness in her heart. For a woman to prepare food for her husband and fetch a weapon to kill him whilst he was still eating will remain a mystery. This is what bitterness can do to a person.

God who established the institution of marriage expected Christians to uphold it as sacred. However, it appears this is not case. Instead of being an example to the world, it has become a laughing-stock. It is very clear there is something seriously wrong with pre-marital Bible teaching in the Church.

Nevertheless, if we are willing to work with the Holy Spirit and obey what the Scriptures say then divorce will not be associated with the Christian marriage. It is not going to be easy, but if we are determined to make the marriage work no matter the storm that will rise against the marriage, the marriage will hold together.

The problem of divorce stems from the way we choose a future husband or wife. What we pay for is what we bring home. It is said, "He who pays the piper calls the tune." Some of the reasons for bad marriages are based on the type of people we choose to marry. The most dangerous mistake in marriage is to marry your own killer.

In cultivation, the soil condition tells the farmer which kind of plough to choose for the cultivation of the land. Similarly, character and self-control should determine the suitability of your future husband. Marriage is a lifetime commitment and we need to be sure of the person whom we are committing our life.

When it comes to sowing, the farmer chooses his seed according to soil conditions, weather and the adaptability of the seeds to the area. Nevertheless, humans are the only creatures who marry for the wrong reasons. Their choices of spouse are based on selfish interest rather than love.

Again, in farming the farmer treats his soil against soil-borne disease, his crops against air-borne disease and water-born diseases. He sprays his crops with insecticide to prevent pests from destroying his crops. He fertilises the soil for a good crop harvest so that his hard work will be rewarded.

However, humans are the only creatures who do nothing about their marriage. You buy a new car and every year the car goes for annual servicing because the manufacturer's manual recommends it. When it comes to marriage, the marriage vows are the recommended manual for servicing the marriage. It is sad that some spouse do not service their marriage.

Businesspersons take stock of their business every year to see if they are making good progress in the business. When it comes to marriage, some husbands do not take annual stock of their marriage. The reason could be either they do not know how to take stock of their marriage or they are too busy to take stock of the marriage, to see if they are making good progress.

We keep a close check on our business to see if the business is doing well, however, with marriage some husbands do not keep a close check on their marriage. We keep an eagle eye on the cash flow in our business but we never keep an eagle eye on our marriage to see if thing are going well.

We work hard day and night to succeed in our business but we never work hard enough to succeed in our marriage. We work hard to please our employers and make them happy in order to gain their favour but never work hard enough in the marriage to please and make our spouse happy.

Jesus Christ once stood outside Jerusalem and said. "I am the true vine, and my Father is the gardener. He cuts off every branch in me that bears no fruits, while every branch that does bear fruit he prunes so that it will be even more fruitful." John 15:1-2.

Let us be honest with ourselves. When in our marriage did we ever take note of our bad attitude, behaviour and conduct in the marriage that makes things difficult and unfruitful? When did we ever attempt to cut off that part of our lifestyle, which makes the marriage unfruitful?

Just as the problems in our business can only be resolved through dedication and hard work, so marriage only works through dedication and hard work. There are no magical formulas available to resolve marriage problems. The only recommendation available in this book is to examine your lifestyle, then find the source of the problem in the marriage.

When did we ever attempt to address that part of our lifestyle that we know is not bearing any fruit in the marriage? What are we doing about the unfruitful part of our marriage? Cutting off that unfruitful part can be painful but it is the only way to have a fruitful marriage. Being realistic about your lifestyle is the only way to bring healing into your marriage.

Pruning in this context has to do with getting rid of that part of our lifestyles that create storms in the marriage. It is the way we live the married life that creates problems in the marriage. Therefore, couples should look at the way they lead their marriage life to see if there are any areas of their lives that need changing.

Grandmother once said, "If things are not going well in your marriage, examine your lifestyle to see if you are the source of the problem. If your lifestyle is the cause of the problem in the marriage then change for the sake of the peace and happiness of your spouse." Married couples who take stock of their marriage will know the cause of the problem. In addition, they will take steps to fix it.

Here is a case study of a Christian woman's testimony told at a crusade. This Christian woman withstood all the storms of marriage and prevailed.

She stood still and saw the Salvation of the Lord because she waited patiently on the Lord in prayer. Now let us read her inspiring testimony.

She said, "One hot summer night, I went to the bathroom leaving my wedding ring on my dressing table. However, later I was amazed to find that the wedding ring had disappeared from the dressing table. When I questioned my husband, he denied seeing the ring. Then he helped me search every corner of the room for the missing ring.

When the search yielded no results, he started accusing me of being an adulterous wife. As if that was not enough, he told my parents I was having affairs. When my parents asked him to prove his case against me he told them the proof lay in the missing ring on my finger.

Against this, he started threatening me with divorce. He made life so hellish that I almost moved out of the matrimonial home. Despite this, I told myself divorce is not going to be my portion and I will never go down that road. God heard my prayer and spoke to me through a faint voice.

The sudden change of my husband's behaviour raised so many questions in my mind. Apart from the missing ring, I could find no other reasons for my husband's changes in attitude. My mind was filled with different thoughts. I thought he may have got himself a younger woman and my continued presence in the house was irritating him.

Besides, I thought he wanted me out of the house so the new woman could move in. So many ideas were flashing through my mind as to what to do in this unfortunate dilemma unfolding before my eyes. I never for once thought the man who married me would behave in this manner. Has his love for me suddenly died in him?

Then one day he foolishly gave me this ultimatum: "Produce the ring or the marriage is over." As if this was not enough, he asked his family to tell my parents unless I produce the wedding ring by a particular date they should consider the marriage over between us. At this, I realized my husband was bent on destroying the marriage we both worked hard to make it work.

One day, after my quiet time, for unknown reasons I felt like going to the seaside to buy fish. When I came home, I decided to prepare my husband's favourite food, although I knew he would not eat it. When I cut the fish open, I was gripped with fear and amazement. The missing wedding ring I thought would never be found was in the belly of the fish I bought from the fishmongers. How did it get there?

I took the ring, cleaned it and kept it away from my husband. Then on the day agreed by both families to annul the marriage I walked in to the midst of the family, proudly displaying the wedding ring on my finger for everyone present to see. My husband was shell-shocked after critically examining the very wedding ring he bought and slipped on my finger on our wedding day."

The Christian husband who put his wife through this pain repented and confessed he took the wedding ring while his wife was having her bath. Then he drove to the seaside and threw the wedding ring into the sea. This man underestimates the power of God. God will always intervene in the life of His children to glorify His holy name. From the day her husband hatched his evil plan to throw the ring into the sea, God also prepared a fish to swallow it.

Today the couple are still happily married because of the willingness of a committed Christian wife to forgive her husband. This woman knows and understands what it means to forgive. **The power of forgiveness is what can save your marriage.** Without forgiveness, we will be wasting our time praying, because there are some things God expects us to do before we come to Him in prayer.

If we fail to obey what He expects us to do, then there is no need coming to Him in prayer.

It took the persistent prayers of this Christian woman who knew the spirit behind her husband's horrendous behaviour was the spirit of Satan. The power of divorce controlled by Satan was pulled down by the extraordinary power of forgiveness. The only thing divorce is scared of is the word forgiveness. Try it today and you will see the amazing power behind forgiveness.

This Christian woman demonstrated the extraordinary **power of forgiveness.** She stripped divorce of its power and made a public spectacle of it, by demonstrating how forgiveness can dismantle the machinery of divorce. Only the word forgiveness can shut the marriage door to divorce. Grandmother once said, "Divorce is a sickness. Nevertheless, it can be cured; if only those suffering from the sickness are prepared to be healed."

Forgiveness is the ultimate power that can keep divorce out of our marriage. Forgiveness is one of the cornerstones of marriage. Its power in marriage is formidable, surpassing any of the marriage building blocks. Forgiveness is the crown jewel in marriage or the icing on the marriage cake.

He who knows how to forgive understands the meaning of the word love. It is possible for one to love and yet not forgive but forgiveness sees beyond love. The language of love without forgiveness is not love. Where love reigns, forgiveness reigns supreme. There cannot be peace without forgiveness in marriage.

The woman demonstrated **love in action.** The institution of marriage owes this woman gratitude and respect. She went beyond the point at which other women would have walked out of the marriage. Her patience was tested in the storms of adversity and wavered not. Instead, she weathered the storm by allowing God to take care of the consequences.

What more can we say, she lifted the Christian marriage banner higher for the whole world to see. This woman can stand with her shoulders tall in declaring there are some Christians who are determined and committed to protect the Christian marriage from the shame divorce has caused it.

Sad to say that there are not enough women with this character in marriage, that is why we are experiencing skyrocketing divorce among Christians. Bad temperament is a deadly disease that can destroy any happy marriage. It can be dormant but when ignited it will burn anything in its path; it will only stop after it has burnt itself out.

This woman exercised self-control when she was pushed beyond the limit of her endurance because she wanted to save her marriage. When she was pushed to the wall with nowhere to turn, she encouraged herself and turned to God for help because she knew that with God all things are possible.

How many women encourage themselves in a time of marriage crisis? Unless married couples are prepared to go the "extra mile," in resolving the problems in marriage, they will be overwhelmed by the storm of divorce. The problems we face in marriage are that some people have no room in their heart for forgiveness.

When Christians fail to realize that the devil is behind every break-up of Christian marriage, then Christians will continue to work with the devil to speed up divorce. Do not blame your spouse; blame the spirit that fuels divorce. An unforgiving spirit drives and speeds up divorce.

Lack of forgiveness is the major root cause of divorce today. Unless pastors and marriage counsellors address this issue, every piece of advice and sermon will come to a dead end. A spouse going through marriage problems must be aware the only way to resolve the trouble is through forgiveness.

If spouses cannot forgive each other then how can they expect God to forgive them? God commands us to forgive one another. Jesus once told his audience, "For if you forgive men when they sin against you, your heavenly Father will also forgive you. But you do not forgive men their sins; your heavenly Father will not forgive your sins." (Matthew 6:14-15).

Storms are unavoidable in marriage. However, we should not regard all storms as something inspired by the devil. Some storms come to test us and strengthen our marriage and not to weaken us. Even if the storm is of the devil, God can use it to our benefit and shame those responsible for the storm.

Storms in marriage are meant to be calmed and not create waves that will worsen them. How do we calm storms? We need to go back to the word of God. In Galatians 5:21-22 Paul speaks of "love, patience, gentleness and self-control. Against such things there is no law." Our ability to stay calm in a stormy marriage is what can bring victory and shame bystanders.

How do we pray in marriage storms? The only way to prevent storms in our marriage is to keep the flame of prayer burning in the marital home. Most Christians do not know how to pray in storms because they become disorientated. Then they lose focus and can no longer concentrate on what they are saying.

In raging storms, we need to know how the storm started and why it started. The why and how are the key words. If we can identify how the problem started then we have solved half of the problem. "Then with prayer and supplication if we make our request known to God," the storm will be calmed by Jesus.

"Prayer and holy life are one. They mutually act and react. Neither can survive alone. The absence of one is the absence of the other" (E.M. Bounds). If we need God to answer our prayer, then holy living is what is required of us. Living our married life to please God is the only way to answered prayer.

The ear of God is always attentive to the cry of His children "Who live by the Spirit and are led by the Spirit." The goal of our prayer is to have our prayers answered by God. When God says yes to our prayer, no one can say no. When God says yes, it is done. When God says it is done, then that is it.

"Therefore what God has joined together, let man not separate." Could this be the reason why the institution of marriage is hated by Satan? In addition, could this be the reason why Satan loves divorce? We know from Scriptures that the devil opposes whatever is of God. Therefore, if marriage is a divine institution we should not be surprised that Satan is fuelling the circle of divorce in the world.

Again, could this be the reason why a spirit of unforgiving rules in so many marriages? In a marriage where spouses do not want to forgive, it is because Satan is whispering in their ears not to. The Holy Spirit will have no choice than to leave them at their own peril, because He expects them to know the written word of God.

When we refuse to forgive our spouse, we strengthen the hand of the devil to harden our hearts. This allows the devil to fills our heart with anger, bitterness and resentment. Any of these could lead to murder. We have nothing to gain by not forgiving our spouse; rather we stand to gain when we forgive our spouse.

When we forgive, we make God happy and make Satan sad. On the other hand, we make Satan very happy when we refuse to forgive our spouse. This makes God very sad. He will be sad because Satan will come and accuse you before Him, telling God, "You see your children who call themselves Christians, they have no regard for your commandments. They flout them when it suits them."

The power to stop divorce is not by human knowledge, is not by human wisdom and not by human power but by the **divine word forgiveness.** When we do this then we are working with the Holy Spirit to bring peace into our marriage. We must stop divorce before it takes root in our marriage. Stop divorce before it turns you and your wife into bitter enemies.

Some of the causes of divorce could be lack of commitment on the part of both spouses to dedicate their marriage to God. The other could be forgotten vows. A woman will fast, pray, and in her desperation make a vow to God telling Him, "If you give me a husband I would give you such and such amount and dedicate my marital home as a place of fellowship."

When the LORD answers her prayer, she soon forgets her vows because she got what she wanted. She was on fire for the LORD, praying day and night. Now that she has what she wanted she has turned from hot to cold. We will do ourselves a great a favour if we repent and turn away from our cold attitude towards prayer.

What you have forgotten is that the devil that stood between you and your marriage is not far away from you. He is very close by, waiting for you to grow cold in your prayer life so he can come in. Once he comes, you will have no power to get him out. Do not ask me why, because you know why.

In your desperation, you made a vow to the LORD, and because you have not fulfilled the vows, God will not stop the destroyer from creating problems in your marriage. Now listen to what king Solomon says, "When you make a vow to God, do not delay in fulfilling it. He has no pleasure in fools; fulfil your vows. It is better not to vow than to make a vow and not fulfil it." (Ecclesiastes 5:4&5).

In conclusion, we will take up the story of Dorothy, a young professional woman who married her childhood boyfriend in a colourful wedding. She was a committed Christian and although her husband was a Christian, he was not as committed as Dorothy was. They both worked hard to purchase a three-bedroom house.

The nature of the husband's work took him away from home very often. This often-caused loneliness. As a result, Dorothy demanded he give up his job and look for work that would keep the two of them in their matrimonial home every day. This did not go down well with the husband.

Instead of the husband taking the suggestion to the LORD in prayer, he consulted his mother for advice. The loving mother told his son not to give in to his wife's demand. Was the husband right in consulting the mother? I leave this for reader's discretion and opinion. However, it is obvious she would ask her son not to give in to his wife's suggestion.

To withhold the identity of Dorothy I will not go into details of what happened. In a nutshell, this simple suggestion dragged both families into an uncompromising position. In the end, there was a temporary separation because neither of them was prepared to give forgiveness a chance to work a miracle in the marriage.

Nevertheless, after a lot of prayer and intercession by the Church and friends the husband moved back into their matrimonial home. What Dorothy said before taking her husband back is the reason for using her story in the conclusion to this chapter. She said, "I forgive you but I will never forget the pain you have caused this family."

Can we forgive and still keep a record of the offence in our heart? Can we forgive and still remember what others have done to us? Can we forgive and still be nursing the pain others have inflicted on us? Can we forgive a person for his wrongdoing and yet any time we see the person the memories of the offence keep flashing in our mind?

"Therefore, if you are offering your gift at the altar and there remember that your brother has something against you, leave your gift there in front of the altar. First go and be reconciled to your brother; then come and offer your gift." (Matthew 5:23-24) "In your anger do not sin: Do not let the sun go down while you are anger." (Ephesians 4:26)

16. The Power of a Praying Husband

"The prayer of a righteous man is powerful and effective." (James 5:16). The Greek text might suggest this reading: "The prayer produced by a righteous person will heal." The prayer that results from true faith is effective.

Although it may seem simplistic, the underlying principle for praying is recognizing and acknowledging God for who He is. As you read this chapter, you will see how the praying husband's prayer gives a wealth of insight into what prayer can do for your marriage.

The spirit of prayer should rule over the spirit of married couples and the way they conduct their lives. When married couples are out, they must allow the spirit of prayer to control their lives. The more married couples pray, the more prayer influences their lives. Prayer is the power that stops the enemy from coming into your marriage.

It is what we are in Christ, what we are in our prayer lives that holds the key to our victory or brings defeat to our marriage. If the spirit of flesh rules in our lives, it will reign in our marriage and bring shame to our marriage. Married couples must live for God both in the home and outside the home.

Married couples must listen to the voice of God in public if they want God to listen to their voice in private. There is no need praying to God if we will not listen to HIM. When married couples are out in public, they must allow God to have their hearts. When married couples submit to the kingship of Christ, their marriage is fenced by a ring of fire.

A husband will love his wife better if he behaves better, and a husband who prays better loves his wife better. Married couples who pray better will get more from God. Similarly, a husband who prays more for his family will get more from his wife. It takes the power of prayer to lift the cloud of darkness hanging over a marriage.

The Christian who builds his marriage on the Lord Jesus Christ is like a triangle with Christ at the base, holding the two other sides together. (The two arms of the triangle are you and your wife, or you and your husband.) This is the reason why each of us will be answerable to God for what part we played in destroying or building our marriage.

Marriages held to together by God cannot be shaken by a marriage wrecker. Not even the demon-inspired professional marriage wrecker can shake it. So build your marriage on Jesus Christ. Those who build their marriage on Jesus Christ have him to hold onto in times of raging storms. Build your marriage on the LORD Jesus Christ and He will be the anchor in your marriage (See Matthew 7:24-27).

Those who build their marriage on earnest praying have a happy marriage. It is earnest praying that keeps married couples together. Earnest prayer stimulates the joy of marriage. Earnest praying brings spiritual and physical healing to the marriage. Earnest praying brings quick answers to prayer.

Prayer and devotion build a happy marriage. A marriage that is built on prayer and the word of God during courting will survive any storms that will emerge later in the marriage. This is because God speaks to us by His word and through the Holy Spirit. When the line of communication between God and married couples remains unbroken, the marriage becomes the apple of God's eye.

It is imperative that married couples devote much of their time to prayer and studying the word of God. Do not wait until trouble sets in before you start praying. It may be too late to salvage anything from the irreparable damage. Remember, the couple that prays together stays together.

The Word of God is an attack weapon to defeat the enemy in your marriage. Prayer on the other hand, is a defensive weapon that protects your marriage against an enemy attack. These two spiritual weapons are the most feared weapons in the evil spiritual world because Satan and his demons know they can only be defeated by these weapons.

Therefore, equip your marriage with these formidable spiritual weapons. Since we live in a world where the pull towards temptation is greater than ever, it is through the word of God and the power of prayer that we can overcome the forces that are warring with us. When a married couple is united in prayer, the enemy cannot come between them.

The Holy Spirit speaks to a husband and wife through the word of God, making its meaning clear to them. Therefore, our hearts and minds must constantly be in tune with the Holy Spirit. As they read the Bible prayerfully, study it, memorize verses, God will unveil to them what in the marriage needs to be put right.

We cannot produce the best marriage by our own strength unless we cooperate with the Holy Spirit and cultivate the characteristic of fruits of the spirit, by letting Him control our marriage. Remember God lives in the Christian marriage by His Spirit. Therefore, we must live our married lives to please the Holy Spirit.

Prayer and Bible study binds married couples together in love and in unity. Devoting one day a week to fasting and praying is an antidote to trouble in the marital home. The power of prayer of a faithful servant is unfettered. It closes every loophole in the marriage that will give an advantage to the enemy to let himself in.

Praying husband, do you know that prayer and devotion to God are very important to a happy marriage? Praying husband, do you know that the character of the parents and their example in the home have a powerful influence on the lives of their children? Praying husband, do you know that your children look up to you to inspire them to prayer?

A praying husband is the pillar of the marriage. A praying husband keeps God in the marriage. A praying husband keeps his hands on the helm of the marriage and trains his children in the word of God. A praying husband teaches his family to trust in the word of God. A husband who does not pray invites the devil into his home and keeps God and His word out of the marriage.

A praying husband is a valuable asset to marriage. Praying husbands are needed in marriages. A praying heart sanctifies and purifies the institution of marriage. A praying husband keeps marriage in line with the will of God, and keeps every thought in line with God's Word. A praying husband's heart and mind are controlled by the Holy Spirit.

Praying husbands are the husbands that have kept the institution of marriage pure and without blemish. They are the husbands that have won victories for the institution of marriage that God established. They are the men that spoiled the activities of marriage wreckers. They are the men that have kept the flame of the Holy Spirit in the marriage burning.

A praying husband disarms marriage wreckers and makes a public spectacle of them. A praying husband's marriage is untouchable by marriage wreckers. A praying husband sees trouble before it happens and takes pre-emptive measures. A praying husband's marriage is cleansed by the blood of Jesus Christ. A husband's marriage is purified by the blood of Jesus. A praying husband's marriage is sanctified by the blood of Jesus Christ.

Praying men are the husbands who have built their marriage on the Lord Jesus Christ. Praying husbands are God's mighty men in the institution of marriage. Praying husbands are the master builders of the institution of marriage. Praying husband are husbands who keep a constant vigil over their marriage.

A husband whose prayer life is weak is like Samson when Delilah cut off his locks in their time of spiritual conflict. The only protection and rescue for any failing marriage lies in intense spiritual prayer. The only hope for marriage's survival and existence is through prayer.

In a world where the institution of marriage is crumbling, we need praying husbands. We need praying husbands to stop the canker that destroys the institution of marriage. Praying husbands are needed to cure and heal the disease that spread divorce. It takes intense prayer to keep divorce out of any marriage.

In the Christian marriage, prayer is the ultimate weapon that helps a husband and wife accomplish their task. Through prayer, the believing husband is enabled to pull down enemy strongholds around the marriage. (2 Corinthians 10:3-6). The prayers that pull the enemy's stronghold down are not just ordinary prayers. It is intense prayer and earnest praying.

The praying husband's prayer casts out the spirit of divorce from the marriage. A Praying husband's prayer breaks the yoke of divorce in the marriage and a praying husband's prayer brings deliverance to marriage undergoing divorce. A praying husband's prayer acts as a protective shield or covering against divorce.

The praying husband's prayer runs parallel to the promises of God in the marriage. The praying husband's prayer opens an outlet for the promises of God concerning the marriage. The praying husband's prayer removes every hindrance in the way of the marriage. A praying husband's prayer acts as a permanent seal around his marriage.

A praying husband's prayer makes his marriage watertight. A praying husband's marriage is impermeable by the devil and his demons. A praying husband's prayer is a flaming fire that keeps the enemy away from his marriage. A praying husband's prayer is a defensive shield that blocks evil arrows shot by the enemy.

Love purifies the heart of a praying husband from all the elements that weaken marriage. A praying husband makes love his supreme condition for prayer. A praying husband's love for his wife inspires him to pray for the family. **Love is the power that keeps the praying husband on his knees day and night, interceding for his family.**

There is no limit to the praying husband's power of prayer. A praying husband's prayer keeps his children from being corrupted by the children of the world. Without the fervent prayer of a praying husband, his wife will be robbed of the sweetness, joy and beauty of the Christian marriage.

The praying husband's prayer removes all obstacles in the way of the marriage. A praying husband's prayer changes the purpose of God. Yes it does. Let us take some classical examples from the Bible. "After forty more days Nineveh will be overturned." This was God's message for them.

The people of Nineveh believed God. When the people of Nineveh repented, it changed the purpose of God. Your prayer can also change the purpose of God in your marriage. Try it today and see how prayer changes things. If things are going wrong in your marriage, then let the power of prayer work miracles in your marriage.

Praying husband, do you know that prayer can change your circumstances? Jonah is a classical example. "From inside the fish Jonah prayed to the LORD his God." Now listen to his prayers. He said, "In my distress I called to the LORD, and he answered me. From the depths of the grave I called for help, and you listened to my cry."

If from the inside the fish the LORD heard the prayer of Jonah, if from the depth of the grave Jonah prayed and the LORD answered him, then would God not answer you who are on land? Would God not listen to you who are not in the grave? Our realization that God can do anything if only we put our trust in Him holds the key to all our troubles.

Praying husband, do you know that there four spiritual weapons at your disposal? These spiritual weapons are, Godly Desires, Prayer, Submission to God and Dependence on God. These were the very weapons Jacob used when he struggled with the angel. Praying husband, you to can make use of these weapons and prevail against your enemy.

Praying husband, your prayer can change your circumstances. Yes, it can, do you know that Jacob, in his struggle with the divine being, stood his ground and cried out, "I will not let you go unless you bless me." Then the angel replies,

"Your name will no longer be Jacob, but Israel, because you have struggled with God and with man and have overcome" See Genesis chapter 32:27-32.

Praying husband, do you know that when God gives you a new name, it indicates a changed spiritual character or a new standing before God. A praying husband does not give God rest until He blesses him (Isaiah 62:7). A praying husband's home is a fortress and witches and wizard know that, so they keep away.

Moses changed the purpose of God and saved Israel. The prayer of King Hezekiah changed the purpose of God. In addition, God said, "I have heard your prayer, I have seen your tears; I will add unto you fifteen years." It was the intense prayer of King Hezekiah, which made God change his purpose for the king. See 2 Kings 20:1-6.

The power of the praying husband can bring a dead marriage back to life. Do you doubt this? Do you know that the prayer of Elijah brought back a dead child? Do you know that Elisha did the same and restored to life the son of the Shunammite? If God can restore life to the dead child, He can restore your dead marriage to it former glory.

Praying husband, what else can we say of the Apostle Peter? He knelt down and prayed for Dorcas and she opened her eyes. What about Paul, he prayed for Publius, and he was healed. The prayer of Hannah gave Samuel to Israel. Hannah was so resolute and passionate in her request for children, that the priest accused her of being drunk.

The Scriptures are filled with men and women of God who prayed earnestly and witnessed the result of their prayers. Praying husband, do you know that, the faith that brings pleasure to God and gains His attention is that faith which motivates its possessor to move towards God."

Praying husband, do you know that God answers prayer, but He does it according to His will. Nevertheless, the praying husband who is diligently seeking God puts his marriage in the arms of God. And allows his family to know God's will and put their faith in Him to fulfil His plan in the marriage.

Rebecca had no children and she became pregnant as a direct result of Isaac's prayer. Isaac's prayer was a prayer of faith. God was moved because of the intense prayer of a concerned husband and father. You too can intercede for your family by intense praying and God will answer your prayer today.

Praying husband, do you know the tragedy of childlessness drove Isaac to prayers, and do you know that nearly twenty years would pass before the answer came? Nevertheless, he kept on praying. Praying husband, do you know what kept Isaac praying for twenty years? For a man to wait to for that number of years takes faith and courage.

Isaac was a man who knew that besides God there is no hope anywhere. This man knew that outside God there is no hope. Isaac fixed his eyes on God and trusted God to open the womb of Rebecca. Isaac's prayer was based on faith. Praying husband, do you know that God honours prayer that is according to His will and perseveres in spite of delays? See 1 John 5:14-15; Luke 18:1-8.

Praying husband, what would you do when things are happening in your marriage that are beyond you? Do you know that Rebecca also had a problem and decided to take it to God? Our ability to realize that something is wrong in our marriage holds the key to the problems in our marriage.

When Rebecca was faced with similar problems, she decided to find what was happening to her. She decided to find out why. Therefore, she wisely decided to take her question to the LORD. God answered her prayer. Praying husband, if you would also take your prayer to God today He will surely answer your prayer.

Praying husband, grandfather once told me that, "when faith gives way to fear, we are likely to do the wrong thing." Praying husband do you know that human weakness can be tested by danger? Praying husband, do you know that faith alone in the LORD is what can get us out of danger?

There is not enough space to talk about Jacob, Rachel, Zechariah and Ezra. All these men and women's prayers changed the purpose of God. Your prayers can also change the purpose of God about your marriage if only you believe. Do you remember what the woman in Mark 5:28 said? "If I just touch the helm of his garment," and within the twinkle of an eye she was healed.

The men who have done mighty things for God have always been mighty in prayer. These men knew that, "the prayer of a righteous man is powerful and effective" (James 5:16). They knew the power of prayer and made use of the power prayer to their advantage. It is also available to you.

Do you now believe that the power of prayer can move God to grant you your heart's desires? Yes He can, lets take a classical example of the story of

Jabez in 1 Chronicles 4:9-10. His mother named him Jabez, saying, "I gave birth to him in pain." Jabez was a man who knew the power of prayer.

He cried out to God, saying, "Oh, that you would bless me and enlarge my territory! Let your hand be with me, and keep me from harm so that I will be free from pain." Guess what happened. God granted his request. This prayer is what is called intense and earnest praying of a man who is determined to move God to change what his mother had said about him. Praying husband, tell God, "I am not going anywhere until you grant me my request."

The key words in Jabez's prayer are "Let your hand be with me." If you know how to use a weapon in your hand effectively, then you will win the battle. The problem with most Christians is they fight a defensive battle, instead of fighting an attacking battle. Defensive weapons do not win battles. We win battles when we are on the offensive. Battles are not won with defensive weapons or armour; rather battles are won with offensive weapons.

For example if we look at Ephesians 6:10-18, Paul makes a list of the battle armour of God. If you study the list carefully, you will observe that all of the armour listed is defensive except for one item.

The armour Paul listed is protective armour, and you cannot defeat the devil with protective armour.

The offensive or attacking weapon Paul mentions in the passage is, "The sword of the Spirit, which is the Word of God." You can only defeat the devil by the Word of God. The Word of God is the most formidable weapon in the hand of a Christian who knows how to use it effectively.

Defensive weapons are good, but you cannot defeat demons and witches with them. It takes only the Word of God to overcome Satan and his wicked, evil spirits. Let us look at Revelation 12:11 and see by what means the saints overcame the devil. "They overcame him by the Word of God and their testimony."

Again, see Revelation 19:13 "He is dressed in a robe dipped in blood, and his name is the word of God." Compare this with John 1:1 "In the beginning was the Word, and the Word was with God." Again, turn to Revelation 12:11, "They overcame him by the blood of the lamb."

You may have the greatest weapon at your disposal, however if you do not know how to use it then it will be useless in your hand. Our ability to master the weapon at our disposal is the key to our victory against Satan and his demonic forces. You may have as many Bibles in you house, but they cannot win victories for you if you do not know how to use them effectively.

Praying husband, do you know that you cannot win a battle with a blunt weapon? Because a blunt weapon is less offensive and as such cannot do any damage to the enemy. An offensive weapon must have a sharp edge or pointed end. Similarly, a Bible covered with dust and cobwebs is an indication of neglected spiritual life.

Praying husband, if the Bible in your home is in this state, then you are in serious trouble because devil can walk into your home and sit with folded arms and say, "How wise is this man to play the game my own way. Go on; I will reap the benefits of your foolishness." However, if the devil sees you reading the Bible, then he knows that will spelt disaster for him.

This is what Paul says the Bible is. "For the word of God is living and active. Sharper than any double-edge sword, it penetrates even to dividing soul and spirit, joints and marrow, it judges the thoughts and attitude of the heart." A Bible in your home covered with dust and cobwebs will have no power over demons.

Praying husband, do not put your Bible under you pillow or sleep with the Bible by your side thinking it will scare the devil and his demons away from you. Satan is not afraid of the Bible, what Satan fears is the spoken Word of God. It is only when the Word of God is spoken that Satan and his demons are sent running for their life.

Praying husband, the devil and his demons are not afraid of the cross around your neck as you see in Hollywood movies. Remember they are only movies. It does not work in real life. In real life confrontations with Satan and his demons, we need the Living Word of God to overcome them.

Praying husband, be warned that, unless you are led by the Spirit, except you keep in step with the Spirit, and finally unless you are living in obedience to the Word of God, Satan and his demons will not be afraid of you. It is only by holy living you can overcome Satan and his demons with the Living Word of God.

Praying husband, Satan and his demons know who a spirit-filled Christian is. Beside Satan and his demons, know you are no match for them as long as you are not living a holy life. Therefore, praying husband let holy living be part of your married life so that in time of spiritual battles you can overcome them.

Praying husband, are you a prayer warrior? Does your prayer conquer the enemy? Is your prayer a miracle working prayer? If the answer is no, then let me remind you of someone whose prayer does. Joshua's prayers were miracle-working prayers that exposed sin and stopped the sun.

Praying husband, there are hindrances to prayer but keeping the flame of prayer burning is the only thing that can surmount the hindrances. There are toils but endurance is what makes the strongest prevail. The praying husband must always keeps the flame of prayer burning in his home to keep the enemy out.

When prayer stops, the enemy prevails. When the flame of prayer fails, marriage loses its divine characteristics. When the praying husband stops praying, marriage loses its divine power. When the praying husband stops praying, the marriage sinks to a low level. When the praying husband stops praying earnestly, the enemy walks into his marital home without any resistance.

Praying husband, take note of this, what Satan does not want us to think about is what we are in Christ Jesus. What we are in Jesus Christ is what makes the devil panic, therefore praying husband, stand your ground and tell Satan who you are in Christ Jesus. Praying husband, Satan will try to put you down because he knows the power in you is greater than his power.

This is the reason why Satan will try to make you believe that he is to be feared, because fear is Satan's greatest weapon. If you entertain the fear of Satan in you then you are down and out. Satan rules by fear and that is the reason he wants every Christian to believe he is to be feared.

It takes the whole of a praying husband to pray until the storm in the marriage calms down. It takes the whole of a praying husband to pray until the wind and the wave in the marriage cease. It takes the whole of praying husband to calm the storm in a marriage. It takes the whole of a praying husband to pray until troubles are kept out of marriage.

Luther once said. "If I fail to spend two or three hours in prayer each morning, the devil gets the victory through the day. I have so much business I can't get on without spending three hours daily in prayer." The praying husband that prays well wins the battle. The intense praying husband knows when he his praying less because the Spirit of Christ speaks to him.

A husband who does not pray will never learn God's truth. A husband who does not pray will never be able to teach God's truth to his family. It takes the power of prayer to allow the full flow of God's spirit into marriage. Lazy, short prayers will cut the pipeline of God's full flow. A dead prayer will draw the devil's interest to your marital home.

The praying husband watches and prays to cover and guard his conduct. The praying husband is vigilant and watches over his family to drive troublemakers. The praying husband is vigilant and guards over the life of his family. The praying husband knows how to use the power of prayer effectively.

A praying husband will not wait until his marriage suffers before he starts praying. Worldly things do not mar a praying husband's life. A praying husband is quick to repent. A praying husband seeks nothing but holiness. A praying husband is constantly in touch with the Holy Spirit.

Are you looking for a happy marital home? You can find one in the arms of a praying husband. Are you seeking a peaceful marital home? Then seek for a praying husband, for the God of a praying husband is a God of peace. Praying husband may, "the LORD bless you and keep you, the LORD make his face shine upon you and be gracious to you, the LORD turn his face towards you and give you peace." (Numbers 6:24-26).

Are you looking for a battle-free marital home? You will find one in a praying husband's home. Are you looking for a husband who will love and cherish you? Then look for a praying husband because in the arms of a praying husband you will find love, joy, happiness and a peaceful marriage.

A praying husband has spiritual warfare as his highest priority. He fights the family's battle against Satan and his minions. He stays awake in times of spiritual conflict, interceding for his family. The praying husband prays and fasts for his family. The praying husband has God the Father, God the Son, God the Holy Spirit watching over his family.

A praying husband does not hold a grudge against another person if he expects God to answer his prayers. A praying husband has no reason to hold a grudge against anyone. Grudges are hindrances to prayer therefore the praying husband must stop the seed of bitterness being sown in his heart. When a grudge has given birth to bitterness, it can lead to murder.

Are you looking for a husband? Then do not just look for a Christian, rather look for a praying Christian. Looking for a Christian to marry is not enough, rather seek a husband who prays with God, seek a husband who prays with Christ and finally, seek a husband who prays with the Holy Spirit.

During courtship, take particular interest in the prayer life of your future spouse. Look for signs of spiritual weakness; find out how long he or she spends praying. The prayer life of a man should be very important to every woman. Prayer is a spiritual weapon that married couples have to wage spiritual battle with in time of marriage crises. Therefore, every woman must make sure her future husband knows how to use the weapon of prayer effectively.

Spending time praying with your suitor is the ideal way to assess his or her prayer life. If during this assessment you notice signs of laziness, weakness and lack of desire to pray, I suggest you put a temporary hold on any arrangement until his prayer life has improved. Be watchful and do not be fooled by deception. **Prayer is the power that holds marriage together.**

Again, watch out for deception. Some people can become praying warriors overnight for the sake of getting what they want. Some Christians can pray like Elijah when they need something from God. Once the need is granted, they forget about God. Christians like this forget that the enemy is not far away from them.

It is far better to marry a praying husband than to marry a Christian who do not know how to pray. The security of your marriage rests in marrying a praying husband who prays with God instead of a Christian who does not know how to pray. **A praying husband knows that the success of his marriage depends on the power of prayer.**

A praying husband must know that Power with God is the highest attainment of the life of prayer. Praying husband, it is only when you give yourself to holy living that you can expect the power of Christ to manifest itself in your marriage. God rejoices in the prayer of a praying husband. **The power of God is placed at the disposal of the praying husband.**

When we pray, we expect an answer from God. After all, that is why we pray! Yet sometimes, even though we know we are praying according to God's will, the answer is delayed. This can be very frustrating and many people give up before the answer comes. There are many possible reasons for the delay, but we must trust that God has a purpose. He will answer our prayer, but in His own time.

We do not know all the circumstances surrounding any situation that we pray over and we have no idea of the kind of timing required to see that situation resolved in the best possible way according to God's will. Sometimes, even though we pray, the situations are not resolved in the way that we pray, but we must trust that God has everything under control.

Sometimes the more we pray, the more the problem is gets worse. The fact the problem is getting worse will not move God to intervene and answer your problems quickly. In prayer, you cannot leapfrog the waiting period just because you have an urgent request. Prayer always requires a response of some kind. Sometimes we need to rest in God's promises and wait for Him to answer. Sometimes, God expects us to be obedient to His command and act on it in response to prayer.

Praying husband, do you know that sometimes God must be petitioned for a long time before He answers. Do you know that other times; He answers the humblest prayer immediately? Praying husband, circumstances will not move God to answer your prayers.

Praying husband, do you know that by studying the prayers of Isaiah will give you a wealth of insight into what prayer can do for your marriage? Praying husband, do you know that, even though Peter had denied the Lord, Satan could not keep him away from the risen Lord. Do you know that Jesus' prayer for Peter was effective?

Praying husband, if your marriage is failing turn to Jesus for He will never fail you. Just as His prayer for Peter was effective, His prayer for you too will be effective, if only you will turn to Him. He lives to pray us. (Hebrews 7:25) Praying husband, turn to Jesus with your marriage problems and all will be well.

Praying husband, do you know that when King Saul prayed, God was silent. When King David prayed, God answered him immediately. What do you think the difference was? The difference is not in the words that the men used, but in something else, that set the two men apart from one another, something that made their reigns very different.

Praying husband it is not the words you use in your prayer that will make God answer your prayers. It is the condition of the heart, it is the intended purpose and it is love and submission in marriage that move God to answer a married spouse's prayers. Love and submission sets apart the Christian marriage and makes it different from any other marriage.

You cannot expect God to answer your prayer if you do not love your wife, because love is the foundation for every marriage. How can you stop loving your wife and claim you love God? A husband who loves God will surely love his wife sincerely. The only prove that a man loves God comes from loving his wife. From the day, your love for your wife dies in you; your prayer hits a dead end. As long as you love your wife sincerely, God keeps answering your prayers.

The more affectionate you are towards your wife, the more the LORD keeps answering your prayers. The more you walk faithfully in your marriage vows, the more the LORD watches over your family. Praying husband, if you want God to answer your prayer, then love your wife and seek her highest interest.

You cannot stop loving your wife and expect God to bless you. The blessing in marriage comes with a condition, and that condition is love and submission. Every marriage rests on two pillars, which are love and submission. Without either one of them God will withhold the blessing in the marriage.

Praying husband, give a wealth of insight into what prayer can do for your family and then watch God open the windows of heaven to release the showers of blessing upon your family. In conclusion, prayer is the means by which the

Christian married couple can remain in constant communion with God.

17. The Power of United Prayer in Marriage

"Until now you have not asked for anything in my name. Ask and you will receive, and your joy will be complete." (John 16:24).

"Again, I tell you that if two of you on earth agree about anything you ask for, it will be done by my Father in heaven. For where two or three come together in my name, there am I with them." (Matthew 18:19-20).

Prayer is the ultimate weapon to help us accomplish our task. Through prayer, the believer is enabled to pull down the enemy stronghold. See Paul's second letter to the Corinthians, Chapter 10:3-6. In this, Paul describes how prayer can shake the foundation of divorce to its core.

Prayer is the only power that can hold marriage together. Prayer is the only weapon married couples need in their war against divorce. Divorce is not fought with money or with power of words but with prayer. The court should never be an arena for Christians to fight marriage battles. The only people who benefit from divorce battles are lawyers.

When Christians are tempted in using money and words as weapon in settling divorce then, they are doing the devil's dirty work for him. This allows him to turn his attention elsewhere. Christians are blessed with the most formidable weapon there in this world. Why should Christians be tempted to use the weapon of the devil in fighting an institution God established?

This reminds me of what Martin Luther once said, "Do you know what the devil thinks when he sees men use violence to propagate the gospel? He sits with folded arms behind the fire of hell, and says with malignant looks and frightful grim, "Ah, how wise these madmen are to play my game! Let them go on; I shall reap the benefits. I delight in it" But when he sees the Word running and contending along on the battlefield, then he shudders and shake for fear.

For the Christian, marriage without prayer is a dead marriage because it has no life. A marriage without prayer is like an empty gun, which cannot win any battle. A marriage without prayer is like a man going into battle with a children's toy gun. However, children's toy guns are for play and not for battle.

A marriage without prayer is weightless because it can be blown away by the winds of adversity.

Marriage without prayer in times of crises would have nothing to hold onto. There are four main reasons for ineffective prayers in marriage: laziness, quick and short prayers, dead prayers and careless praying.

What are the hindrances to marital prayers? Married spouses who are too busy to pray are busy fighting a losing battle. Whatever prevents married couples from praying will eventually affect the marriage and kill it off. Marriage is bound to fail when praying stops because it is being hindered by the worries of this world.

When a busy, married life becomes occupied with the affairs of this world, it neglects marriage's spiritual life. Some married couples allow other duties to become pressing issue in the marriage. This chokes marriage to death. If you are too busy to pray, you will find God too busy to listen to you.

When you allow a busy life to choke your marriage to death, the verdict from the coroner after an inquest will be death by misadventure. A busy life is one of the contributing factors in marriage failures. Married couples who are too busy for each other will find themselves drifting apart.

Similarly, a busy life is one of the hindrances to married prayer life. If we allow our married life to be so busy that we neglect our spiritual life, DIVORCE will take its rightful place in the marriage. A busy life wrecks a happy married life. A busy married life is one of the quickest ways to temptation.

Satan would prefer our marriage to become busy so that our prayer lives become dead to the spirit and alive to the flesh. A dead marriage means it has gone out of business. Therefore, both spouses go their separate ways to find a new husband or new wife. Then they put up this sign in front of their homes: **This marriage is under new management.**

Christians who forget or do not know that prayer and the word of God are what keep the devil away from their marriage would find they are no match to the devil. Unless our prayer lives are refined by the Holy Spirit, our marital home would become Satan's playground. However, if we allow our prayer to be refined by the beauty of Jesus it spelt disaster for Satan and his demons.

In Matthew 18:19-20, Jesus taught his disciples the power of united prayer. This prayer, if followed by all Christian married couples will dismantle the divorce machinery that has plagued this generation and the generation before. In these verses, Jesus gives us a very special assurance for the united prayer of a married couple.

In the verse, He talks about prayer that two (married couple) or three people should agree on and ask together. Here it implies having one mind or having one opinion concerning a specific request. Let us now turn our attention to the text. "Again, I tell you that if two of you *(a man and his wife)* Italicize mine, **on earth agree about anything you ask for, it will be done for you by my** Father in heaven."

It is worth studying the text for its intended meaning. The bond that unites a man and his wife is no less real and close than that which unites both of them to God. Both husband and wife should depend on each other. Their dependency should be through the union and cooperation of the Holy Spirit.

In the union of husband and wife, the Holy Spirit can manifest His full power. Remember that husband and wife are joined in union by the Holy Spirit. Therefore, when the husband and wife come together in prayer, the Spirit of God is with them. The Holy Spirit is the power that draws married couples together in unity of prayer.

The mark of true prayer in the unity of husband and wife is when they are in agreement concerning the things they ask. They must be very specific and very clear in what they ask. Asking here should be centred on two things: asking according to God's will and believing they have received what they have asked for.

One thing is certain; the Lord does not want our asking to be in vain. When we pray, we expect an answer from God. After all, that is why we pray. However, sometimes we know we are praying according to God's will, yet the answer is delayed. The delay can be very frustrating, and could cause some people to give up before the answer comes.

Giving up because of a delay in answering prayers is for immature Christians and not for the mature. Sometimes certain delays to unanswered prayers could be a test of faith. In such delays, we should remember the words of Jesus Christ in the parable of the persistent widow: "Always pray and never give up" (Luke 18:1). Persistence in prayer holds the key to unanswered prayers.

There are many reasons for the delay, but we must trust that God has a purpose for the delay in answering our prayers. God will answer our prayer, but in His own time. This is the problem with most of us. Inability to wait can cause us to quit before the answer comes. We live in an INSTANT age where everything is instant.

We want it and we want it now. God does not work this way. Demanding something instantly from God is not part of His nature. God demands that his children must wait for His own timing. We do not know the circumstances surrounding any situation that we pray over. If God were to reveal to us why He delayed in answering our prayer, we would ask for His forgiveness. The problem with us is that we have not the slightest idea of what is happening in the spiritual world.

Again, we have no idea what kind of timing is required in seeing that situation resolved in the best possible way, according to God's will. God does not owe us explanations as to why He is silent over certain issues in our lives, which we deem very important. If we demand an INSTANT answer to prayer, it will not come.

If God were to answer every prayer instantly, there would be more chaos in this already chaotic world. The prophet Isaiah once told his audience "They that wait upon the Lord shall renew their strength." Let us live our prayer life according to the word of God. One thing is for sure, if our prayer is not answered, there must be something in the prayer that is not as God would want it.

We cannot hold a grudge against another person if we expect God to answer our prayer. A Christian has no reason to hold a grudge against anyone. Married couples who hold grudges against each other should not expect answers to prayer until the issues are dealt with first. God always seeks the honest and sincere marriage.

If God is happy with married couples, He withholds nothing from them. Love and unity in marriage draws Jesus' infinite attraction. The presence of Jesus in the fellowship of husband and wife bestows the unity of prayer and power in a marriage. Remember this: "It will be done by my Father in heaven."

Marriage that is united in faith, love and the Spirit allows the power of the name of Jesus to flow freely and the answer to come. The sign that there has been an answer to true united prayer is the fruits of receiving what we have asked. God rejoices when the prayer of married couples are answered by Him.

If a believing husband and wife know they have been joined together in the name of Jesus Christ to experience His presence and power in the unity of prayer they will shout Hallelujah every moment of their life. The proof of a good and happy marriage is the unity of their faith in the power of united prayer.

The unity of prayer by husband and wife can conquer the power of Satan and dismantle his stronghold. Married couples must never allow their unity to be shaken by outside forces. Marriage is part of prayer; you cannot separate the two of them. Marriage and prayer are constantly in tune, inseparable, and are intimate companions. They walk and talk together. Married couples who give all to God in prayer will get all from God.

Today people talk about marriage but many of them do not know its alphabet. There is a peculiar affinity between marriage and prayer: both of them recognize God, both submit to God, and both have their aim and end in God. Prayer is that which can stop problems in marriage.

The central trouble in a Christian marriage is a lack of effective prayer. People can do excellent things in their marriages but excellent things without prayer are of no use to marriage. God cannot deny married couples who wholly dedicate themselves to prayer. Prayer is the means by which married couples communicate with God.

A desire for God that cannot break the chains of sleep is a weak thing and will do little in moving

God to grant our request. The way to ensure God makes our marriage strong and far beyond Satan's reach is to start praying from the day we get married. If you want to keep your marriage out of trouble, then keep talking to God.

Our laziness in praying to God for things to work well in our marriage is what will make the devil catch up with us. Most Christians do not know how to pray because their prayer lacks substance and earnestness. We pray as if we have other options so that if God does not answer the prayer, we fall back on what we already have in mind.

The Scriptures tells us that Elijah prayed earnestly and God answered him. Hanna prayed earnestly and God answered her prayers. What about Isaac? He earnestly prayed and God opened the womb of Rebecca. If your prayers are not answered, then they are not answered because God does not see any urgency in your prayers.

Heaven is too busy to listen to half-hearted married couples' prayers. Our experience and the revelation of God are born of costly sacrifice, our costly storms, costly conflict and above all, our costly praying. Wrestling all night to defeat the enemy in our marriage should keep us awake from 03:00 to 05:00 everyday of the week.

It is very costly for married couples to go a day without praying, knowing the enemy is not far from us. Married couples must pray "with all perseverance." They must hang on to prayer because by it your marriage will wax strong. Prayer is the only thing that can solidify your marriage. Therefore, keep talking to God.

The heart and soul of married couples are in prayer. Without prayer, love in the marriage will die out. Therefore married couples must "pray and never faint," the more severe the trial and the longer the waiting, the more glorious the results. The answer may not be instant but keeping talking to God.

No marriage is perfect, but through prayer, the obstacles in the marriage can be removed. No matter how hopeless, importuning brings hope from the realms of despair, and creates success where neither success nor its preconditions existed. The Christian marriage is a union of two imperfect Christians brought together and held together by God's grace. This is the reason why our imperfection should bring us in communion with God every day of our life.

The Christian is helpless without prayer. Therefore, the Christian planning to get married should know that marriage could not survive without prayer. Because we are not perfect and never will be. Two imperfect people marrying would not produce perfection in any marriage. Only God is perfect. The sooner we understand this the better it will be for us.

Do not go into marriage looking for perfection, you will not find it. Rather go into marriage with Christ and Christ alone. Christ is the foundation of Christian marriage; this is the reason why married couples must relent in their prayer to make their marriage strong in the LORD.

Nothing but prayer can bring God and married couples into happy communion. Married couples who know prayer have a purpose and are definite and direct. If they know their utterances have the ear of God; they can achieve great things in their marriage. God's ears are close to those who talk to him in earnest.

18. Broken promises

"Do not judge or you will be judged. For in the same way as you judge others, you will be judged, and with the measure you use, it will be measure to you. Why do you look at the speck of sawdust in your brother's eye and pay no attention to the plank in your own eye? How can you say to your brother, 'Let me take the speck out of your eye,' when all the time there is a plank in your own eye?" (Matthew 7:1-5)

Love is a very confusing concept in this modern society. Nevertheless, the Bible is not confused or vague about the powerful concept it calls love. The Greeks have four distinct words for love, each with its own meaning.

(1) Eros denotes the relationship between male and female, including physical desires, craving, and longing. That word for love is not used in the New Testament. (2) Stergos describes affection, especially mutual love between family members. (3) Philos reflects the care and concern that friends have for each other, what we call brotherly love. See John 21:15-17.

(4) Agape describes a unique type of supreme love involving a conscious and deliberate choice to do good for another, a commitment based on the decision of the lover, not the qualities of the person receiving the love. Agape is perhaps best seen in God's love for the world (John 3:16) and in the love that God calls on believers to display (1 Corinthians 13:1-13).

If you look for love in the wrong place, you will never find it, the reason why we are faced with so many divorcées among young men and women in the Church. Do not go looking for love in the wrong place. Finding love in the wrong place will become a thorn in your flesh. Love creates interest in marriage, and then brings married couples into a union of one flesh.

Marriage in this state becomes a subject of delight. Love is the only thing that makes marriages work, if only we understand what love means. The understanding of the true meaning of Biblical love and marital love is very important in a world in which some people marry for the wrong reasons.

With marriage, many Christians are aimless because they have no patterns through which conduct and character can be shaped. They just move on aimlessly, their minds in a cloudy state, no pattern in view, no point in sight, and no standard after which they would strive to make their marriage work.

There is no standard by which to gauge and value their effort when things are going wrong in a marriage. Marriage believes in love so it will seek the very highest form of love before committing itself. The marriage institution is not self-centred, nor does it seek its own interest; instead, it seeks the interest of the husband and wife in the marriage.

Love is the precondition for marriage. Love shows the way of marriage. Love is vital, so essential, and so far-reaching that it enters the very core of marriage. In fact, love itself is a very definite thing that aims to make the marriage work for the glory of God. Another word for marriage is **love.**

Grandmother once said, "The love atmosphere that the husband initiates will permeate the whole home. In the long term, it will not only bless the members of the family but also those around them and the community as a whole." This is an area where real Christianity is lived and where hypocrisy cannot thrive.

The next example we will look at is that of a Peruvian woman called Lucia. The layout of this story is quite different from all the above because of its nature. The story does not flow in sequence, as you would expect in life story writing. The reason for this is that some of the characters in the story provoke issues that necessitate an immediate response.

This allows the writer to respond with Scriptural verses and then expand the verse with clearer understanding. As a result, you will find the story of Lucia is fragmented. The fragmentation of the story of Lucia is designed to challenge the attitude of some of the character's views about Lucia.

The writer has chosen to write the story in this style to stimulate interest and arouse curiosity. The story is both challenging and confrontational. The story exposes the hypocrisy of some Christians who sit in the church, pretend they are holy, and are without sin. Again, it exposes Christians who have summarized the Ten Commandment into one.

That is, "You shall not commit adultery." In their small mind, they think it is perfectly right to break all the other nine, as long as you keep the Eighth Commandment you are right with God. Until you study carefully how Jesus summarized the Ten Commandments, you will end up walking with hypocrites.

The problems we encounter in married life have nothing to do with God. Rather it is due to decisions we made that were not in accordance with to God's plan for us. If we keep God out of our decision-making then the devil will walk in and become part of the decision-making. What Satan may suggest to us in terms of decision and choice may appeal to our hearts and minds.

However, Christians must subject such thought to the word of God, which forms the basis of a decisive test. Only the word of God can expose Satan's lies. As believers we must test every dream, every vision and prophecy against the word of God. Christians must be sure the source of every revelation is the Holy Spirit.

If we make the mistake of being carried away by what we see and like in some revelations then we will only have ourselves to blame. The devil is very good at deception so we must test every revelation for flaws and inconsistency. Our ability to discern the voice of the God Shepherd from the hired Shepherd is what will save us from wolves.

Before we take up the story of Lucia, let us look at the following examples of how some Christians can be deceived through false prophecy, vision and dreams. The Scriptures warn us not to believe all prophecies. The most likely reasons why some

Christian believes every prophecy is that they like what they are hearing.

The story of Kimberly is an unfortunate one and must serve as a warning to all Christians who are looking forward to a happy marriage. The mistake most Christians make is that they think pastors who preach from the pulpit are all men of God whose prophecies are under the inspiration of the Holy Spirit.

If you are one of these Christians, then you are a sitting duck. A Christian who fails to study the Bible but depends solely on sermons coming from the pulpit is likely to accept and believe all that he or she hears from the pulpit. Some of the pastors who preach from the pulpit are nothing but "wolves in sheep's skins."

Their poisonous sermons are laced with witty stories to evade detection. Do not just listen to the sermon from the pulpit; instead discern the spirit speaking through the man in the pulpit. Look out for its trademark. **Jesus Christ is the centre of our praise and worship.** Pastors who love to be in the spotlight turn to draw the attention of their congregation away from Christ to themselves.

One Sunday morning a visiting pastor came to preach in their Church whilst their pastor was away visiting another Church. The visiting pastor was an excellent communicator and the congregation was charmed by this gift. During the sermon the visiting pastor paused, then pointed in the direction of Kimberly and said "Young woman, get up and look behind you. The man sitting directly behind you is your future husband."

This is a cheap prophecy perfectly articulated to put him in the spotlight. Then he turned his attention to the young man and said, "Young man, this young woman is the wife you have been praying for." Prior to this cheap prophecy, there had been many prophecies concerning Kimberly and Kevin. Whilst some saw visions, others dreamt of them getting married.

One of their friends remarked, "Well, what else are you two waiting for? The confirmation is now very clear." They hurriedly married without putting all those dreams, prophecies and visions to the test. It does not matter who is prophesying, we must still expose those prophecies to the Word of God. Those who fail to study the Scriptures will find themselves at the mercy of pastors with questionable characters.

The marriage was a disaster. Three months after the wedding, they were fighting each other in a divorce court. What had gone wrong after the colourful wedding? This couple failed to seek God's counsel. Moreover, today many Christians blindly follow the same path. A Christian who is too lazy to study the Bible will believe whatever a pastor is teaching.

What the flamboyant pastor did not know was that the young man he was prophesying about was already married. Did God really speak through this pastor? We know from Scriptures that God is not an author of confusion. This smart man was careful in keeping his married life very discreet. Nobody in the Church knew he was married except God.

Yet the church married them without finding out any information about his past life. If the church had done its homework, this situation would have been avoided. What happened to Kimberly is bound to happen to any body who fails to seek God's counsel. When it comes to marriage, we must find enough information on our fiancé before committing ourselves.

Being extra careful will bring out what we do not know about our spouse. It difficult to find out information in one sitting, but if we persist in our quest to know the other side of our fiancée we will find the information we are looking for. Marriage is one thing we do not have to rush into.

Would you say this prophecy was divinely inspired? We must allow Scripture to speak for itself. "God is not a man that He should lie." It is clear from Scriptures that divinely inspired revelation and prophecy does not contradict itself. What about the channel through which the prophecy came? Well, that is not for us to judge.

For it is written, "Only God knows those who are His." Again, John writes, "many false prophets have gone out into the world." Let us take an example of true revelation from the word of God. Turning to Acts chapter nine, verses 11 and 12 you will notice how Luke describes vividly an account of a revelation that confirms how we can discern false visions from Satan.

Luke writes that the Lord told him (Ananias), "Go to the house of Judas on Straight Street and ask for a man from Tarsus named Saul, for he is praying." Now note very carefully how the Holy Spirits confirms revelations. In verse 12, the Lord told Ananias, "In a vision he has seen a man named Ananias come and place his hands on him to restore his sight."

Who saw the vision? It was Saul. This implies that God was telling Ananias that He had revealed to Saul that he was sending a man named Ananias to restore his sight. You will note that there are two people involved in the revelation. Whilst Ananias was receiving his visions, Saul was also receiving his to confirm the word of God.

Both Ananias and Saul received visions to confirm or validate the revelation. Beware, the devil is very good in using Scriptures to make you believe the decision you are about to take is definitely according to God's will. He may even use dreams, visions and prophecy to confirm that God is leading you in the decision you are about to make.

The people around you become his instrument in accomplishing his purpose in your life. Remember, the devil cannot operate without using people. Therefore, he has to posses and use people to achieve his aims. Satan operates within an unseen world that is invisible to our naked eyes. The earlier we know this, the better it will be for us.

God is pure and holy and He wants to bring us into His presence. This requires that man be regenerated. The Scripture says, "Without holiness no one will see the Lord" (Hebrews 12:14). David also said, "The man who shall stand in God's holy place must have clean hands and a pure heart and not approve deceit or falseness." (Psalm 24:3-4)

The story of this young Peruvian girl you are about to read will make you wonder whether some people really understand what marriage is all about. God's intended purpose for Christian marriages is to glorify His name and be an example to the rest of the world. However, the story of this young woman and the pastor and others continue to shame the Christian marriage.

The rampant divorce rate in Christian marriage should remind us that God's intended purpose for marriage is to glorify His Holy name and not bring shame to His name. To days, rampant divorce rate among Christians should serve as a wake-up call to the damage divorce is doing to the Christian marriage.

The story of Lucia begins in Peru and ends in London. We will take up the story from London and end it in Peru. Her story should serve as a lesson and warning for the reasons why some people want to marry.

People marry for various reasons without making their evil intentions known until you become a victim. This kind of deception is bad for marriage and bad for the Christian faith and puts the Christian marriage institution in the limelight. Oh! How I wish we could see the deceptive character of some people, but it is so sad that this is our spiritual blind spot.

Today some people marry because of money; others marry because of the status of the man or the woman. Others marry to avoid sexual sin. If burning sexual desire will lead them into an immoral life then they would rather marry than fall into sexual sin. Unfortunately, some Christians marry to avoid sexual sin. This is what the Church is faced with; therefore, the church must endeavour to expose this bad attitude.

Marrying to avoid sexual sin should never be the reason we marry. Those who go into marriage for the wrong reasons will never have God's approval. We get God's approval when our desire to marry fits perfectly into His will for us. Only then shall we get His blessing in the marriage.

We must marry for the right reasons and not for the wrong reasons. Marrying for the wrong reasons will eventually lead to the breakdown of the marriage. People who marry for the wrong reasons are more likely to walk out of the marriage if the reasons for which they married no longer exist or if what attracted them to the marriage suddenly begins to fade.

The subject of marrying for the wrong reasons is why Sister Lucia allowed her life experience in an unholy marriage to be written down to warn other women from being caught in the same trap. Her inability to discern the genuineness of a dream, vision and prophecy cost her happiness.

Our inability to discern some people's evil intentions in marrying can cause problems later on in marriage and lead to bitterness and anger. Deception is the way some people in the Church live their lives and those who fall prey to them come out wounded and badly shaken and the healing process can take a long time.

Some people are insensitive to the pain they inflict on others. They simply do not care if others are suffering because of their actions. They marry and divorce when it suits them without caring about the feelings of those involved in the marriage. These are the very reasons why we must be careful of the people we choose as our life partners.

Most divorce cases are based on selfishness, greed and self-centeredness instead of the desire to make the marriage work. No matter how we try to conceal the reason for which we got married, it will eventually come out when it finally burns itself out. A burnout marriage would have nothing to hold on to except divorce.

If marriage were like a crystal ball we could gaze at and see the beginning and the end, some marriages would not be experiencing the problems they are facing today. Besides, couples would be able to eliminate those who come into marriage with the wrong motives. Sometimes we may feel that way about life, wishing we could have seen the problem coming.

If only we could have known how certain situations were going to turn out. Sorry, we do not have a marriage crystal ball to allow us gaze into the future to sieve out undesirable suitors. However, while we do not know the outcome of tomorrow's troubles, believers in Christ by faith can see where the trouble is going to come from if they are willing to wait on God in prayer.

Sometimes our problems stem from our inability to wait on the LORD. Again, God has given us the Holy Spirit which if relied on can help us to make a godly choice that will make the joy of marriage fulfilled in our lives. Some Christians play with words for their own selfish interest without caring about the feelings of those they are hurting.

People who fall in this category glean through the Scripture for verses that would justify their actions. Do not be deceived by some Christians who seem to have memorized many Biblical verses and use them to their advantage. There is nothing spiritual about memorizing so many verses in the Bible.

In 1 Corinthians 7:10 the apostle Paul writes, "To the unmarried I say: It is good for them to stay unmarried, as I am. But if they cannot control themselves, they should marry, for it is better to marry than to burn with passion." Some Christian men and women, who cannot control their high sexual drive, use this verse as a reason to satisfy their burning passions for sex. Therefore, they marry for no other reason than for sex and sex alone.

People who marry for sex express love and affection toward their spouse when they need sex. Once the sex act with the spouse is over, the love, attention that every woman cherishes in the marriage disappears into thin air. The only time they see it again is when they want sex. However, they forget that marriage is not about sex alone.

Marriage is about passion to love each other, to show affection to each other, share ideas together, to share each other's burden, to share each other's thoughts, to cherish and adore each other and to live together "until death do us part." Marriage is looking at your spouse and telling her, "You are the reason I live."

Above all, the reason God instituted the marriage institution was to "multiply and replenish the earth." On this note, I want to advise women who are planning to get married to be aware there are some men who do not want children in marriage. Therefore, it is imperative that women sit down with their fiancé to discuss the issue of children.

If your fiancé makes it clear that he does not want children in the marriage then please, do not compromise for the sake of your love for him. If you are someone who wants children in the marriage, then break off the engagement and walk out before you cry yourself to death in a marriage that will turn out to be nothing but trouble.

Run away from him and never look back or listen to him again. There is nothing morally wrong in breaking off an engagement where an interest of conflict will one day destroy your happiness and lead to divorce. Do not even think that you can persuade him to change his mind once you are married.

I know of a lovely Christian couple who married in 1986. What Patrick did not tell Pascal before the wedding was that he never wanted children. Sometimes it is difficult to tell what goes on in the minds some Christians when they are faced with issues that affect others lives. Being honest and truthful is supposed to be one of the marks of the Christian faith.

Whilst Pascal's sister is married with seven children, she has none. Her parent tried to talk her husband into changing his mind, but Patrick will not change his mind. He never gave any convincing reasons why he did not want children in the marriage. People like this do not care if others are suffering because of their actions or decisions.

Nevertheless, Pascal, being submissive, went along with her husband wishes. She never showed any remorse for her husband's selfish views of marriage without children. Pascal loved children and she desperately wanted to have her own children, but the person who stood between her and her desire to have children was her own husband.

The story of Pascal parallels that of Lucia. Whilst Pascal weathered through storms and wrote a wonderful book about marriage without children and infertility in marriage, Lucia's life took a different twist. Both of these women are wonderful Christians. They each faithfully gave their love to the man they loved. However, they both went through different trials in a marriage they thought would bring them the joy.

Lucia is an exceptional Christian woman with a God-given gift that most Christians would say,

"Thank you God but I don't want this kind of gift." She calls her exceptional gift her ministry. Her God-given gift is a test of faith that would shame most money grabbers in the ministry.

She wakes up every Saturday morning at 5:00. Then out of her small monthly income prepares breakfast and lunch for homeless people living in and around Victoria and King's Cross Stations. She hires a Taxi to take her to these two train stations in the city of London. Once at the station she distributes the food to the homeless people.

After they have their breakfast, she would open the Scriptures and present them the word of God, which is the spiritual food these people hunger for and really need. Her charm and smiles captivated the hearts of the homeless people. Some men of God would avoid this group of people because they know once these homeless people found their way into their Churches they would have nothing to contribute financially, a situation they would want to avoid.

Lucia is a unique Christian with a burning passion for the spiritual and physical needs of the destitute. She lives for Christ and Christ alone. Her entire life revolved around her work among the homeless and a passion to go where others would not want to go. It takes the wings of faith for a man or woman to go this far with the message of Salvation.

Some of the homeless people she cared for were alcoholics and drug addicts. Others were driven there by circumstance. Some of them too were dangerous and hardened criminals with tattoos all over their bodies. One look at some of them would make you run for your life. On one of her visits, she asked me to drive her round so that we could distribute the food and evangelize.

I must confess one look at of some of them brought the thought of my wife and three lovely children flashing through my mind. Do not take me for a coward. In situations like this, God's special gift supersedes anything else. What you must know is that women can go where men cannot go. Even the Scriptures tell us that it took three women in the Bible to change the course of history that eventually led to the coming of the Saviour. See Joshua chapter six and the book of Ruth.

One smile from Lucia will soften and melt any stony heart. She was beautiful and used her beauty to walk into the heart of hardened criminals with the message of Salvation. Through the power of the Holy Spirit, she conquered and set free Satan's captives. This set her on a collision course with Satan.

This young woman made sure her God-given gift benefited those for whom God had called her to lead out of darkness into the light of God. So that when she stands before her maker, she can faithfully account for what she did with her talent. The gifts of God are meant to benefit both the saved and unsaved.

Lucia was a woman with the heart of Barnabas. Today, the Church needs men and women with the heart of Barnabas. The Church needs this special gift to enable Christians to reach the untouchable with the message of Salvation. We as Christians must pray for God to give us this unique gift.

In addition, we must seek a special gift that will enable us go where under normal circumstances we would not want. Remember, the Church has no legs so it will need to use our legs to take the message of Salvation where Christ wants us to go. Would you today allow the Church of Jesus to make use of your legs?

Again, the Church has no hands and it will need our hand to take gifts of God to those in need. The Church has no mouth and it needs our mouth to proclaim the message of Salvation to the lost that

Christ died for on the hills of Calvary. Today, God is calling you to make use of your legs, hands and mouth for the sake of the unsaved.

We know from Scriptures that the devil has a cunning way of pouring cold water on our spiritual life. He does this by using the worshipers in the Church. The devil has so many willing accomplices in the church that he has no time looking for anyone outside the Church to quench your burning spiritual life.

Watch out before it is too late, because the devil has so many willing friends in the Church who are always eager to work with him to pull you down. The fact is that those who bring Christians down are from within the Church and never from outside. This is where it hurts. We call them the "the enemy within."

Whilst Lucia was busy working for LORD, the devil was watching her closely and devising plans to derail her work in setting free those he was holding captive. Therefore, he started grooming someone in the Church to derail her work for the Lord Jesus Christ. The enemy seeking to pull you down is in the Church and not outside the Church. The enemy in Church are invisible making it very difficult to unmask them.

The person the devil hired to carry out his evil assignment was no other person than the assistant pastor. Are you surprised? You do not have to be. The Holy Scriptures speak about them. The devil works with those who are willing to cooperate with him to bring Christians down. There are only two places to look for the enemy: in your family and inside the Church.

These two places are where a Christian is likely to come face to face with his or her killer. It may take many sittings to make a good picture of why the assistant pastor did the devil's dirty work for him. The behaviour of this pastor should not surprise you because the Scriptures speak about such people.

He was recruited to destroy Lucia's happiness. It was a complex assignment because the devil needed someone with a good knowledge of the Scriptures, someone with authority, who was well respected. The assistant pastor met all these criteria. When it comes to service for the devil, he knows whom to choose.

There are some assignments the devil will never recruit a novice to carry out, and Lucia's story is a typical example. Therefore, the devil needed someone the congregation could go to for spiritual and physical advice. Such a person must be someone who commands respect in the Church.

One day when Lucia asked the assistant pastor to remember her in his prayer in the choice of a husband, the devil seized the opportunity. This was it. Now or never, this is where the drama unfolds. The stage was now set for the devil to put his plans into action. Time wasting is what the devil has no interest in. Perfect timing is one of his evil qualities.

If you end up speaking to the wrong person about your problems or your prayer request, then be sure you may end up with a catalogue of failures and disappointment in your life. People you speak to about your problems could be the very people the devil will use to bring you down. Satan has no clue to what is in your mind or what your problems are except to you tell him. His agents, with their listening ears are so close to you to relay the information to him.

Knowing the right person to talk to about your personal problems will play a crucial role in helping to put you on the right path. You will never know the real person you are speaking to until you realise you have signed your death warrant. Therefore, we need to pray for the Holy Spirit to lead us to the right person to seek advice.

It is rather unfortunate Lucia spoke to an opportunist who was lying in wait for the likes of Lucia. This was a bachelor pastor looking for a woman like Lucia for a wife. If one came to him with a prayer request, would he let her slip out of his hand? No, he would not. For the perfect place to get a wife is in the house of God.

From that moment, he loved her. Could this be true love? No, it was lust at first sight and not genuine love for Lucia. The reason he wanted to marry Lucia was for her beauty. He saw in Lucia a woman of stunning beauty that satisfied his lustful desires. Is this a reason a man should marry?

A generation that is bent on marrying purely on good looks will kill their marriage before they walk down the isles. Grandmother once told me "Men who marry because of beauty will kill if someone else shows interest in their wife." An unattractive man who marries a beautiful woman walks with jealousy as his companion.

The assistant pastor is not alone in this type of choice of a wife. When it comes to choosing a wife, many Christian men are caught in these types of lustful desires. I am not against choosing a beautiful woman for a wife but the Christian's motives should not be that of lustful desire when it comes to choosing a wife or husband.

Christians must understand that there is a difference between lust and love. Lust does not lead to love. Lust fades but love does not fade. Lust is possessive but love is not possessive. Lust is artificial but love is natural. Lust does not lead to happiness, instead it leads to regrets and misery but love brings happiness.

Lust, when satisfied, leads to hatred and rejection. See second Samuel 13:1-22. Love, on the other hand, unifies a relationship with the joy of the Lord. Lust is temporal but love is everlasting. Lust speaks of self-centredness and possessiveness but love seeks the other person's highest interest.

Lust runs away from responsibility but love accepts responsibility. Lust fears responsibilities, love shoulders responsibilities. Lust walks in darkness but love walks in light. Love shines but lust dims. Again, whilst lust lives in constant fear, love lives in the spirit of boldness. Lust cannot wait because of greediness but love can wait no matter how long it takes.

One day Lucia came to visit me for advice. From our discussions, it was clear she was in love with the assistant pastor. The stage was now set for the pastor to achieve his aim. He really succeeded in working his way to Lucia's heart. She was young and beautiful in her early thirties, with long hair to her waist. He was in his mid-forties.

The twisted web in this love story is that Lucia needed someone she could work with in her ministry and the assistant pastor needed a woman who could meet and satisfy his lustful desires. Spiritual things and physical things do not mix. These two were so blinded by love they thought it was possible to mix water and oil and produce a different substance.

Mixing other substances and water results in a new association but does not result in a change in composition. Sugar may be dissolved in water, but the water is water and the sugar remains sugar. The same is true of oil and water, which do not dissolve in one another. They may be shaken together, but they remain oil and water.

Likewise, when a number of people enter a room and are together, they might be considered a mixture in the physical sense. Nevertheless, no one has lost any of his or her individual characteristics because of being together with other people. A wolf in sheep skin is still a wolf and cannot change its nature.

For Lucia, the pastor was definitely God-sent. A word of caution, if we fail to include God in our decision-making we open ourselves to all sorts of problems. For an example, see the Gibeonite Deception in Joshua Chapter 9. Watch out, for there are some Christians in the Church with angelic appearances. Beneath that angelic appearance is the very nature of Satan. Do not be surprise at this, because in every congregation you will fine some members with the spirit of Satan.

Do not be fooled by their cheap public show of holiness, it is all faked: that holiness is a black void. After briefly courting, the senior pastor announced the wedding between the assistant pastor and Lucia. This did not go down well with some women in the Church who had their eyes on the assistant pastor. They got so close yet were not noticed.

The assistant pastor lives in Corydon. He lived in Corydon because he was not a paid pastor, which meant keeping his secular job. The assistant pastor had to travel every Sunday for Church service and then journey back to his home. When a branch of the Church was opened where he lived, he had to combine his secular job with pastoral work. This means Lucia had to travel to spend some weekends with her fiancé.

When desire cannot wait, when lust cannot wait, when feeling cannot wait, it opens the door for sin.

The perfect moment the devil is looking for. The devil is an opportunist who waits patiently to seize on the slightest opportunity to bring down Christians if he spots the slightest indication of weakness.

Grandmother once told us; "Putting petrol and a burning flame in close proximity is a recipe for disaster. Similarly keeping gun powder and fire in the same container is a deliberate attempt to set off a series of explosions." This is a scenario every Christian must avoid to shame the devil.

God does not make mistakes and He does not lie. Therefore, it will not be long before a man's evil intentions are exposed and everyone will know that God was not part of a union initiated from the beginning by the devil. This was what happened between the pastor and Lucia.

Do not allow the devil to play a leading role in the search for your future wife or husband. That role is for Christ. Christians who love the Church more than they love Christ will always deny Christ the leading role in their lives. Courting couples who put God out of their relationship will certainly put God out of their marriage.

When Lucia came for advice, she was questioned about the frequent visit to her fiancé's house. She said they were part of their marriage preparations. Again, when asked about the number of rooms in the house, she said there were three rooms. At this, I asked about the sleeping arrangements. She said she slept in one of the guest rooms. I felt there was something wrong with this constant visiting.

Nevertheless, I told her there was nothing morally wrong with the sleepover visits, as long as she went with a female friend but if this arrangement was not convenient for them, she should consider an alternative form of visits. At this, she asked what kind of alternative arrangement would be suitable.

I advised her to consider day visits instead. This would mean going in the morning and leaving the same day. In addition, she should avoid any close contact that would lead to temptation. She was told the best advice was for them not to be in an enclosed place alone because courting couples who are fond of being alone behind closed doors are likely to fall into temptation.

However, they can be in a public place alone where everybody could see them. The reason for this is to avoid temptation. Temptations are stronger when the opposite sexes are left in close proximity for a long period. Sexual sin is like an open wound that attracts flies. Therefore, the only way to keep the flies away is to cover the wound.

Whether this advice was heeded or not, only time will reveal what has been going on behind closed doors. Then one day she walked into my office with tears in her eyes. A look into her face and her countenance said it all. She ran into my arms like a schoolchild running away from a gang of school bullies into the arms of her father. For the next five minutes, there was silence except for the wiping of her tears with a handkerchief.

She broke the silence saying the first night at the assistant pastor's house was nothing but rape. Her fiancé walked into the guest room and told her there was nothing morally wrong in sleeping together in the same bed. After all, they are getting married soon. Sorry, the fact that you are about to get married is no excuse for you to sleep in the same bed as your fiancé.

It should be noted that some people's view of marriage desecrates the spirit of the marriage institution. Keep this in mind. **God's plan for sex is through the implementation of the marriage institution. Anything short of this is a direct violation of God's law concerning sex.**

Be warned the lust of the flesh is one of the temptations, which can make a person forget he or she is a Christian. The lust of the flesh is what can lead a Christian to break the eighth commandment. The lust of the flesh can blind and harden the Christian's heart against the consequences of disobeying God.

Do not allow yourself to be fooled by the devil into breaking the eighth commandment. Because when the game is over, he will desert you to face the consequences alone. Besides, you need to weigh carefully the shame and disgrace your selfish actions can have on those around you.

In the moment of his passion, this man forgot he was a pastor. As a result, he sinned against God. This is what the lust of the flesh can do to the Christian. It makes us forget who we are in Christ. It can make us forget we are the temple of God. It can make us forget the Holy Spirit cannot dwell in the throne of a redeemed man's heart if the body is defiled.

There are three great temptations: **Money, Power and Sex.** Watch out, one of them can easily overcome you. The strongest among the three is Money; he who has it can control Power and Sex. At the top of Power is Money and behind Sex is Money. These three are like dynamite in the hands of Satan. He unleashes them with such power that even the champion Christian can easily be blown away.

This is the reason why all the great men of God, both past and present that fell, fell because of one of the above. Yet, both Christians and men of God continue to fall under the force of these three weapons of Satan. Great political leaders, film stars, sportsmen, Kings and rulers have had their knees bent by either one or two of the great three temptations.

Lucia's fiancé was a well-built and physically strong man that gave Lucia no chance of fighting back. Besides, he told his fiancée the marriage would be off if she continued to resist his advances. The problem here is that she also needed the marriage to legalise her stay in the United Kingdom.

This man carefully planned and played with words because he could not wait until after the wedding to consummate the marriage. This man found himself in a room alone with an attractive young woman. Could this man of God have prevented this sinful act? Oh! Yes, he could, but he allowed the desire and craving for Lucia's body to draw him into sexual sin.

The devil will always tempt us at the time when we are most vulnerable. Waiting for that vulnerable moment, he lures us with a bait of seductive suggestion that create lustful desires in the mind. Seductive suggestion is a mind game the devil uses to make us sin against God. This tactic is one of the oldest and yet most powerful tools the devil employs to weaken our resistance against the lust of the flesh.

When we are faced with such seductive suggestions, it important to follow Jesus' example, which is to throw the Bible at the devil. When Jesus was faced with suggestive worship of the devil, he responded, "Away from me, Satan! For it is written; 'worship the Lord your God, and serve him only.'"

The Scriptures are full of verses about lust, greed, lying, stealing and gossiping. If we burn the stories into our memory, we can use them against the devil's seductive suggestions. The rule is that when Satan strikes at you, strike back with the Word of God. Then sit back and watch him run like a frightened schoolchild.

A second look at Lucia and your heart will start beating fast. God might have spent a lot of time shaping her body beautifully. To have such a stunning woman like Lucia alone in your bedroom you would require the power that helped Joseph resist and run away from his tempter leaving his cloak behind.

After the night of passion, the subsequent visits were like a married woman visiting her husband. They were virtually living like a married couple. The problem with the lust of the flesh is once you yield to it, it sets off an uncontrollable chain reaction that holds you captive. It just continues without stopping because the lust of the flesh weakens a person's resistance to sexual immorality.

No matter how hard you try, you find it difficult to stop. The lust of the flesh works its way into our heart and mind, paralyzing our resistance to sexual sin. This is the reason why the longer we stay in our sins, the more difficult it is for us to come out of it. Sin does not easily give up on its victims.

The pastor and Lucia's nights of passions gave birth to a baby. She was excited about the pregnancy but he was furious. You may ask why he was furious. Well the answer is simple. What he did in secret was about to be exposed publicly. An embarrassing situation he did not want to be in the public domain.

Against this, he told Lucia to have an abortion or the marriage plans were over. This man was nothing but a control freak, a domineering husband in waiting. What is shocking here is that the person demanding the abortion is no novice in the word of God. For a pastor to demand his fiancée abort the baby in her womb raises more questions.

This shows the extent some Christians will go to, to hide their shameful deeds. It is not surprising that people bound by sin love the darkness and do not want the light of the gospel to expose their sinfulness. The problem with sin is that people want to hide it rather than confess it. The worse the sin is, the more we want to hide it.

Even if killing is the only thing to help hide some people's sin, they will do exactly that. In a world where nobody wants to own up to his sins, some people will do anything to hide it even if it means killing. Christians who what to hide their sins are spiritually sick from the top of their head to the soles of their feet.

Sin must be confessed, before one can be forgiven. Only then can a person be ready to respond to a new life in Christ. To confess your sins and be right with God is far better than to hid your sins and be right with men. The only way a fallen Christian can break the yoke of sin is to expose the sin before Christ. The only way a sinner can break free from sin is total surrender to Christ, who alone has the power to set the sinner from his or her captivity.

The problem with some people is that when they sin, they want to hide it instead of confessing it. The only way to restoration and healing for our sins is to cry out to God by confessing our sins before Him. There may be some repercussions, but the result will be a renewed fellowship with God.

If a person knows your weakness, he or she will play it to his or her advantage. In this case, the assistant pastor played the game fully to his advantage. When we were growing up our father always told us that, "I don't trust my own pocket so can I trust you?" What this saying implies is that apart from God, never trust a man born of a woman.

This pastor knew very well that sex before marriage is a sin. Therefore, he had no excuse for his sins. However, to tell his fiancée to have an abortion would be a deliberate violation of the sixth commandment. Can a Christian justify abortion? What message would we be sending out to a morally degenerated world?

Life is life; it does not matter whether in the womb or outside the womb and it does not matter whether a clot of blood or a fully formed baby. The sixth commandment that states that, "You shall not murder" does not say it is applicable only to life outside the womb. The Scriptures state clearly that life is in the blood.

Therefore, the seed conceived in the womb is blood irrespective of how long it has been since conceived. In the sight of God, the person who commits murder in the womb and the person who commits murder outside the womb are both guilty of murder. A clot of blood as a result of conception is life, therefore abortion is murder: there are no two ways about it. Abortion has left so many women depressed in our society.

On the other hand, it is known that women who have abortion face double the risk of having mental problems, which is a serious problem we are confronted with in our society today. Besides, 10 percent of all mental problems in women are linked to abortion that goes to confirm that abortion is an evil thing in our society.

Our quest to hide our sins from the rest of the world is what can lead us to murder. If murder is the only option that will prevent others from knowing the sins we have committed, then some will not hesitate to go that far. So many people have gone down this route and have resulted in innocent blood being shed.

This reminds me of news that appeared in the local newspaper. The story has it that a former Army bomb disposal expert tried to murder his pregnant wife by planting a hand grenade in her car after she confronted him about his affair. As a result, the wife, who is a nurse, suffered extensive leg injuries in the blast.

Her eight-year-old son escaped unscathed while her unborn child was also unharmed. Sometimes one wonders if some people know what marriage is all about. Did this man ever love his wife? Why did he marry her? Does the marriage vow state that husbands have the right to murder their wives if their unfaithfulness is exposed? This man is not alone in this treachery.

When I asked Lucia if the senior pastor knew about the pregnancy, she said no. I told her the senior pastor must know about the pregnancy immediately. The assistant pastor was by now threatening Lucia that if the senior pastor heard of the pregnancy, then there would not be any marriage.

Finally, she summoned up her courage and told the senior pastor of the unholy relationship. This infuriated the junior pastor. As a result, he told Lucia "I am not going to marry you." His love for Lucia suddenly changed to hate. This was a pastor possessed with the spirit of Amnon. See 2 Samuel 13:15.

The senior pastor intervened, giving the assistant pastor an ultimatum. "Marry your fiancée or consider your ministerial career in the Church over." Is the senior pastor right in imposing a woman the junior pastor no longer loves as a precondition for continuing his ministerial career?

What Lucia did not know was that a great storm was building around her, a storm that would overwhelm her. The shocking thing about the storm was that it was going to come from her trusted friends. In a world where there are very few people to trust, it hurt to see the people you thought you could trust deliberately pull the seat from under you.

Her relationship with the junior pastor created envy among those who wanted the pastor's attention. As a result, there was so much attention around her that everyone had reasons to dig the dirt on her. Even her flatmates became embroiled in the storm because two of them were vying for the junior pastor's attention.

How Lucia's flatmates knew she was two months pregnant before her wedding day will remain a mystery. There were only two people who knew about the pregnancy, so who told Lucia's flatmate she was pregnant? They threw her out of the flat and called her all sorts of names. Is this a good reason for throwing Lucia of the flat?

Certainly not, I am not implying what Lucia did was right. What she needed was love, affection and understanding from her flatmates. They told her she was not fit to live in the same flat with them. On the contrary, God would not agree with their way of thinking and their condemnation of Lucia. Someday Lucia would stand before her maker and answer Him.

The raging storm has just begun, and for her to survive the storm she will need the help of the Holy Spirit. Christian love has no room for hatred. After all, there is heaven on earth when Christians are one, in one body and bound by cords of love. In times of crisis, we need people who are in touch with God, who can lift us from where we have fallen and dust the dirt from our soiled cloths. And not Christians who are out of touch with God.

Does Lucia's action warrant her being stoned? Was there anything to be gained by humiliating her? The reader is obliged to draw his or her own conclusion from whatever angle they view the fall of Lucia. Sometimes we forget we are also subject to sinful desires, and this desire can remain dormant. All it needs is a spark to ignite it.

The real culprit in this whole saga is the assistant pastor. He is the one these sinless women should direct their anger toward and not the poor woman. For these women to single out Lucia for ridicule gives reason to believe they had other hidden motives against Lucia. The manner they unleashed the storms against Lucia suggests they envied her.

Their reaction was that of a lynch mob. These women deliberately set out to lynch a fellow Christian. They had only one aim: to strip her of her dignity. Only Christians who are out of touch with the Holy Spirit will behave in this manner. Whether this will make them feel good and self-righteous, only God who sees beyond what goes on in our hearts can tell.

They deliberately set out to destroy the good reputation of a fallen Christian sister because they had hard evidence to drag her to the cross. Armed with the evidence of the pregnancy they set out to nail her to the cross. The attitude of Lucia's friends shows they loved the Church more than they loved Christ.

Christians who love the Church more than Christ are always on a moral crusade and they will mow down anyone who dares to stand in their way. Their behaviour stems from two things, lack of sound Biblical teaching or a desire to appear spiritual. Grandfather once said, Christians who love the Church more than Christ would kill in defence of the church rather than dying for Christ.

They are like the Sanhedrin and the Pharisees in the day of Jesus who obeyed and held on to the traditions of the elders instead of what God required of them. A Pharisee would kill in defence of the Temple in Jerusalem rather than die for God. Similarly, a Pharisees would kill for the defence of the tradition passed down to them rather than obeying the written Word of God or dying for God.

Similarly, the modern day Christians who hold to the traditions of the Church will die for the Church rather than for Christ. The attitude of these women is nothing but a cheap moral crusade, from which nothing can be gained. The behaviour of these women reminds me of Hannah's rivals in One Samuel 1:6-8. It is true certain qualities about us can provoke others to jealousy.

It would have been useful for them to use their time and energy more profitably in reaching out for the lost sinners around them than going round with a placard with the inscription, "Stone the adulterous woman." What these Christian sisters do not know is that even though people fail us, God is still in control of our life.

To achieve their aim they became her judge and prosecutors. They made sure no stone was left unturned in their zest to humiliate her publicly. Christians with critical attitude are of no use to the Kingdom of God because their behaviour and attitude do more harm than good. Finally, these young women succeeded in doing just that. Whether this brought excitement and joy, nobody can tell.

What these Christians failed to realise is that on judgement day God is not going to ask them any question about the behaviour of Lucia. Rather God will be asking them to account for their attitude, behaviour and the way they live the Christian life. Lucia will have to speak for herself.

God will never ask us any question about anybody else; neither will He need us to testify against another person. On that faithful day, it will be about you and God alone. Besides, you will be expected to answer for yourself. If this is true as the Scriptures say, why try to play God? Do not try to be what you are not in the eyes of God.

Their quest to destroy her moral character reminds me of what the prophet Obadiah told the people of Edom. "The day of the LORD is near for all nations. As you have done, it will be done to you; your deeds will return upon your own head." (Obadiah 1:15)

I am not writing in defence of a very good friend. No, far from it. However, if you think that is the case, you are entitled to you opinion. The fact is that when a child of God falls through sin our attitude towards him or she should be about nursing them to recovery through care and love as directed by Christ.

I am not questioning their attitude and action towards Lucia. However, the issue that raises concern is the motive behind their attack on a fallen sister in Christ. In every situation where someone is ridiculed in an attempt to humiliate him or her there could be a conflict of interest. The reasons for their actions must be critically examined and questioned.

However, if the motive is aimed toward correction that will lead to healing and restoration, then it is good and must be accepted in good faith. On the contrary, if the intent is based on envy then it is very wrong. Again, if the intent directed toward utter condemnation that will make the person walk away from the faith then it is wrong.

Frankly, no one has the spiritual right to condemn a Christian who has fallen into sin. The Scriptures do not condone sinners neither do they encourage sin. Sin is sin and God hates sin. However, God loves the sinner and He wants them to turn away from their sinful ways. What is repulsive to God is the sin His children commit.

Some Christians in the Church are nothing but wolves in sheepskin. If you step on their toes, they will draw blood from your toe. Christians like these are the reason why some people have left the Church. As Christians, we must make room in our heart for those who fall into sin. The young woman in this story did not deliberately set out to sin against God.

There comes a time in a Christian's life where difficult circumstances can tempt him or her to sin. However, the Bible does not give us any excuse to sin against God. Sin is sin, irrespective of the circumstance. It only takes the grace of God to overcome such difficult circumstances that cause us to sin.

What hurt Lucia was when they told her a sinner like her was unclean and not fit to live among Christians lest she pollute them. Well, all sinners are unclean, if clean Christians withdraw themselves from them, how then can they get the gospel message to them? Like the Pharisees in the days of Jesus Christ who withdrew themselves from sinners, so are Christians with a critical attitude, they would have nothing to do with Christians who fall into sin.

"We are saved by grace and not by works." The sinner and the person who condemns the sinner have both sinned before God. For the person who condemns the sinner becomes an obstacle in the sinner's way to Salvation. What would you benefit if you action towards a fellow Christian makes him or her to walk away from the faith. Would you receive a crown from God?

Lucia's behaviour in this whole saga had strengthened the hands of enemies who appeared to be consumed with jealousy and envy in the way God had been using her in the Church. The Scriptures makes it clear that we have all sinned and come short of the glory of God. Therefore, let God be the one to judge us.

Her behaviour gave her enemies the opportunity to soil her good reputation. She was living with natural-born enemies without knowing. The knives were out to slash her face to leave lasting scars they hoped would haunt her for the rest of her life. Sorry, there will not be any prize waiting for them in heaven for exposing Lucia.

These three Christian sisters became a thorn in her flesh. They told everybody who knew Lucia that she had fallen from grace to the status of the worst sinner. They saw themselves as saints, and should not be near Lucia in case they themselves become corrupted by her lustful desires. This is a question of when God has not condemned the sinner, the sinner condemned the sinner.

The arrogance of these three friends of Lucia reminds me of what the apostle Paul wrote to the Corinthian Church. "So if you think you are standing firm, be careful that you don't fall." (1 Corinthians 10:12). We are human and subject to weakness, failure and temptations. Being Christians does not make us super-human and above temptation.

They drove Lucia to the brink of suicide. One of them who worked with Lucia made sure that everyone who knew Lucia as a Christian heard about her sinful ways. She succeeded in painting a picture of Lucia as a daytime Christian and nighttime sinner. Christians with bad motives always have a critical attitude.

This woman set out to tarnish the good image of a Christian woman who was well respected at work by her bosses and co-workers. The question we should be asking this holy woman is what would she gain by going this far? For a Christian to ridicule another Christian before unbelievers who have a high regard for that Christian goes beyond the Christian norm.

As a result, Lucia became a subject of ridicule at work. Whenever she walked past her colleagues, they would burst into laughter and call her names. The behaviour of Lucia's flatmates proved there was more to their actions than the accusations. Envy, it is said, can make a Christian behave like unbeliever.

The attitude of these Christians reminds me of what the Apostle Paul went through at the hands of his enemies the Galatians. They charged him with walking, "according to the flesh" (Gal 10:2). They said that he was a coward, for he wrote letters that resounded like thunder but in actual presence he was about as authoritative as a mouse (Gal 10:10). He did not maintain himself in dignity by taking support from the Churches, but demeaned himself by working (Gal 11:7). They claimed that he was not one of the original apostles, and so was not qualified to teach (Gal 11:5; 12:11-12), and that he had no credentials that he could show (Gal 3:1).

They attacked his personal character by saying that he was fleshly (Gal 10:2), boastful (Gal10:8, 15), and deceitful (Gal 12:16), and they insinuated that he embezzled the funds that were being entrusted to him (Gal 8:20-23). The Christian should not look for his enemies outside the Church and his home.

It looks as if Lucia had something they wanted. They wanted the assistant pastor and he would not give them his attention. Beside, they simply could not compete with her for the assistant pastor. They were consumed with envy when they heard Lucia and the assistant pastor were still going to be married.

The question everyone should be asking these three saintly Christians is, have they any problem with Lucia's proposed marriage with the assistant pastor? Their attitude towards Lucia changed from the day the engagement was announced. This made them intensify their moral crusade against Lucia.

If these three saints had listened to Lucia's side of the story that led to her present circumstances, they would have buried their knives deep beneath the earth. Envy can cause us to be blind to the truth. When people are consumed with envy, they do not want to know the truth and would not ask why.

The attitude of these so-called Christian friends of Lucia reminds me of what the prophet Obadiah wrote about Edom: "Though you soar like the eagle and make your nest among the stars, from there I will bring you down," declares the LORD. These girls behaved and acted as if they were without sin and could not be tempted.

These three Christians are definitely not the type of Christians who obey the Word of God. Their behaviour desecrates the spirit of worship and fellowship. In addition, it creates disunity among Christians. Envy is the cause of disunity in the church, and the reason why some sit in the Church, eat at the Lord's Table and yet do not talk to each other.

There is not a single verse in Scripture these Christian women can quote to support the barrage of insults they inflicted on this young woman. Christians like these think they are acting in defence of the Bible. In their blindness, they wandered away from what the Bible stands for, just like the Pharisees in the days of Jesus.

If a Christian falls into sin it is nobody's business, rather it is God's business. Our business in the fall is spelled out clearly in the Scripture. Our business is to help raise the fallen Christian gently by restoring him to his position before the fall. (See Galatians 6:1). If we do this, then we have God's favour.

A critical, faultfinding attitude toward our friends and loved ones can be the main thing that keeps them away from accepting Christ. God works in us, in others, and in circumstances when we pray for others. Christians who become obstacles in the path of sinners should not consider themselves a friend of Jesus Christ.

Christians are suppose to demonstrate the power of the Cross, which is love, and not demonise each other. What message would we be communicating to the world we are supposed to evangelize? Christians devouring one another is never part of the message of the Cross. If the people we were supposed to evangelize see us devouring one another, will they accept the message of the Cross? Even if they will, they will think twice before accepting the message of the Cross.

Christians who come from Churches where sermons are based on Biblical stories are more like to expose their hypocrisy when speaking in defence of the Bible than Christians who come from expository Bible preaching Churches. When students fail their exams, the teachers are held accountable, when business fail, the man at the top is held responsible and similarly when the congregation is behaving badly, the man who stands behind the pulpit is the culprit.

When Lucia could no longer withstand the barrage of insults, she gave up her job. Then the shameless Christian sisters called for a toast to celebrate the resignation. This made her homeless so she went to stay with one of the female drug addicts she won for Christ. Her short stay with the drug addict was as if she had been cast into hell's fire.

Lucia once said to a friend, "I just feel like going somewhere where no one can see me." This reminds me of King David when he was being pursued by his enemies who were seeking to take his life, who cried out to the LORD; "Oh, that I had the wings of a dove! I would fly away and be at rest."

I caught up with Lucia again when her health started deteriorating because of the problems with her fiancé and the roommates. One of her friends who stood with her throughout the crisis once remarked, "The attitude of these friends can be described as sinister, a devious plot made more horrific by that fact that it is coming from childhood friends we thought we knew."

We spent sometime praying. During the prayers, I kept asking the LORD to give me a word of encouragement for Lucia. After ten minutes of praying, the Word of the LORD came for Lucia. After praying, we sat over a glass of cold water. The LORD led us to read Micah chapter 7 verse 7 to 9. I told her to read the verses several time and meditate on them. After reading the passage, I saw a different Lucia. Her downcast countenance had changed from sorrowful to that of a happy and joyful woman.

In the days of Israel's misery, the Word of the LORD came to Micah for His children who were being mocked by their enemies. "But as for me, I watch in hope for the Lord, I wait for God my Saviour; my God will hear me. Do not gloat over me, my enemy! Though I have fallen, I will rise.

Though I sit in darkness, the LORD will be my light. Because I have sinned against Him, I will bear the LORD'S wrath, until he pleads my case and establishes my right. He will bring me out into the light; I will see His righteousness. Then my enemy will see it and will be covered with shame."

A Christian who sins weakens his defences against his enemies. When a Christian sins, he opens the door of his spiritual life for the enemy to come in, instead of shutting the door of his spiritual life to the enemy. Sin harms both our spiritual life and physical life; therefore, we are to run away from sin.

Lucia's short stay in the house of the drug addict was hellish. Some days she stayed awake the whole night for fear of being attacked by her host. Sometimes the drug addict would stay all day in town and come home late. By the time she came home, she was high on drugs. Poor Lucia would have to protect the drug addict's daughter and herself.

Lucia interceded for the drug addict's deliverance from drugs. She prayed that the Lord would deliver her from the bondage of alcohol and drugs. God heard her prayers and delivered this poor and helpless woman from alcoholic and drug addictions. Where the Church and her tormentors failed, she succeeded.

What the Church and her tormenters could not do for the drug addict she was able to do. Who then will receive the LORD'S favour? Before she left the house, the drug addict gave up her life of drugs and alcohol. Today she has been set free through the prayers of one sinner some Christians rejected. That sinner was Lucia. When the world rejects us because of our failure, the LORD takes control of our life.

The action of these three Christian saints reminds me of John 8:1-11. When some Pharisees came to Jesus with a woman caught in adultery and asked Him what should be done with her, He knelt for a moment and wrote in the sand. We have no idea what He wrote. However, when they continued asking Him, Jesus responded in one short sentence:

"If any one of you is without sin, let him be the first to throw a stone at her," (7:8). This was a conditional command. Since none of them could meet the condition, they began to go away one at a time, and the woman was left alone with Jesus. His few words accomplished much in confronting the Pharisees with their own sin, for they walked away one by one.

Grandfather once said, "Sin is like a hill. You stand on it to see others' sins." Christians who judge others are in fact standing on their own sins while judging others. When you stand at the foot of a mountain, it is difficult to see what is on top of the mountain. However, the person who stands on a mountain of sins sees the sin of others.

Lucia's tormentors viewed her sins as means to justify her treatment as an outcast. Nevertheless, Jesus sees her as a free woman to be respected. Jesus looked beyond her sins and focused on the future of a young woman who would be an effective instrument in His hand.

They treated Lucia heartlessly with malice and cruelty. While they subjected her to utter humiliation, the assistant pastor was kept out of the ridicule. They saw the assistant pastor as a victim and Lucia as the villain. Let us be honest with ourselves: a search of the Scriptures will reveal whose responsibility it is to judge. If the Bible does not give us the right to judge, then let us not allocate to ourselves what is exclusively God's responsibility.

God has not called us into the kingdom to be judges but rather to be his followers. Jesus calls people to be his followers and not to act as judges. If you search the Scriptures, you will notice that each time Jesus calls a person, He says, "Follow me." On the day of Judgement God will not need us to testify against our brothers and sisters.

If we were to testify against fellow believers, the testimony coming out of our mouth would condemn us to hell's fire. When Jesus told Peter, "When you are old you will stretch out your hands and someone else will dress you and lead you where you do not want to go." Jesus said this to indicate the kind of death by which Peter would glorify God.

Peter turned and saw the disciple whom Jesus loved was following them. Then Peter asked, "Lord what about him?" Jesus answered, "If I want him to remain alive until I return, what is that to you? You follow me" (John 21:19-22). Knowing what is going to happen to John is none of Peter's business.

Similarly, what happed to Lucia should never have been the business of these saintly Christians. It is strictly God's business. We have been saved to follow Christ and that is the bottom line. It will be worth it if these three supposedly saintly Christians turn to the prophet Obadiah and heed the warning he gave to the people of Edom.

"Be sure God's judgment will surely fall on all who have harmed God's children." Perhaps while reading this concise prophecy you too might pick up the warning the prophet is sounding. It is up to God to deal with our rotten lives and not for us to do that. Our past sins are God's business and nobody else's business.

I am not in any way writing to make Lucia look innocent. Far from it, a spade must be called a spade. Yes, she was wrong and we all know that. Demonizing a Christian for her sins goes beyond what the Scripture teaches in relation to our attitude towards those who fall into sin. The main culprit behind this whole saga has been forgotten.

He has disappeared into thin air and the three saintly friends of Lucia seem to have lost track of him. We will put him in the spotlight later. For now, we will concentrate on Lucia.   During the course of Lucia's stay, she applied to the Home Office for the right to stay in the United Kingdom.

Because her application was turned down, she had to sign a form at the police station every Friday morning. Then one Friday morning when she arrived at the police station to sign the forms, she was ushered into the waiting arms of immigration officers. The grim-faced immigration officers told her she was being moved to a detention centre to await deportation.

She was driven from the police station to the deportation centre. At the centre, she found herself among thirty women awaiting deportation. She felt very sorry for some of the women at the deportation centre because some of them had children. When Lucia arrived at the centre, she saw an open door for evangelizing through which she could lead these detainees into the waiting arms of Jesus.

Without wasting time, she quickly turned the sombre mood of the detention centre into praise and worship that lifted the spirit of the detainees. The first night was turned into singing and praising. The officers were shocked and surprised because they had never seen anything like that. From their office, they saw how she gathered all the women around her.

Then she stood in the middle, opened the Scripture and started expounding the word of God to the women. By the end of the first week, three of the women gave their life to Christ, one of whom was a devoted Muslim from Nigeria. When Lucia was released from the detention centre, she brought this young girl to my office.

Upon Lucia's recommendation, the girl was offered a temporary employment in our office. Lucia was able to put her in a Bible-teaching Pentecostal church. She left at the end of her six-month contract. Lucia gained the confidence of the officers at the detention centre so that they allowed her some limited freedom, something denied to the other women.

By the end of her third week, another five of the women gave their lives to Christ. By now, the atmosphere in the centre turned from the fear of being deported to that of resting in the everlasting arms of the Living God in whom they all put their faith. Every morning she led the women in praise and worship before having their quiet time. She became a spiritual mother to all the women.

Lucia was stigmatized as the worst sinner and not fit to live among some holy Christians. Yet in the eyes of God, she was not what her accusers thought she was. What God saw in Lucia, her accusers could not. God saw an instrument He could use to accomplish His work at the detention centre.

There is something interesting we can learn from The Valley of Dry Bones. "The hand of the LORD was upon me, and he brought me out by the Spirit of the LORD and set me in the middle of a valley; it was full of bones. He led me back and forth among them, and I saw a great many bones on the floor of the valley, bones that were dry.

He asked me, "Son of man, can these bones live?" I said, "O Sovereign LORD, you alone know." (Ezekiel 37:1-3). Ezekiel was right when he said, "O Sovereign LORD, you alone knows. "Can a dead man's dry bones become alive again?" Can a fallen Christian ever find restoration again?

Is there any hope for a fallen Christian in a hopeless world? Only the Sovereign LORD knows. Just as the Sovereign LORD made flesh to come on those dry bones and put breath in them, so can the sovereign LORD restore the likes of Lucia by His Spirit and make them new.

As you read this book, I do not know what your dry bones are. However, one thing I do know is that the Sovereign LORD is able to restore you again. Your flesh may have been eaten away in disgrace and shame, and you have nothing to hold onto. Nevertheless, remember what the prophet Joel said; "I will repay you the years the locusts have eaten." (Joel 2:25.)

However, do not despair, for the Sovereign LORD is able to restore all that has been eaten away: whatever you have lost in your ministry, your marriage, or your business and your enemies are rubbing salt in your wounds. Do not be worried about those dry bones, for the Sovereign LORD can restore them again.

God sent Lucia to the detention centre to lead those women to Christ and not the immigration officers. God looked around and did not find anybody qualified to reach out to those perishing souls at the detention centre other than Lucia. Her short stay at the detention centre put joy on the faces of angels in heaven. God placed Lucia at the very place where the fruits in the farm were ripe for harvest.

If God had placed any other Christian there, that Christian would have been nothing but a fruit inspector instead of a fruit harvester. God is not interested in fruits inspectors because they are of no use to Him. God looks beyond our limitations and our sins when it comes to sending out fruit harvesters. God is more interested in those whose heart is right before Him than a self-righteous Christian who is only interested in fruit inspections.

It is not what people are saying about you that matters, it is what God say about you that matters. It is not what people think about you that matter, what God thinks about you is what matters. God, who sees the heart of men, knows those who are His. What Lucia's accusers were saying did nothing to change Gods mind.

By the fifth week, another two of the women gave their lives to Christ. By the sixth week, she was told her circumstance at the detention centre had changed so she was free to go home. They told her the Home Office would communicate with her. When God has not finished with you, no one can touch you.

The sudden change of decision from the Home Office amazed everyone close to her. The answer is simple; she had accomplished the mission God sent her to do at the detention centre. God had specifically chosen her to use her to bring those women at the detention Centre to Christ and that work had been accomplished.

The short stay of Lucia at the detention centre should remind us of Paul's trip to Philippi in Acts 16. The apostle Paul went to Macedonia because of a God directed vision (vv.9-10). How would Paul have known that his journey to Macedonia would end in prison? Was God behind the prison sentence?

Oh! Yes, the trip was planed by God because of one sinner and his household God wanted them saved. God used Paul to bring Salvation to a jailer and his family. You may ask why God would have to put Paul through hardship and inconveniences to bring one lost sinner to the redeeming grace of Jesus Christ. God can use inconveniences in our life for His own glory.

Once her mission was accomplished, there was no reason to hold her at the centre any longer. God always uses the most unlikely people. People we think are not as holy as we are the very people God will use to shame us. Jesus Christ once stood outside Jerusalem and said, "It is not the healthy who need a doctor, but the sick. I have not come to call the righteous, but sinners." Mark 2:17.

After a lot of soul-searching, the junior pastor gave in to the senior pastor's demand and married Lucia. Events preceding the wedding and after the wedding told Lucia the kind of man she was about to be married to. Everyone drew his or her conclusions about the motive of the assistant pastor's marriage to Lucia.

One month after the wedding, this man sent Lucia packing out of their matrimonial home. He told her she was free to come back on condition she get rid of the pregnancy, which was by now six months. The pastor's insistence on abortion as a pre-condition for Lucia to return to her matrimonial home should have been awake-up call for Lucia.

A husband who thinks about nothing but murder is a sick person. For a man of God to ask his six-month pregnant wife to have an abortion is beyond human understanding. People who stand behind the pulpit sometimes kill the Word of God by what they say and what they do. Jesus once said, "By their works you shall know them."

The Church members tried intervening but this man would not listen. When persuasion failed, Lucia was taken in by a middle-aged widow. Shame and depression made her develop high blood pressure. As a result, one of the twins in her womb died. She herself was very lucky to have survived, considering what she went through during the pregnancy.

From the pregnancy to the birth of the baby girl, this man refused his responsibility as a husband and a father. As a result, Lucia had to depend on mercy of those the Lord used to help her financially. When the baby was born, instead of sending a congratulatory message with flowers, this man sent a text that read, "Give up the baby for adoption if you love me so that we can be back together."

Examining the text, will reveal he never loved Lucia. The key words in the text are "If you love me." Love is not selfish, Love is not self-seeking rather Love is seeking a person's highest interest. If this man really loved Lucia, he would have demonstrated **love in action.** The aroma of love is affection but the text did not give up that aroma.

One thing stands clear, this man married for sex and nothing else.

His love was centred on the flesh, because of the message he send to Lucia. When a man's wife gives birth to a beautiful baby girl, the best thing the husband can do is to show his love and affection to his wife with a beautiful bunch of red roses with the words "I love you, and thank you for making me a proud father." This man did none of that. Instead, he send a text message that read, "Give up the baby for adoption so that we can live happily as husband and wife."

Lucia turned down the offer. At the time of writing this book, the baby is four years old. Moreover, the man has not seen the baby or contributed a penny towards Lucia and the baby. When questioned about his strange behaviour, his answer was always "it is Lucia I love and not the baby."

A person who marries because of sex will walk away when things go cold. The heart of a husband who turns his wife into a sex slave is filled with greediness, selfishness and jealousy. He has no confidence, always suspecting his wife and does not trust his wife. He will react violently when he sees another man talking to his wife.

It is a shame that these words are coming from a Christian who knows the mark of Christian husband is to love his wife affectionately. For a Christian father to make such a comment about how he feels about his own daughter is beyond understanding. People who give up their children for adoption do so because they are under age, they have financial difficulties, sickness or mental health problems.

When the man realised he could not convince Lucia give up the baby for adoption, divorce became his last weapon to end the marriage. This man is not alone in the act of changing women at will. My heart goes out to the unfortunate woman who will be the next victim to walk in the path of this man.

Lucia never thought she would someday have to go through divorce. However, it has happened and she cannot change it. She came out of the divorce worse-off. Her only consolation in this drama was her British citizenship. She won the battle to live in Britain but lost the marriage battle.

The man has filed for divorce on the grounds of irreconcilable differences. This is what he wrote, "Lucia and I have decided to divorce. We love each other deeply and pray for each other's happiness." I find it hard to understand what he meant by "we love each other deeply."

This reminds me of a woman who once remarked in a divorce court, "I am not going to let this go. I thought I married for love. But I married to be punished and have everything stolen from me." Lucia can be seen in the words of this woman. Lucia never allowed herself to be consumed with the bitterness of the divorce.

Deep down her heart, she forgave her husband. I think that the words "I love you" are probable the most seductive words used in this world. It is amazing how gullible people can be. If this man really loved Lucia, as he claimed in his text message, he would have put his love into action.

People who see love as a language for sex are very confused. Lucia's husband made the marriage impossible by his controlling behaviour. He was vindictive and very unpleasant. My heart goes out to the woman who will be his next victim after divorcing Lucia. Like Lucia, many women will fall prey to his charms.

In marriage we do not think about divorce, we do not plan for divorce, it does not form part of pre-marital preparations and is not enshrine in the marriage vows, so why is divorce so rampant in our generation? Is divorce unexpected in marriage or does it just happen? How do we face it when it comes?

Divorce is nothing but pain in the heart, which creates lasting pain and bitterness in marriage. It turns spouses who are passionately in love into bitter enemies. It turns families against families. In addition, it either turns children against their father or mother. Love is the only thing that can heal wounds caused by divorce.

The love of God is rooted in marriage because He set up the institution of marriage. On the other hand, the language of Satan in any marriage is divorce. It is a burden he carries into every marriage that is driven by the wheel of bitterness. **We marry because of love and we divorce because of hate.**

We must ask ourselves whether Christian marriage is advancing the marriage institution. This is not a vain and speculative question. It is practical, pertinent and all-important. The thought of standing before an angry God who created the marriage institution should send shock waves through those contemplating divorce.

How hard are Christians working with God to save and preserve the institution of marriage? The problems of the Christian marriage are rooted deeply within our reasons for marriage and attitude towards marriage. Until we critically examine our reasons for marriage and change our negative attitude towards marriage, the divorce circle will continue.

The Christian view of marriage is not the same as the worldly view of marriage, because Christian marriage is guided by the Scriptures. Today we are faced with so many single Christian parents within the kingdom community of believers. These are facts and those of us in the kingdom community must accept them.

Alternatively, will anyone dare say they are impertinent and out-of-place? Let us ask the large and important class of people in our Churches. They are the hope of the future Church. To them all eyes are turned. Can they restore the dignity of the marriage institution? On the other hand, will they also go down the same road?

19. Providential

"The blessing of the LORD brings wealth, and adds no trouble to it". (Proverbs 10:22)

The story of Rachel is a very intriguing. It has a mixture of doubt and uncertainty at the beginning but a wonderfully happy conclusion. The story tells of a young woman who was very careful not to make a decision without including God in her decision-making process. Her story confirms that a happy marriage depends on including God in our decision-making concerning the choice of our future spouses.

We must never forget the fact that God instituted marriage. Therefore, any decision concerning marriage should include Him. It will be unwise to keep God out of our choice of future partners. Keeping God out of the choice of a future husband or wife may be one of the reasons why some marriages, although they have a happy beginning, end in divorce. What God cannot do is lead us in making the wrong choice, because He knows that marriage is a covenant relationship.

The most likely reasons why some Christians choose their future husbands or wives without including God in their decision could be their inability to wait on God for answers. God sometimes does not give instant answers and this could be a problem for people who are in a hurry to get things done quickly.

If God does not give an instant answer, it may be because there are certain issues surrounding your choice that have to be dealt with before an answer comes. God will never answer until those issues are dealt with. Sometimes this may take a long time and we have to wait, however, those who wait upon God get the best from Him.

On the other hand, those who have problems waiting on God very often turn to go their own way before the answer comes. Against this, if we walk away from God on a crucial issue that concerns our future life partners we will only have to deal with the consequences later in the marriage.

When it comes to marriage, we must be ready to wait on God no matter how long it takes. The waiting may be for your own good: do not walk away before the answer comes. Countless Christians have walked into marriage before the answer came, only to find out that they married the wrong person.

The waiting time can be exciting to those who are willing to wait for the outcome. On the other hand, it can create anxiety in those who are in haste to see the outcome resolved. Remember it is said, "Hasty climbers have a sudden fall." The thought of what the answer could be should stimulate our interest in waiting for the LORD.

Being married to the wrong person is something we all dread. We must pray earnestly and seek God's counsel in making the right choice to avoid our marriage ending in divorce. Sometimes our inability to wait on the LORD is the reason we wake up with a troubled marriage that leads us to the dark road of divorce. The dark road of divorce should never be the portion of any Christian.

Today some Christians wish they had waited on the LORD. The consequences of disobedience can be found in our inability to wait on God. Against this, if we are not careful it can lead us down the dark road of divorce, and never see a glimpse of light in the distant future. It is the wish of God that none of His children's marriages ends in divorce.

However, the reason for our troubled marriage can be found in our decision and choice. This reminds me of a story of a young man who walked into the house of a young Christian woman he had never met. When the young woman opened the door, he was captivated and bewitched by her beauty and charm. She was charmed by his good looks. The chemistry between them was not compatible, yet they wanted it to work. They hurriedly married after six months, without checking each other's background.

For some unknown reason, this young couple both appeared in hurry to get married. I warned the young woman to be sure it was the will of God. At this, she told me she loved the man and the man loved her. If love is the precondition for marriage, then what are the criteria on which we determine what is genuine from deceptive?

What this young woman should have been be thinking of, is whether the man would be trusted to obey the marriage vows. It was obvious these two did not understand what love really means. Their understanding of love was vague. Love is the virtue in marriage that brings glory to God who established the institution of marriage.

Less than three months after the marriage, the young man was seeking to divorce the woman he married in a colourful wedding. Today, they barely can stand to be in each other's presence. Two lovely Christians have suddenly forgotten what Christian marriage is all about. This is a story of a young man who sees marriage as "cut and paste."

This young man was seeking to divorce his wife because she discovered his dark side and this infuriated him. The irony is that instead of breaking from his past life he still wanted to hold on to it and on other hand, hold on to his marriage. Marriage is like blending two metals together, and this young man was doing the opposite.

Although his faithful and loyal wife was willing to forgive him if he turned away from his past life, he was standing by his willingness to go ahead with the divorce, just because his wife taped-recorded his conversation with a mystery woman. This man's understanding of marriage is vague.

The decent thing this young man should have done as a Christian, was to go down on his knees and pray this prayer: "Spirit of the Living God invade my life and take control of me and grant me the power to overcome the lust of flesh. Oh, LORD my God, take away from me the lust of the flesh and grant me the will to overcome the lust of the flesh."

He never prayed. Instead, he allowed his heart to be hardened by the devil. This happens when we refuse to admit our sins and confess them before God who alone has the power to forgive. This attitude shames the institution of marriage and betrays the Christian ethics of marriage. This is the grim sad story our youth are facing in the Church.

The Church must pick up some of the blame for failing to put together experts who can counsel and adequately prepare the youth for marriage. Pastors cannot claim to be ignorant of the problems the youth are facing in marriage. Pastor should be well advised that by making the issues of marriage problems part of their sermons would restored some dignity to the Christian marriage.

The marriage of this young couple brings back to memory the story of an army officer wanted for staging a failed coup d'etat. While travelling, he failed to check his flight destination. As a result, he was arrested, court-marshalled and sentenced to death by firing squad.

If this young army officer had taken time to check his flight destination, he would be alive today. The carelessness of this army officer may hold the answer to the reason some Christian marriages are failing. They are failing because we fail to check for character and the genuineness of our fiancés' faith in Christ.

Just as the hospitals are filled with people with different sickness, so are the Churches filled with different kinds of Christian. If we fail to seek

God's counsel regarding our suitor, we will end up with the wrong person; a situation we must try to avoid if we want our marriage to be a happy one.

We must exercise caution when it comes to choosing a spouse in the Church. In the second Timothy 2:20-21, Paul writes, "In a great house there are not only vessels of gold and silver, but also of wood and of earth; and some to honour, and some to dishonour" (NKJV). We must be alert, and watchful of people who parade themselves in the Church dressed in Scripture.

We are responsible for our attitude in our marriage. We must change our bad attitude for the better, for the sake of our marriage. If we cannot change then it is because we think too much of egotism and are not mindful of working towards the good of the marriage. Marriage is a learning process; therefore, we must be willing to learn with submission and humility.

This is the problem with many of the youth of today. Most people's understanding of love is sex. Therefore, they marry for nothing but for sex. Do not be deceived in thinking the only way to control your passion for sex is to marry. No, marriage is not about sex alone, it goes beyond that. Marriage is companionship for life and its genuineness sometimes can be tested in the storm of adversity.

The youth of today needs to be educated on the institution of marriage. This is where pastors, Christian marriage counsellors, Church elders and parents should play a greater role in the education of the youth on the subject of marriage. The youth must know that there is a lot more to marriage than what they perceive.

The youth must know the following about marriage, what marriage is, what it involves, marriage is a journey without end, what it is to be married and what is required of a married person. Once they embark on it, there is no turning back except death. They must understand what the Scriptures say about marriage.

The story of Rachel is a classic example of a woman who understood what marriage is all about. She was the kind of woman every Christian man would like to have as a wife. One look at her and you would be charmed by her submissiveness and politeness. Rachel took God by His word and waited for His will to be made perfect in her choice of a life partner.

Spiritually well matured with good Christian values, which may have been due to her Christian upbringing, she was an example to all the girls in the college, to both Christian and non-Christians and well respected by both staff and students. In this young woman, you would find good virtue.

She had a childhood sweetheart whom she planned to marry after graduating. She was very beautiful and he was very handsome. They were both devoted to each other, and love held them bound together. The young man was a devoted Christian, the kind of husband any woman looking for a godly husband would want.

This is how the story of Rachel unfolds. One day the Scripture Union travelling secretary who was to speak to members of the Scripture Union in the polytechnic failed to turn up and did not inform us. However, whilst we were waiting for his arrival, one of the students drew my attention to a young man waiting outside to speak to me.

The young man introduced himself, and said he had been asked by the Scripture Union travelling secretary to come and speak to the Christian students in the college. This was welcome news because we were kept waiting for a long time without knowing if the speaker would turn up.

After the meeting, Rachel prepared light refreshments for the guest speaker. Was this a mistake or was it a question of providence? Rachel was a woman any young Christian man looking for a bride would find difficult to resist. On the other hand, the young man felt fate had brought them together.

As we sat down talking, the young man kept stealing looks at Rachel. At this, I smiled. Rachel interrupted. "Why are you smiling?" "A piece of cake went down the wrong way" was the reply. She was now aware we both knew what was going on. The young man simply could not resist Rachel's good looks.

Do not be surprised at this, because any young man looking for a bride will behave in this manner. The expression on Rachel's face showed she did not like the whole scene. To avoid embarrassment I told them I had other things to catch up on. Therefore, we ended the meeting and she left hurriedly in the direction of waiting friends.

On the way home, the young man said Rachel's face looked very familiar. He asked if Rachel had sister and brother. I told him yes. At this, he asked me if a meeting could be arranged the following weekend at my house. I was surprised at this because the young woman was in a boarding institution and it would not be easy to arrange the visit.

For a moment, I thought this was a messenger sent to deliver a message and not to look for a bride in a college pasture. I pondered over his request and wondered whether inviting Rachel would be appropriate or inappropriate, knowing she lived in a hostel and under the control of a housemistress. This would involve written permission, however thing tuned out well without any objection by the housemistress.

That weekend I asked Rachel if she could come and cook. She was not told who the guest of honour would be. When she finished cooking, we heard a knock at the door. She answered the doorbell and was dumbstruck with amazement, and then she turned and smiled at me and said, "That was a pretty dumb thing to do."

She was speechless, but politely invited the guest in, with her usual lovely smile. After lunch, the two of them were left to get to know each other. The young man was right when he said Rachel's face was familiar. Sometimes our human instincts can lead to what we are looking for; therefore, we must not ignore them.

It emerged that Rachel's elder brother and the young man went to the same secondary school. In addition, he and Rachel's elder sister met several times at the town's Christian fellowship. Rachel's elder sister knew that their brother and the young man were very good friends. After college, Rachel's brother went to the military academy where he graduated as an officer cadet.

On the other hand, the young man went on to university where he studied Banking and Economics and became a banker. After their brief encounter, Rachel asked me to tell my newfound friend to look for a bride elsewhere because she had a boyfriend and they were looking forward to getting married.

The message was not passed on to the young man for obvious reasons. Something within me told me to say nothing. Why, I cannot tell, but I allowed events to dictate the future. Sometimes the Holy Spirit speaks to us in a way we do not really understand. As Christians who have the Holy Spirit in us, we need to obey such a voice without question.

Every weekend my friend would bring foodstuffs to my house then ask me to invite Rachel to come and cook for us. She never refused any of the invitations, because of the respect she had for me. Why the housemistress never refused her permission to visit is something difficult to explain. The explanation for this could be God had granted Rachel a favour.

The weekend cooking became bait for the two of them. Therefore, I kept an eagle eye to see which of the two fish would be attracted to the bait and swallow it. As fate would have it, Rachel's childhood sweetheart failed his 'A' level exams. It was bad news and decision time. Could this be perfect timing or providence?

History has taught us that God sometimes uses world events to accomplish his purpose. This could be the reason why prayers are delayed sometimes in each individual's life for a purpose that is hidden from us. Therefore, for every delay, God has a reason to use certain events to fulfil His promises. The Scriptures are full of such events.

On one hand stands a young handsome Christian bank manager. On the other hand stands a childhood sweetheart who has just failed his 'A' level exams. This beautiful young woman was caught between two young men who were vying for her love. She had to make a decision, a decision that would not only dictate her future but also change her life.

Frankly, both young men were very handsome and God-fearing men. This posed a dilemma for Rachel. Her mind was occupied with so many thoughts. Thoughts like this open the floodgate to all kinds of indecision and if care is not taken, our emotions can override our judgement. In our quest to look for a spouse, we should never allow our emotion to dictate to us.

In my heart, I wanted Rachel to marry the bank manager because we became very close friends. However, both of them were top of my prayer list. Although I desperately wanted Rachel to marry my friend, nothing was done or said that would influence Rachel's decision. Sometimes I had to fight my emotion from influencing Rachel.

Marriage is a long-term commitment and love should play the crucial role in any decision taken. Any outside influence is bound to create problems later in the marriage. This I wanted to avoid, allowing her to make her own decision. For once, I was afraid I was getting involved with an arranged marriage.

Those of us that were involved in the life of these three young Christians kept praying and waiting for the decision of this young woman who was caught between two men. We prayed that love would be the deciding factor, especially for Rachel who was faced with the choice; in addition that the will of God may be made known to all.

Before I knew, what was going on Rachel and Hughes were holding secret meetings in his office.

Now it was no longer weekend in my house but at my friend's house without me. I had been sidelined, no longer in the picture. Was I jealous? No! Envious? No! Overjoyed? Yes. Yes, because I played a crucial role in the life of these two friends.

I kept praying that God would make His will known to both of them. It is the responsibility of married Christians to pray for young Christians looking for a spouse. The only time I appeared in the picture was when Hughes asked me to accompany him to their engagement ceremony.

When my friend was leaving for England, he left his pregnant wife with me. She stayed with me until the baby was due. She joined her husband after he got a job with an international organization based in Switzerland. The choice she made turned out to be a happy one. They are happily married with three lovely children.

Did she regret? No, she made the right choice! Did she include God in her decision? Yes, because she depended wholly on God. Their marriage is a good example of a happy Christian marriage. She made a godly choice and it ended well with her. Was God in that decision? Yes. Her decision to marry the banker was God's will for her.

Nobody walks into marriage with God and comes out disappointed. What God demands is absolute obedience when it comes to our choice of our spouse. Prayer is the only gateway in looking for a spouse. If we ask God who instituted the marriage institution, He will give us what is best for us.

20. In obedience to God

Teach me to do your will, for you are my God; may your Spirit lead me on a level ground. (Psalm143:10)

"Call to me and I will answer you and tell you great and unsearchable things you do not know." (Jeremiah 33:3).

The story of Gertrude is breathtaking and worth reading. She is one among millions of women. If you have never seen a woman with the beauty of Jesus, then here is one. The truth is that if you searched the whole world, you will find very few women like her.

If you look through the mirror of Scripture, you will surely see her face in Proverbs 31:10- 31. Again if you look for her in Ephesians 5: 24 you will find her there. You will find this woman all over the pages of Scripture, especially where women of obedience and good morals are mentioned.

When Gertrude started praying for a husband, God answered her prayers by telling her where to find a bridegroom. Where she was asked to find her bridegroom would send shockwaves through and raise the blood pressure in women with pride. Let us pause here and reflect over where she was asked to look.

It is the most unlikely place from which any woman will want to seek a bridegroom. Most women will resist going to that extent to look for a bridegroom. Here we are dealing with an unusual woman who took God at His word. You will see the face and character of this woman in Ruth 1:16-17.

Have you read about the Syro-Phoenician woman's faith in Mark 7:24-30? We can see this woman's faith in Gertrude. I have no shred of doubt in my mind that if any other Christian woman was given the same revelation she would surely say, "This revelation is definitely not from God." A word of caution: Sometimes-good things can come from the devil but be warned, it could be nothing but a decoy.

Most Christian women would have walked away and turned their back on such a revelation. I have spoken to a number of Christian women on this issue and this is what they told me. It is doubtful if these women thought carefully before giving me these answers. This is what one Christian woman said.

"This is the last place any decent woman would look for a bridegroom." Some even went further to say, "Even a desperate woman would not look for bridegroom where she was asked to look for one." Whilst love is the only thing that can pull down barriers, pride on the other hand can build barriers and deprive us of God's perfect blessing.

In a dream, God showed her a particular railway station where homeless people sleep and beg for handouts. God did not give her the description of the man. She was only told to pass by that particular station each time she was going to work and when she left work. Sometimes it is very difficult to understand God because His ways are not our ways.

For such a beautiful academic to be asked to look for a bridegroom under a railway bridge raises more questions than answers. Would that mean stooping too low just for a bridegroom? This young woman was never desperate for a husband, but being faithful, obeyed God and did as she was told.

What makes the revelation look doubtful is that the underground train station in question was far away from her place of work. This meant taking her miles away from her normal route. Does this make sense? Yes, because we are dealing with a woman who knows God never fails.

As she passed the station every day to and from work, she noticed one particular scruffy-looking man kept asking her for money. It happened that they became so attached to each other that every evening she stopped by and spent about five minutes witnessing to this homeless man.

Then one day she took the man to a barber to have his hair cut. From the barbershop, she took the man to her flat for a hot bath. This homeless man had never had a bath for years and now was lying in a hot perfumed bath. He went into the bath without his tattered clothes and came out of the bath a new man.

From the bath, he became a new person, his old way of living replaced with a new way of living. This happened from the moment he stepped out the bath. Why a University lecturer would risk her life based on a revelation will remain a mystery. She put her reputation and her life on the line for a man who had nothing in this world except cardboard from which he made his home at an underground railway station.

However, this man went into the bath as an unmarried man but came out of the bath a married man. Had this drug addict been a dangerous man, this beautiful lecturer would have stood no chance in overpowering him. This was a man of six foot eight inches and a weight of about twenty stone.

He was a gentle giant yet he was tamed by the hospitality of the young woman. Conversation between them revealed two things about the man, which the lecturer did not know. One, the man was a university graduate who had a promising career in banking. Second, he became a victim of his own making when he fell in with the wrong group. As a result, he lost his job and his home.

The lifestyle of this man drove his father to an early death because he could no longer live to bear the shame of his son's lifestyle. This young man had been the pride and joy of his parents who put him at the very centre of their hearts. The problem with so many parents is that they show so much love and attention to their children that they fail to see the warning signs.

Surely, we must all love our children but we must also know where to draw the lines, and know when and where to use the rod. After several years away from his mother, he finally got in touch with his mother because of pressure from Gertrude. The mother was overjoyed to hear from a son she thought was dead.

When they arrived, his mother was more eager to know the mystery woman he brought home than to see her lost son after so many years. Seeing her son come with a woman for the first time erased her worst fears. Now she knew her son was not what she had thought he was. This brought exceeding joy to the mother who breathed a sign of relief that one day she would become a grandmother.

God used Gertrude, a young Christian woman who took God by His word, to turn the life of a young man from rags to riches and from captivity to freedom through Salvation in Christ. She succeeded because she was standing on the promise of God that cannot fail. Only Christians who are standing on the promise of God will triumph in this dark world of sin.

Today they are happily married and their home is an example of Christian marriage. I have great respect and admiration for this unique young Christian woman who shut her ears to friends and opened her ears to God. She refused to listen to the voice of her friends and instead listened to the voice of God.

She put her faith in the God whose eyes are on the righteous and His ears are attentive to their cry. See Psalm 34:15. Only God can direct you to where to find the man you are looking to marry is or where the woman you are looking to marry can be sought.

Today, countless young beautiful women are desperately looking for husbands to no avail because the kind of husbands they are looking for may not be found in the Church. Therefore, they look outside the church for spouses, hoping they can lead them to Christ after marriage. Be warned, if you take what belongs to the devil, then do not be surprised when he comes knocking on your door.

Some women in the Church sample and sieve the men in the Church the way grains are sieved. These women appear to have a series of grading sieves like that of a combine harvester. As the grain passes through the threshing drum, they are threshed and graded according to size.

This is how some women in the Church look for future husbands. Although the Bible does not tell us how to choose husbands and wives, it tells where to find a bride and bridegroom. Our choices of future partners are entirely in our hands. Be careful, a happy marriage depends on whom we choose as our spouse.

As we make these choices, we must remember that we live in an artificial world. In a world where artifice has been incorporated into everyday lives, we need to keep our eyes open to discern what is artificial and what is natural so that we are not deceived. Therefore, trust in God alone to make your marriage happy.

Bibliography

Paul B Hoff. *Genesis. An Independent study Textbook;* Fifth Edition 1999.

William F. Lasley. *Paul's Salvation Letters: Galatians and Romans. An Independent-Study Textbook.* First Edition 2002.

Jack V. Rozell; *Christian Counselling. An Independent-study Textbook.* Fourth Edition 2000.

Peter Kuzmic. *The Gospel of John. A study Guide.* Sixth Edition 1979.

Louise Jeter Walker; *Evangelism Today. An Independent-Study Textbook.* Fourth Edition 2004.

Raymond T. Brock; *Introduction to Psychology: A Christian Perspective. An Independent-study Textbook.* 2006 Global University First Edition.

T. Burton Pierce. *Ministerial Ethics.* Third Edition 2004.

John W. Kirkpatrick. *Guidelines for Leadership. An Independent-Study Textbook.* Second Edition 1999.

Eleazer E.Javier. *The work of the Pastor. An Independent-study Textbook.* First Edition 1989.

Paul W. Smith; *Biblical Theology of Prayer. A study Guide.* Third Edition 2003.

E. M Bounds. *On Prayer,* 2006, By Hendrickson Publishers.

Andrew Murray. *With Christ in the School of Prayer.* .2007 By Hendrickson Publishers.